D0427795

Lapse of Time

by Wang Anyi

Introduction by Jeffrey Kinkley

CHINA
BOOKS
& Periodicals, Inc.

San Francisco

Panda Books

Beijing, China

S

Address inquiries to China Books,
2929 24th Street, San Francisco,CA 94110
ISBN 0-8351-2031-7 (casebound)
ISBN 0-8351-2032-5 (paperback)
Printed in the United States by CHINA
BOOKS
& Periodicals, Inc.

in cooperation with   Panda Books, Beijing, China

Contents

Preface

The early 1980's, when these stories were written, was a time that the revolutionary toughness and group hatreds left over from Mao's last years were beginning to fade. Writers of diverse backgrounds (and differing degrees of implication in Mao's old order) trumpeted "Humanism!" as the ideological alternative. Meanwhile Wang Anyi (pronounced 'wong ahn ee'), an innocent young woman in her late twenties, unobtrusively embodied such a humanism in works of fiction.

When we read her stories, that humanism appears far older than the author herself. Wang Anyi is not one simply to condemn or write off "The Ten Lost Years" (1966-76). In her creative world, authentic human feelings live on through the darkest days of the Cultural Revolution. They are perpetuated along with—perhaps in tandem with—the old class relations, with all their old prejudices, suspicions, and tolerances, too. Wang Anyi analyzes China with an imagination that seems nourished by both pre-revolutionary and post-revolutionary culture. Her stories are alive with such tensions and contrasts. A humanist on the outside, she is a warrior on the inside, believing that "we are our own worst enemies." And it is good that she is spiritually armed, for although her works are not outstandingly political, feminist, or artistically difficult, they have drawn fire from the old guard.

Most of us outside observers are likely to think first of the exterior Wang Anyi. She was born in 1954, to a father who three years later was proclaimed a Rightist. Because of the Cultural Revolution, she only got to graduate from junior high school (in 1969) before being resettled as a farmhand, at the age of 15, on a commune in northern Anhui. It was in a poor area by the Huai River noted for its famines, one of the least desirable places to which a Shanghai young person could be sent, as we learn from the realistic and quietly understated family talk about the traumatic rustication movement in "Lapse of Time." In 1972, Wang Anyi came a step closer to home by being assigned to a cultural troupe headquartered in Xuzhou. Hence, when she writes about such outfits, as in "Life in a Small Courtyard" and "The Stage, a Miniature World," she knows whereof she speaks. Wang Anyi began publishing short stories in 1976 and finally got to return home to Shanghai in 1978, to serve as an editor of the magazine *Childhood.* After that, her rise was meteoric. The Chinese Writers' Association gave her further professional training in 1980, and within a few years she was winning, and retaining, national acclaim as one of the new talents salvaged from the sacrificed generation, along with Bei Dao, Zhang Chengzhi, Zhang Xinxin, Zhong Acheng, et al. "The Destination," a story about the betrayal of that generation's ideals, and "Lapse of Time," also included in this anthology, are two of her several works that have won literary prizes in China.

Yet, no more than her young characters is Wang Anyi obsessed by "lost years." The outer world of Wang Anyi, according to the author herself, is rather a sheltered environment of nurture and privilege. She did spend her childhood in a place just like Lane 501 of "The Base of the Wall," in a well-to-do neighborhood of Shanghai, China's most fashionable city. There she could read her fill of books from East and West, her imagination nourished by freedom from worry, yet evidently hemmed in by walls of loneliness and protection. Moreover, she had Ru Zhijuan, a major author and member of the Communist Party, as her mother. Ms. Ru was already famous for her fiction in the 1960's, despite indignities that came from association with her husband. After the Cultural Revolution she re-emerged as a post-Mao writer of conscience, boldly criticizing deception and materialism in contemporary Chinese life. For both mother and daughter, it has been a high-profile life of new creative challenges, peer and reader recognition, professional-writer status in writers' associations, and trips abroad. In this world of the literati must lie much of Wang Anyi's link to China's bedrock humanistic tradition—except that she tells us in her stories, the tradition dwells within the Shanghai proletariat, too.

The inner Wang Anyi still wrestles with the special problems and faults of her generation, and the often still less fortunate young people below her, but in the collection she appears to be struggling even more with guilt about her past comforts. Her stories strike one first of all as noteworthy for their realism. They are about everyday urban life, and a grimy, gloomy, overcrowded, and therefore utterly exhausting life it is. In "Between Themselves," we see the underclass living in their shacks (as in Xia Yan's "Under the Eaves of Shanghai," written a revolution ago), gobbling down their food as if there were no tomorrow and asserting their will for its own sake, as if that might win them one last bit of self-determination before they must succumb to the world of order and of schools, where even the little children do their recitations "dragging it out, knowing it by heart." Wang Anyi does not stint in describing the brutalizing density, the rude jostling, the interminable and often futile waiting in line that accompany life in the Chinese big city. Such a life takes its toll of body, mind, and spirit. Accordingly, Wang Anyi probes the mental illnesses that strike the few, and the fatalism, loss of hope, and accommodations to unemployment as a way of life that afflict the many. Yet, strangely in view of all this, she has been hailed as a writer of positive "Shanghai" consciousness. That was during the mid-1980's, when writers of Wang Anyi's young generation tended to classify each other in groups according to the regional "roots" their fiction probed or celebrated. Works such as "The Destination" and "Lapse of Time" do convey a sense of the Shanghai mystique and the superiority Shanghainese feel over people with "rustic" manners, even over famed port cities of the last century, like Ningbo that fell on hard times under Mao. According to the former story, one can be "Shanghai" about the very way one squeezes into a bus, for there is a knack to it that divides the initiated from the hick. Yet this also symbolizes the city's precarious existence just above the line of barbarism. Wang Anyi has captured not just an overcrowded patch of the Chinese earth but a lapsed moment in time, for prestigious Shanghai is already yielding pride of place to technologically advanced Guangzhou/Hongkong as China's city of the future.

The pre-Cultural-Revolution Shanghai aristocracy and its spectacular downfall are now known to Western readers through Nien Cheng's shocking *Life and Death in Shanghai*. A couple of steps below Nein Cheng and her late actress-daughter would be the former capitalist Fan family, with its two concubines, of "Lane 501." Some distance below that would be Wang Anyi's own family. Nien Cheng's stratum, of course, was as rare as its manners were rarified. What surprises one, in Wang Anyi's rather more subtle accounts, is the pervasiveness of class identity, class images, and prejudices, in a society that once dreamed of abolishing classes. The working class in Lane 499 are have-nots who can only dream of the sofas, extra rooms, telephones, and pianos of Lane 501. They wear hand-me-downs, quarrel, drink, pick their toes in front of guests, and consider shutting oneself in one's room to be aberrant behavior. Even after Red Guards have stripped them of all their movable possessions, the upper class still lives in finer rooms than the proletariat. The lower class envies them, fears them, pretends to look down on them as was sanctioned by ideology, yet secretly admires them still, recognizing that "they're not the same." They risk tarnishing themselves with the bourgeois political curse itself to have their sons baby-sat by people of superior manners. The upper class, meanwhile, is presented by Wang Anyi as badly divided against itself. Families do not visit each other, and professors look down on old capitalists—not because of how they got their money, but because they lack culture. Though the Cultural Revolution has brought the lower class into upper class homes to strip them of their "reactionary" possessions, more often it is not people with names (or at least nicknames) from Lane 499 who do the robbing, but the Kafkaesque figures who only show up to cart things away. Paradoxically, then, the upper class ends up as far above the hoi polloi as ever. It has learned to lock its doors and cease going out in public, and so become an object of mystery, of mystique. Only when a "proper lady" like Ouyang Duanli in "Lapse of Time" joins the masses out of necessity do the latter realize how very low "leftism" has brought such people. At that point, the old humanism of this really not very political society reasserts itself.

But outer worlds are not always the point, where Wang Anyi is concerned. Beneath each domestic surface lie wild, unrestrained passions waiting to break through. Children of the old bourgeoisie long to go out of doors, even if only to market, to see the sun and find out how the other, more dangerous half, lives. Once outside, they are disappointed by the drabness and monotony, but this only intensifies their yearning for something "more to life" not yet discovered. Young A'nian, from the other side, catches his first glimpse of what a private emotional life can be like when he confiscates a secret diary kept by a professor's daughter. Amid the dreary, oppressively public life in the "Small Courtyard," it is the secret amour of a humble carpenter and the heroine's belated confrontation with a romantic might-have-been that provide breakthroughs into new worlds of feeling. And for Ouyang Duanli, who enjoyed making-up and shopping before the Cultural Revolution, but now sells old clothes to keep her family from hunger, productive labor itself offers both release and self-determination—up to a point. The inner passions of these stories do not culminate in raw exuberance, however, but find expression in quiet and confidential mutual understandings.

Wang Anyi considers herself to be driven by repressed inner passions, and in her later works she furthers the individualist cause with characters who are clearly repressed by the old, pre-Mao society. We get just a hint of that social concern in the stories of this volume. They provide, for instance, more than one depiction of the awkward meetings and negotiations that go into arranged marriages. Characteristically, Wanh Anyi is less interested in the oppression than in the greed and opportunism that accompany the process—schemes to "marry into a spare room," rid the family of an emotionally disturbed daughter in the guise of curing her, and so forth. On the other hand, "The Stage, a Miniature World" is a funny satire of the inefficient, you- scratch-my-back-I'll-scratch-yours old China in head-on collision with the new era of Deng Xiaoping. "Feudal" habits are cut to the quick, yet even in this piece Wang Anyi is so even-handed as to make corruption itself appear, at times, like a benevolent and in any case unshakable godfather. I judge the story to be realistic and topical satire of just how things were in the entertainment profession as troupes for the first time became responsible for their own profits and losses in the early 1980's.

Wang Anyi's Chinese readers call her language refined and "beautiful," her style elegant and restrained; emphasize the already implied quality of unaffectedness, and the hidden excitement beneath the introvertedness, and one could become convinced that the style is a direct reflection of the author. "And the Rain Patters On," the most complex narrative of this collection, with three remembered encounters and four streams of time, ironically is the earliest story of the collection (1980). In "The Base of the Wall" (1981) and "Lapse of Time" (1982), Wang Anyi has put aside her flashbacks and more complicated ways of revealing inner consciousness in favor of more straightforward tales about the subtle human changes (still including psychological changes) that went on during the Ten Lost Years. Three stories from 1983 develop further her device of encapsulating all society in a small community, but they lead back to one more journey into unfathomable inner worlds and private channels of communication (which nevertheless terminate in a Chekhovian standoff) in "Between Themselves" (1984). But this is far from going in a circle; the last work strikes me as both the most refined and the most open-ended of the collection. Wang Anyi does not rest on her laurels. As of the mid-1980's she has already entered other literary realms—explored the "deep structure" of Chinese culture, and the sensitive subject of sexuality.

Wang Anyi's inner restlessness and outer capacity for growth doubtless are partly responsible for the fact that she has so many loyal Chinese readers. She is still young and still writing, so ultimately the stories in this volume may signify but one phase of her career. Yet this neat little volume will always fulfill one goal that Wang Anyi once set for herself: "I hope that my fiction has this effect—that people will read it and say, 'Yes . . .this is the way things were once upon a time. These are the lives that people led.'"

Jeffrey Kinkley
Edison, New Jersey
June 1988

The Destination

Over the loudspeaker came the announcement, "The train is arriving at Shanghai terminal. . . ."

Dozing passengers opened their eyes. "We're arriving in Shanghai."

"We're nearing the terminal."

The impatient ones removed their shoes and climbed onto their seats to reach for their luggage.

A group of middle-aged men from Xinjiang began making plans. "We'll take a bath as soon as we check into a hotel. Then we'll call the heavy-machinery plant and go out to a Western-style restaurant."

"Right. We'll have Western food." Their spirits rose. They had gone to work in Xinjiang after their university years in Beijing, Fuzhou and Jiangsu. Though they retained their accents, their appearance and temperament were "Xinjiangized," weather-beaten and blunt. When Chen Xin asked casually about Xinjiang after he got on the train at Nanjing, they gave him a detailed and enthusiastic account of the region: the humor and wit of Xinjiang's different ethnic minorities, the beautiful songs they sang, the graceful dances and lively girls. They also described their own life there, how they fished and hunted. Expressive and eloquent, they painted an appealing picture.

"How long will you be in Shanghai?" one of the group, a man from Beijing, asked, patting Chen Xin on the shoulder.

With a smile, he turned around from gazing out the window. "I've come back for good."

"Got a transfer?"

"Right."

"Bringing your wife and children?"

"I haven't any," he blushed. "I couldn't have come back if I'd been married."

"My, you must be determined." Chen Xin's shoulder received a heartier slap. "You Shanghainese can't survive away from Shanghai."

"It's my home," Chen Xin said, justifying himself.

Chen Xin smiled.

"One should be able to find interesting things anywhere. You skate in Harbin, swim in Guangzhou, eat big chunks of mutton with your hands in Xinjiang and Western food in Shanghai.... Wherever fate lands you, you look for something interesting and enjoy it as best you can. Maybe that's what makes life interesting."

Chen Xin only smiled. Absentmindedly, he kept his eyes on the fields flitting past his window, fields carefully divided into small plots and planted like squares of embroidery—there were patches of yellow, dark and light green and, beside the river, purple triangles. To eyes used to the vast, fertile soil of the north, the highly utilized and carefully partitioned land struck him as narrow and jammed. But he had to admit that everything was as fresh and clean as if washed by water. This was the south, the outskirts of Shanghai. Oh, Shanghai!

The train hurtled past the fields and low walls and entered the suburbs. Chen Xin saw factories, buildings, streets, buses and pedestrians.... Shanghai became closer and tangible. His eyes moistened and his heart thumped. Ten years ago, when classes were suspended during the Cultural Revolution, he and other sent-down youth left for the countryside. At that time, as Shanghai faded into the distance, he had not expected to return. No. He probably had thought about it. In the countryside, he plowed, planted, harvested wheat, dredged rivers, and tried to get a job or admittance to a university.... He finally enrolled in a teachers' college. After graduation he was assigned to teach in a middle school in a small town. Able to earn his own living at last, his struggles should have ended; he could start a new life. But he felt he had not arrived at his destination. Not yet. He was still unsettled and expectant, waiting for something. He only realized what he had been waiting for, what his destination really was, when large numbers of school-leavers returned to Shanghai after the fall of the Gang of Four.

In the past decade, he had been to Shanghai on holiday and on business. But with every visit he only felt the distance between him and Shanghai grow. He had become a stranger, an outsider, whom the Shanghainese looked down upon. And he found their superiority and conceit intolerable. The pity and sympathy of his friends and acquaintances were as unbearable. For at the back of that lay pride. Still he was forced to admire Shanghai's progress and superiority. The department stores were full of all kinds of goods and people dressed in the latest fashions. Clean, elegant restaurants. New films at the cinemas. Shanghai represented what was new in China. But above all there was his home, his mother, brothers, and dead father's ashes. . . . He smiled, his eyes brimming with tears. He would make any sacrifice to return. He had acted as soon as he learned that his mother was retiring and that one of her children could take her job. He had gone here and there to get his papers stamped, a troublesome and complicated business. He had fought a tense and energetic battle, but he had won.

The train pulled into the station. As Chen Xin opened the window, a cool breeze—a Shanghai breeze—rushed in. He saw his younger brother, now grown tall and handsome. Seeing him, the youth ran beside the train calling happily, "Second brother!" Chen Xin's heart shrank with regret. He calmed down, remembering how, ten years earlier, his elder brother had run beside the train too at his departure.

The train came to a halt. His younger brother caught up, panting. Chen Xin was too busy talking to him and handing him his luggage to notice that the cheerful group of middle-aged men were bidding him farewell.

"Elder brother, his wife, and Nannan are here too. They're outside. We only got one platform ticket with your telegram, saying you were coming. Have you got a lot of luggage?"

"I can manage. How's Mom?"

"She's OK. She's getting dinner ready. She got up at three this morning to buy food for you."

A lump rose in his throat; he lowered his head in silence. His brother fell silent too.

They moved quietly out of the long station. At the exit his elder brother, his wife, and son, Nannan, took his suitcases from him. They struggled under the weight for a few steps and then gave them back to him. Everybody laughed. His elder brother clasped him around his shoulders while his younger brother took his arm. His sister-in-law followed, carrying Nannan.

"Have you got all the necessary papers?" his elder brother inquired. "Tomorrow I'll ask for leave and take you to the labor bureau."

"I can take him. I haven't got anything to do," offered his younger brother.

Chen Xin's heart trembled again. He turned to him with a smile. "OK. No.3 can take me."

It took three buses to reach home. His mother greeted him, lowering her head to wipe away tears. The three sons were at a loss for words, not knowing how and also too shy to express their feelings. All they could say was, "What's there to cry about?" It was his sister-in-law who knew how to stop her. She said, "This calls for a celebration, Mum. You should be rejoicing."

The tension lifted. "Let's eat," they said to one another. The table was moved from his mother's six-square-meter room to the big room his elder brother and his wife occupied. Chen Xin looked around. The room where he and his two brothers had once lived had a different appearance. The light green wallpaper was decorated with an oil painting and a wall light. Smart new furniture had been made to fit the room. The color was special too.

"What do you call this color?" asked Chen Xin.

"Reddish brown. It's the fashion," answered his younger brother with the air of an expert.

Nannan moved a stool over to a chest of drawers, climbed on it, and turned on the cassette player. The strong rhythm of the music raised everybody's spirits.

"You live well!" The excitement in Chen Xin's voice was obvious.

His elder brother smiled apologetically. After a long pause he said, "I'm glad you're finally back."

His sister-in-law carried in some food, "Now that you're back, you should find a sweetheart and get married."

"I'm old and ugly. Who'd want me?"

That made everyone laugh.

More than ten different dishes were placed on the table: diced pork and peanuts, braised spareribs, crucian carp soup.... Everybody piled food onto Chen Xin's plate. Even Nannan copied them. They went on serving him even when his plate was like a hill, as if to compensate for the ten hard years he had spent away from home. His elder brother almost emptied the stir- fried eel, Chen Xin's favorite dish, onto his plate. Though younger by three years, Chen Xin had always been his brother Chen Fang's protector. Chen Fang, tall and slender, had been nicknamed String Bean. His school marks were high, but outside of school he was poor at sports and had slow reflexes. His legs always got caught in the rope when it was his turn to jump. When playing cops and robbers, the side he was on was sure to lose. Chen Xin always fought for him when no one wanted him. "If you don't want my brother, I won't play either. And if I don't play, I'll make sure there'll be no game." And he meant what he said, so the boys compromised, fearing the terrible havoc he'd wreak on the one hand and hating to lose a popular, funny playmate on the other. Later, when Chen Fang had to wear glasses, he looked so scholarly that his nickname became Bookworm. For some reason Chen Xin considered this even more insulting than the previous one. He brought an end to it by bashing anyone who dared to utter it. When classes were suspended during the Cultural Revolution, he had finished junior middle and his brother senior middle school. The government's policy was clear; only one son could work in Shanghai, the other must go to the countryside. His heartbroken mother had mumbled tearfully, "The palm and the back of my hand.... They are both my flesh and blood." Feeling sorry for her, Chen Xin volunteered, "I'll go to the countryside. Brother's a softy; he'll get bullied. Let him stay in Shanghai. I'll go...." when he set out, Chen Fang had seen him off at the station, standing woodenly behind a group of friends, not daring to meet his eyes. As the train pulled out, Chen Fang moved forward to grasp Chen Xin's hand and run beside the train even after the speeding locomotive pulled them apart.

Chen Xin had finally returned. Overcome by all sorts of emotions, no one was particularly good at expressing them, so they transformed them into action. After supper his elder brother served tea while his wife made up a bed in the hut they had constructed in the courtyard. His younger brother stood in a queue for Chen Xin to go to the public bathhouse. When Chen Xin had eaten his fill and bathed, he lay on the double bed he was to share with his younger brother, feeling as relaxed as if he were drunk. The clean, warm bedding had a pleasant smell. The lamp on the desk beside the bed gave the simple hut a soft glow. Someone had placed a stack of magazines beside his pillow; the family knew and had remembered that he always read himself to sleep. Oh, home. This was home! He had returned home after ten years. Feeling a peace that he had never felt before, he closed his eyes and dozed off without reading. At dusk he woke up. Someone had come in and turned off the light. He opened his eyes in the darkened room and peacefully drifted back to slumber.

* * *

Early in the morning Chen Xin and his younger brother went to the labor bureau to start the formalities. The triangular lot beside the bus stop was filled with tailors' stalls and sewing machines. A young man with a measuring tape hanging round his neck accosted them. "Do you want something made?" They shook their heads and walked away. Curious, Chen Xin turned to look back at the young man who was dressed up like a model, soliciting customers.

His brother tugged at him. "The bus's coming. They're all school-leavers waiting for jobs. Shanghai's full of them." Chen Xin was astonished. His brother, shoving his way onto a bus, stopped at the door and called out to him, "Come on, Second Brother."

"Let's wait for the next one." The bus filled to bursting and the crowd at the bus stop made Chen Xin hesitate.

"More people will come. Get on quick." His brother's voice seemed to come from afar.

Chen Xin was strong. He could push. He shoved and squeezed until he caught the door handle and placed his feet on the steps.

Then he mustered his strength and, amid cries and curses, pushed deeper into the bus to stand beside a window where he could hang on to the back of the seat. But he was crammed in and uncomfortable, bumping against people's heads or backs, having a hard time fitting in. All round him the passengers grumbled.

"Look at the way you're standing!"

"Just like a door plank."

"Outsiders are always so awkward on buses."

"Who're you calling an outsider?" An indignant No.3 squeezed his way over, ready to pick a quarrel. Chen Xin tugged him. "Don't mind them. It's so crowded. Don't fight."

Softly, No.3 gave him a tap. "Turn this way. Right. Hold the seat with your left hand. That's better. See?"

It was true. Chen Xin heaved a long sigh. He finally fitted in with his chest pressed against a back and his back against someone else's chest. At least his feet touched the floor. He turned his head to look and noticed a silent understanding among the passengers. Facing in the same direction, they all stood in a straight line, one behind the other. This way, the bus could fill to capacity. He thought of the remote town he had lived in where passengers squeezed in any old way, no scientific method at all. The bus held fewer people while the crowding and discomfort were the same. Shanghainese could adapt themselves to smaller spaces better.

The female conductor's voice came through a loudspeaker in Beijing and Shanghai dialects: "The next top is Xizang Zhong Road. Those who're getting off please get ready." With royal airs, these women looked proud and disdainful, like strict disciplinarians. But these announcements helped passengers. He recalled again the buses and women conductors in that little town: battered, dusty buses shooting off before their doors were closed; unenthusiastic conductors never announcing stops, closing doors on passengers and catching their clothes in them. They had no rules at all. Things were shipshape in Shanghai. In that sort of environment, you had to do things properly.

When they got off the bus, No.3 took Chen Xin down a street to one of the city's free markets. There were vegetables, fish, poultry, woollen sweaters, sandals, purses and hair clips, and stalls with fried food and meat dumplings. Below a placard announcing folk toys were paper lanterns and clay dolls. Seeing a market like that, Chen Xin had to laugh. What a strong contrast with Shanghai's wealthy, modern Nanjing Road.

"There are a lot of markets like this in Shanghai," explained No.3. "The government encourages school-leavers to be self-employed."

The mention of the unemployed youth made Chen Xin frown. After pausing, he asked, "What was the matter with you, No.3? Why did you fail the university entrance exam again?"

No.3 lowered his head. "I don't know. I guess I'm stupid."

"Will you take it again next year?"

After a long silence, No.3 said haltingly, "I might fail a third time."

That made Chen Xin angry. "You've no confidence in yourself."

No.3 smiled honestly. "I'm not cut out to study. I forget what I learn."

"Your elder brother and I didn't have the chance to continue our studies. You're the only one in the family who can attend a university. But you've no ambition."

No.3 fell silent.

"What are your plans then?"

No.3 gave a laugh but said nothing. Just then someone called out behind them, "Chen Xin!"

They turned to face a woman leading a handsome little boy. She was in her thirties, with long permed hair and stylish clothes. Chen Xin couldn't place her.

"Have I grown so old that you don't recognize me?"

"Why, it's you, Yuan Xiaoxin! You don't look older, just prettier," Chen Xin laughed.

Yuan laughed with him. "Come on. We were in the same group in the countryside for two years, and yet you couldn't place me. What a poor memory!"

"No. It was just that I didn't expect to see you. Weren't you among the first batch to get a job? Are you still at Huaibei Colliery?"

"No. I came back to Shanghai last year."

"How come?"

"It's a long story. How about you?"

"I returned yesterday."

"Oh." She didn't show surprise. "Zhang Xinhu and Fang Fang are back too."

"Good," Chen Xin said excitedly. "So half the group has returned. We must get together sometime. Our hard times are finally over."

She gave a faint smile, revealing fine wrinkles at the corners of her eyes.

"Uncle," chirped the little boy. "You've got white hair like my grandpa."

Chen Xin laughed, bending down to take the boy's hand, "This is your son?" he addressed Yuan.

"He's my sister's son," she explained blushing. "I'm not married. If I were I couldn't have come back."

"Oh." Chen Xin was surprised. Having graduated the same year as Chen Fang, Yuan must be thirty-three or thirty-four. "But why didn't you marry after your return?"

"Well, how shall I put it? One has to wait for an opportunity."

Chen Xin said nothing.

Caressing the little boy's fluffy hair she said softly, "Sometimes I felt that the sacrifices I made to return to Shanghai weren't worth it."

Chen Xin tried to console her, "Don't say that. It's good to be back."

"We'll be late for the film, Aunty," cried the boy.

"Right, we ought to be going." She looked up and smiled at Chen Xin. "Sorry if I dampened your spirits. But you're different. You're a man, and you're young. You'll find happiness."

Chen Xin's heart grew heavy as he watched her disappear into the crowd.

No.3 commented, "She's a dead crab."

"What do you mean?"

"She's over thirty and hasn't got a boyfriend. She's like a dead crab. No hope."

"It isn't that she can't find one. She said she was waiting for someone to come along. Don't you see?"

Whether he understood or not, he answered disapprovingly, "Whatever you say, she's got a big problem. Men in their thirties are married, or else handicapped or ineligible. Eligible ones are hard to please and like young, beautiful girls. There are handfuls of twenty-year-old girls up for grabs."

Chen Xin meant to say that some people were waiting for love. But then he had second thoughts. That was beyond No.3. Youngsters like him were so different from his generation. Throwing a sidelong glance at his brother, he said instead, "You really know a lot."

No.3 looked very proud. The sarcasm was lost on him. Feeling apologetic, Chen Xin added in a kinder tone, "What do you do every day?"

"Nothing much except watch television, listen to the radio and sleep."

"What are your plans?"

He said nothing. When they were walking up the steps of the labor bureau, No.3 confided, "I'd like to get a job."

Chen Xin halted. No.3 turned to urge him, "Come on." His eyes were frank and sincere. Still Chen Xin avoided them.

* * *

He started work at his mother's factory, which was a long way away. It took him an hour and twenty minutes and three buses to get there. Assigned to work at a lathe, he had to learn from scratch; mockingly, he called himself a thirty-year-old apprentice. What he found hard was not the lathe but the adjustment to the new life and the fast pace. He had to run from the first bus to catch the second and then the third. . . . He mustn't miss any of the connections, which meant no smoking or daydreaming. He also found it hard to adjust to three rotating shifts. After a week on night shift it took more than two weeks to catch up on his sleep; as a result he was always tired. Within two months his face grew thinner. People said he looked better that way for the weight he had gained before he came home was not healthy. It was the result of the flour and stodge he had eaten in the North, whereas in Shanghai people ate rice.

Still he was glad he had returned to Shanghai even though his contentment was marred by a feeling of emptiness. Something was missing. The longing of the past ten years, an ache that had affected his sleep and appetite, had come to an end. But it had given him a goal to fight for. Now he was at a loss and felt empty. Maybe he was too happy being back? He must start a new life even though he had not given much serious thought to what it should be like. Things were only just beginning.

Ending the early shift, he dragged his legs, numb after eight hours' standing, to the bathroom, had a bath, changed, and left the factory. At the bus stop passengers spilled from the pavement onto the middle of the street. At least three buses were late. He waited for ten minutes but there was no sign of a bus. The passengers complained, assuming there must have been an accident. Losing patience, Chen Xin started to walk the few stops to catch the second bus. Li, a worker a year younger than he, had once shown him a shortcut. Relying on his memory, he went along a lane to a narrow cobbled street where people on both sides were washing honey buckets, cooking, knitting, reading, doing homework, playing chess or Ping-Pong, or sleeping on door planks, making the little street even narrower. The houses lining it resembled pigeon coops or the squares of a harmonica. Through the small, low windows he saw only beds, large and small, two bunks and camp beds. So, recreation, work, other activities, all had to take place outdoors. What would they do when all those at work came home, or on rainy and snowy days? Suppose a grown-up son found a wife? If . . . behind the colorful shop windows, dazzling billboards, glamorous clothes and the latest film posters, there existed streets that narrow, rooms that crowded, lives that miserable. Shanghai was not as wonderful as one imagined.

It took him half an hour to reach the second bus stop. He shoved in and fitted his six-foot-high body into the smallest space as he had now learned to do, so that he wouldn't be taken for an outsider. It was already six when he got home, hungry and tired, expecting to find steaming hot food waiting for him, but supper was not ready. His mother had been shopping on Huaihai Avenue and had got home late, as it was impossible to rush through the teeming crowds on the streets, in stores, on buses. His sister-in-law had started to cook when she returned home from work. His mother helped wash and chop the vegetables.

"No.3 does nothing but sleep and listen to his transistor radio," his mother said, showing her annoyance. "You could have sliced the meat for me, you layabout."

Frustrated, Chen Xin went over to his dark hut. A transistor radio was buzzing jarringly, half-talking and half-singing between two stations. He jumped in fright when, groping over toward his bed, he almost fell over a leg. His brother sat up and said, "You're back, Second Brother?"

Chen Xin turned on the desk lamp. "You're too lazy, No.3. Why don't you give Mother a hand when you've nothing to do?" he stormed.

"I bought the rice and mopped the floor this afternoon," No.3 said, defending himself.

"So what? When I was your age I was ploughing and harvesting in the countryside."

No.3 fell silent.

"You're twenty this year. You should use your brains and do something useful. Get up. How can you while away your time doing nothing? Pull yourself together and act like a man."

No.3 walked out silently. Chen Fang, just back from work, joined in. "You're an adult, No.3. You should behave like one. We all need some rest when we come home from work. You should've helped."

Chen Xin added from the hut, "If you were studying for the university entrance exam, we wouldn't blame you, but would let you have as much time as you needed. . . ."

No.3 remained silent. His mother interrupted to make peace. "It's all my fault. I didn't tell him what to do before I left. Supper'll soon be ready. Eat some biscuits first. Go and buy some vinegar for me, No.3." When No.3 had left, she told her two elder sons, "I'd rather he stayed at home and didn't roam around and get into trouble. Of all these unemployed youngsters, he's one of the nicest."

Supper was at last ready at half past seven. They ate in his mother's small room. No one felt like talking after the episode with No.3, and with no chatting, no one enjoyed the meal. In an attempt to liven up the atmosphere, the sister-in- law broke the silence by saying, "My bureau has set up a club to help young bachelors who want to get married. Shall I get a form for you to fill in, Chen Xin?"

Chen Xin forced a smile. "Certainly not. I don't want to get married."

"Nonsense," his mother piped up. "Everyone gets married.

With your looks, I'm sure you'll find a wife."

"Tall men like you are very popular nowadays with young girls," said a smiling No.3, who had forgotten all about the reproaches he had received. He was still young.

"Getting married's no joke," his sister-in-law added. "You need to have at least a thousand yuan."

"We'll help even if we go bankrupt. Right, Chen Fang?" his mother asked.

"Hmm," his elder brother mumbled stupidly.

"But even if you've money, but no room, it's still hopeless," his sister-in-law went on.

"If we can't find a room I'll move out and sleep in the lane if he's getting married. Right, Chen Fang?" his mother asked again.

"Sure," his elder brother agreed.

"You mean what you say, Mum?" asked his sister-in-law, smiling.

His mother laughed. "Haven't I always meant what I said?"

"What sort of a joke is that?" Chen Xin put down his bowl. Although the three of them smiled, he sensed they were serious and full of hints. It was highly unpleasant.

He watched television in his brother's room. Before long he felt drowsy and could hardly keep his eyes open. He had to get up very early to go to work so he rose and retired to his hut where No.3 was already in bed listening to the transistor radio, laughing at a comedy show, looking happy and comfortable.

"Bed so early?" Chen Xin asked.

"The television program was awful," No.3 answered, but only when the program ended in applause. He reluctantly turned off the radio.

As usual, Chen Xin read for a few minutes and then switched out the light. In the darkness he heard his brother say, "I wish Dad was still alive. Then you could take his place while I took Mum's. Dad had a better job, working in an office.

Chen Xin's nose tingled. He wanted to hold his brother in his arms but he only turned and said hoarsely, "You should have tried to go to university."

After a while No.3 began to snore. But Chen Xin's urge to sleep had vanished.

No.3 could have had his mother's job but for him. . . .

He had called long distance saying, "No.3 is living in Shanghai. He'll have a way out somehow. This is my only chance. . . ." His mother was silent at the other end. He had repeated, "I left home at eighteen, Mum, and I've been alone for ten years. Eighteen, and I've been all alone for ten years. Ten whole years, Mum." Still silence. He knew that his mother must be weeping and repeating to herself, "The palm and the back of my hand . . . Oh, the palm and the back of my hand . . ." In the end, No.3 gave him the chance, which was only natural. Ten years ago, he had done the same for his elder brother. Like him, his younger brother had not complained or grumbled but was nice to him. Turning in his sleep, No.3 stretched one leg across him again. He did not push it away.

His brother was too lazy. Wouldn't everything be fine and everyone happy if he could enter the university? But not everyone could do that or go to a technical college. No.3, ashamed at not having passed the exam, was amiable to everyone and never defended himself when he was criticized.

Chen Xin sighed. Life in Shanghai was not easy.

* * *

One evening, Aunt Shen, who worked in the same factory as Chen Xin's mother, was to bring a girl over to meet Chen Xin. As this had been arranged by his mother, he couldn't give a flat refusal although he found the situation awkward and silly. "You must start building a new life," said his elder brother. The statement had stunned him. When his new life became so concrete, he was not prepared for it and found it hard to accept. But, on second thought, he couldn't imagine a more significant and important new life. Maybe it just means marrying and having a child? Shaking his head, he smiled wryly, while an emptiness filled him. The ten years of longing for Shanghai, though gnawing, had been mixed with sweetness. It was like a dream, a yearning suffused with imagination. Anticipation was perhaps the best state. He remembered that when he was a child Saturday had always been better than Sunday.

But everyone in the family was full of enthusiasm. Preparations started after lunch. His sister-in-law swept and dusted her room, while his elder brother bought cakes and fruit. They planned to put Nannan to bed early in case he made a faux pas. It had happened once before when his grandmother was matchmaking and the young couple met at their place. Having always been present when grown-ups talked and not really understanding what it all was about, he suddenly pointed at the young man and girl and asked his mother, "Are they getting married, Mum?" It had been very embarrassing.

No.3 was the busiest of all. He suggested that his mother cook lentil soup and offered Chen Xin his best clothes to wear. Chen Xin was annoyed by his excitement, which was just because he had nothing better to do.

His enthusiasm dampened, No.3 still helped cook a large pot of lentil soup and made Chen Xin put on his bell-bottom trousers.

The girl arrived at seven-thirty; hiding shyly behind Aunt Shen and moving quickly over to an armchair in a corner, where she picked up a book to read. With her head lowered in the darkness, no one could see her features clearly.

"Chen Xin is a promising young man. The workers at the factory are very pleased with him. The ten years he spent in the small town in the countryside gave him a lot of experience. He's not irresponsible like new school-leavers," began Aunt Shen.

"Yes, It was hard for him, having to stay far away so long, "said his mother, her eyes glancing over to the girl in the corner.

"How do you like working at a lathe, Chen Xin?" Aunt Shen turned to him. "Standing on your feet for eight hours is quite tiring."

"It's OK. I don't mind it. I did all kinds of work in the countryside," replied Chen Xin, his attention fixed on the corner. He could see nothing except her profile, short hair and wide shoulders.

"Where's your son, Chen Fang? He must be a lively boy."

"He's sleeping. He's a nice boy," Chen Fang answered absent-mindedly.

"He isn't so nice," countered his wife. "He's a little scamp. I don't want him."

"Don't talk like that. No one can take him away from you. Naughty boys are clever boys."

"That's true. . . ." Chen Xin's sister-in-law moved over to the corner. "Come and have some lentil soup."

Someone quicker had got to the corner first and switched on

the standard lamp, saying, "You need some light to read." It was No.3 who had slipped in unnoticed. Chen Xin was ready to throw him out, but he was grateful for his clever intervention.

The girl was bathed in light. All stopped talking and turned to her. Then all turned back to look at one another with disappointed expressions. After a while, his sister-in-law collected herself and said, "Don't read now. Come and have some lentil soup."

Very embarrassed, the girl finished her bowl of soup, wiped her mouth with a handkerchief and announced that she was leaving. No one made any attempt to stop her. After some polite remarks— "Please come again," "Take care of yourself"—they all rose to see her to the door, while Aunt Shen saw her out of the lane alone. This was the custom and all scrupulously obeyed it. Chen Xin, recently back, didn't know the rules. But No.3 stood beside him, showing him what to do.

His mother asked, "How did you like her, Chen Xin?"

He laughed in reply.

"She's no good. Her cheekbones are too high. It's a sign that her husband'll die early," said No.3.

"Don't be silly. No one's asking you."

"She's a bit short on looks," commented his elder brother.

"She's not pretty. I wonder what sort of person she is," said his mother.

The comments stopped when Aunt Shen returned. She addressed Chen Xin with a smile, "She seemed to like you. It all depends on what you think now."

Chen Xin remained silent smiling.

Realizing something was wrong, she added, "She's a nice girl, honest and simple. She's twenty-eight. Her parents are well-to-do. They don't mind whether the young man is well off or not, provided that he's nice. If he has no room, he can live with them. They have a spare room. . . . You'd better talk it over and give me a reply as soon as possible. . . . You must trust me, Chen Xin. I won't let you down. I've known you since you were a kid."

The whole family saw her to the entrance of the lane.

When they returned, his elder brother asked, "What's your impression of her?"

Chen Xin gave a frank reply. "Not good."

"Looks aren't important. You can date her for a while," suggested his sister-in-law.

"Looks are very important. Otherwise, my elder brother wouldn't have married you," Chen Xin teased her, causing general laughter.

His sister-in-law punched him on the shoulder, half laughing and half angry.

"I too think you could date her, Chen Xin. You mustn't go by looks alone," said his elder brother.

"Looks are very important when two people are introduced to each other. What would I fall in love with if not with her looks?" Chen Xin had his reasons.

"She doesn't have to be a beauty, but at least presentable." No.3 had to voice his opinion.

"I think she's OK, Mum," his sister-in-law said, turning to his mother. "Besides, she has a room. That's very important in Shanghai."

Chen Xin retorted, "I'm marrying a girl, not a room."

"But it's an important factor. She's not ugly except that her face is a bit wide. Her eyes and eyebrows are all right."

"Forget the eyes and brows. For one thing, she doesn't attract me at all."

No.3 laughed. This was something new to him.

"It's all for your own good. You can't live on attraction," said his sister-in-law.

"I agree," his elder brother added.

His mother broke in, "Let him decide for himself."

"Yes, yes," his elder brother seconded.

"Well, let's leave it at that," cried Chen Xin. It was all so pointless. "Don't bother about it any more, Mum. I'll find my own wife. If I can't find a good wife, I'll remain a bachelor all my life." He retired to his hut.

In his dreams, a pair of eyes smiled at him, a pair of jade black eyes, in the shape of a new moon, eyes that smiled sweetly and gently. He woke up. From his window, only one-foot square, he saw a new moon.

Ah, eyes like a new moon. Where was she? Who was she? In the school where he had taught, every morning on his way to breakfast in the canteen he saw a girl on an old-fashioned bicycle taking a shortcut from the back gate to the front. Elegant and petite, she always turned to look at him with those eyes. . . . He was confident that if he had asked, where are you going? she would have replied. He had never asked, and he would never know where she came from and where she was bound. Many people took a shortcut through his school. The front gate led to a hospital, cultural center, cultural troupe, and a machinery plant. At the back gate were a department store, playground, and cotton mill. She had passed by him hundreds, thousands of times and he had let her go even though he liked her and the sight of her made him happy. But his mind was set on Shanghai, his sole destination. He had finally returned to Shanghai, while she had become something in his past, something that would never return, leaving only a beautiful memory. He had few regrets as Shanghai carried more weight than a girl. Still he was a little sorry.

He remembered his school with its big garden, bigger than any school in Shanghai. The campus had a boulevard and a grove. In summer he iced melons in the well in front of his room. Several students used to bring food to him. But he had left these loyal students without saying good bye, afraid of complicating matters. He missed that school. That part of his life had touched his heart.

* * *

One morning his elder brother surprised them by telling his mother that his family wanted a separate residence card. He stammered, "Then . . . we can have . . . two rations of eggs. . . . Two rations of everything."

He avoided his mother's eyes when she looked up silently. Chen Xin wondered why he stuttered, as if it were something very embarrassing. After all it was a bright idea to get extra rations, which were given according to residence cards. He laughed. "What a brainstorm. How did you ever think of it?"

But his joke had made his brother flee in shame. His mother fixed her eyes on him, saying nothing.

Chen Xin left for work. Following behind him, No.3 whispered as if it were a secret, "You know why elder brother wanted to have another residence card?"

"He wanted more eggs. . . ."

"Of course not," No.3 cut him short. "He's after the room."

"The room?" Chen Xin halted, puzzled.

"Right," No.3 affirmed. "The twenty-two-meter room belongs to him once he has his own residence card. It must be our sister-in-law's idea."

"Let him have it," Chen Xin moved on. "You don't put your brains to good use, yet you're very quick in such matters."

That day, Chen Xin was preoccupied, his brother's suggestion recurring in his mind. He had a feeling it implied something more. Then his younger brother's words rang in his ears: "He's after the room." He also recalled how his sister-in-law had harped about his marrying a girl with a room. Did it really mean that? Instinctively he waved his hand to deny it. "It can't be," he said almost aloud, scaring himself. Then he had to laugh.

When he returned home after work, he heard his mother saying to his elder brother, "You can't separate from us. Chen Xin has a right to that room too. He has been away working in the countryside for ten years. If he marries, you must divide it. Isn't that right?" His mother asked again when he didn't answer, "Isn't that right?" Only then did he echo, "Right." Bringing in a dish, his wife banged it loudly on the table. By coincidence?

A heavy cloud hung over the dinner table. His elder brother and wife sulked while his mother apologetically piled food in their bowls. No.3 kept throwing meaningful glaces at Chen Xin. "See?" he seemed to say. Disgusted, Chen Xin turned away, looking at no one. Luckily Nannan brightened the atmosphere by standing up and sitting down on the chair asking for this and that. He had thrown away his spoon and was grabbing with his fingers. His grandmother caught his hand and spanked him lightly on the palm. No.3 made a face and cried "Hurrah!" while Nannan declared proudly, "It didn't hurt at all."

Everybody laughed. But Nannan's mother dragged him down from his chair and scolded, "You rude boy. You don't appreciate favors. You should thank your lucky stars that you're not kicked out." The laughter froze as everyone wondered whether to continue laughing or look solemn. "Oh, boy!" No.3 said softly to ease the embarrassment.

Chen Xin's mother's face fell. "What do you mean?"

"Nothing," his sister-in-law countered.

"I know what you were driving at." His mother brought it into the open. "It's the room."

"No. I don't care about the room. But when my son grows up, I won't let him marry a girl if he doesn't have a room."

"Don't rub it in. I may be poor but I love all my sons and treat them all equally. The palm and the back of my hand, they're all my flesh. Chen Xin had to leave home because of Chen Fang. You shouldn't dn't be so ungrateful." The old lady wept.

"Ungrateful? When other girls marry, they all get a suite of furniture including chairs and a standard lamp. When I married Chen Fang what did he have? Have I ever complained? And we never failed to send Chen Xin parcels and money every festival. What complaints can you have about such a daughter-in-law?" She wept too.

Chen Fang was stunned, not knowing whom to console.

No.3 fled. He was useless, disappearing whenever a real crisis occurred.

"Don't cry." Chen Xin stood up. He was disturbed and agitated. "I don't want the room, Mother. I'm not marrying. I'm quite happy just back in Shanghai."

His mother was even sadder. Stealing a glance at him, his sister-in-law wept more softly.

At night, when everybody had retired to bed, his elder brother entered the hut smoking a cigarette. "Don't mind your sister-in-law," he said. "She's not mean, though she likes to grumble. I had no savings when we married. We had nothing except a bed and she's never complained. These last years, by scrimping and scraping, we bought some furniture and decorated the room. She was content with the improvement and wants to keep it. She's not bad and knows we should divide the room into two for you but just finds it hard to accept. I'll talk her round gradually."

"Forget it, Brother," Chen Xin stopped him. "I meant what I said. I swear I don't want the room. Please reassure her. Just don't separate from us. The old lady likes to have her whole family together."

His brother broke down, putting his arms around Chen Xin's shoulders. Though Chen Xin wanted to take him into his arms, he pushed him away and pulled the quilt over his head. Ten years had toughened him.

It was not easy to live in Shanghai.

      * * *

Chen Xin, used to a carefree life, was very disturbed. The following morning, his day off, he got up at daybreak and went out, telling no one. He wanted to take a walk. Accustomed to the vast spaces in the north, he found Shanghai oppressive. High-rise buildings blocked out the breeze and the crowds made the air stale. Where could he go? He would go to the Bund.

He got off the bus and moved ahead. He could see the ships anchored in the Huangpu River on the other side of the road. On the bank there were green trees and red flowers, and old people doing taijiquan exercises, children playing and young people strolling and taking photos. He felt lighter. He crossed over to the river, the symbol of Shanghai. It was not blue, as he recalled, but muddy and stinking. Everything should be viewed from a distance, perhaps. A closer look only brought disappointment.

He came to the Bund Park, bought a ticket and went in. A fountain cascaded down a rock into a pool, rippling the water. He recalled that long, long ago, the water didn't fall directly into the pool but onto a statue of an umbrella under which a smiling mother and two children were sheltered. He had liked the sculpture so much when he first saw it as a child that he had stared at it refusing to be led away. It was like a symbol of his life. His father had died early and his mother had brought up her three sons, overcoming many difficulties. By sticking together, they had given one another warmth in hard times. When a typhoon hit Shanghai, the four of them had huddled together on the bed. The lightning, thunder, and howling wind had frightened and excited them. His younger brother had made exaggerated shrieks, his mother playfully blamed the sky, and Chen Xin, acting as a protector, sat beside the light switch, which his elder brother, having just learned something about electricity, was scared of. The storm was frightening and exhilarating. And there was a warmth. It was this that had attracted and drawn him home.

Water, falling on the pond, caused monotonous, empty ripples. A drop fell on his hand. He suddenly realized that it was from his eyes. What was the matter with him? When he had left home and his mother had sobbed her heart out, he hadn't shed a tear.

Today ... he experienced a tremendous disappointment, as if a most precious thing had suddenly been shattered. He turned and left the park.

The stores were opening and salespeople were removing the shutters outside the shop windows, which displayed a dazzling array of goods. The pedestrians on the street, so well dressed they looked like models, made his head spin. Unconsciously he stopped outside a shop window: Plump dolls with enormous heads were shooting down a slide, two others were swinging in each other's arms. In the background several Young Pioneers were flying model planes, which circled in a blue sky.

He couldn't move. It all reminded him of his childhood, his youth and the golden memory he had when he left Shanghai. He had mistaken this memory for Shanghai, to which he had struggled to return. Back home, he found he could never recapture the past.

The pedestrians increased, edging from the pavement onto the street. They seemed to be walking in file, and it was hard to move quickly. Life in such a compressed world was difficult. He remembered the struggles on buses. In restaurants, he had to stand beside tables for seats, and then others waited for him to leave while he ate. In the parks three couples sat on one bench and in the Yu-yuan Park lined up to have a picture taken on a rock mountain. Humans created not only wonders, but also problems. Why must he squeeze in? Why?

People rubbed shoulders, toes touched heels. Though they lived so closely, they were all strangers. Not knowing or understanding one another, they were proud and snobbish. He remembered a song his brother had recorded a few days ago: "People on earth are thronged like stars in the sky. Stars in the sky are as distant as people on earth."

A town was different. It was calm, maybe a little too deserted. One could run and stroll at ease on the streets and breathe freely. And in a small town, the same people meeting constantly knew one another by sight, nodding to and greeting all acquaintances, creating a warm, friendly feeling. So a big city had its drawbacks, while a small town its advantages.

He moved with the stream of people, not caring where he was

heading. He was dazed. The bittersweet yearning in the past decade disappeared, and with it the fullness he had felt in the past ten years. He had arrived at his destination. What was his next step? One must have a destination. Should he follow the new trend and equip himself with Western-style clothing, leather shoes, bellbottom trousers, and a cassette recorder ... then find a sweet-heart and get married? ... Yes. He could start doing that though it required effort and hard work. But would he find happiness if fashionable clothes concealed a heavy and miserable heart? If he married for the sake of getting married and the wife he chose was not understanding, wouldn't he be adding a burden to his life? Again he missed the new-moon eyes and the chances he had lost. A man's destination must be happiness, not misery. He suddenly felt that the destination he sought ought to be something bigger. Yes, bigger.

His spirits lifting, the dark clouds parted slightly to let through a dim light. Dim and hazy, it was still a light.

"Chen Xin."

He halted. Someone had called him.

"Chen Xin." He turned and saw a bus plowing slowly through the crowds on the street. His elder brother was leaning halfway out the window, reaching out to him. Behind him was his sister-in-law. They seemed agitated.

Shocked, he chased the bus. His elder brother grabbed his hands and gazed at him speechless and wooden, as he had done ten years ago when he ran after the train. Chen Xin was touched. His sister-in-law grabbed him too. "Chen Xin, you mustn't do anything drastic." She broke down.

"What nonsense!" Chen Xin laughed, tears rolling down his face.

"Come home," said his brother.

"Yes. I'll come home." Home was, after all, home. Quarrels were caused by poverty. I made you suffer, my loved ones. He was suddenly ashamed of having used the ten years as a trump card. His mother, two brothers and sister-in-law had also endured those difficult years. And besides, life meant joy, fun, pleasure. For instance, the boulevard, tree groves, the well, innocent pupils, and eyes like a new moon. ... He had overlooked them all.

But ahead of him there would be another ten, twenty and thirty years, a long, long time. He must give his future some serious thought.

Another train was leaving the station. Where was it bound? He knew that his destination would be farther, greater, and he would have to wander more than a decade, maybe two or three decades, a lifetime. He might never settle down. But he believed that once he arrived at his true destination, he would have no doubts, troubles, or sense of rootlessness.

Translated by Yu Fanqin

And the Rain Patters On

The rain begins to pitter-patter down, as people waiting for a bus scurry under the eaves of a building. A stylishly dressed girl does not move, however, but draws a collapsible umbrella from her little handbag. A pattern of peacock feathers on the umbrella can be made out under the street lamp. Beneath it the girl looks like a peacock with tail fanned out. Wenwen does not move either. She simply wraps a long white scarf around her head. She looks a rustic figure. Fashionable Shanghai girls have already begun to top their curls with berets set at an angle. But Wenwen doesn't care. She quietly stands next to the peacock-girl, seemingly oblivious to the sharp contrast. All of Wenwen's old classmates who have returned to Shanghai from the countryside with her have been quick to perm their hair and step into high heels. Whenever they see her they say, "You simply don't care enough about your appearance." "Who says?" Wenwen retorts and leaves it at that.

In the distance two yellow headlights emerge from the darkness. The bus comes into sight. The people move from under the eaves toward the curb. The peacock-girl folds away her fantail. Wenwen however steps back. She seems to be hesitating. Does she want to get on the bus?

As the vehicle nears, the sleepy voice of a female conductor sounds loudly over the bus' public address system announcing

the name of the stop. The waiting people surge forward expect-
antly to meet its arrival and then step back again as it slows to a
halt. The bus is quite empty so everyone will be able to get on. But
late at night the desire to return home becomes urgent; only after
actually getting on the bus is the trip home assured. Wenwen
instinctively runs toward the bus. A drop of cold rain splashes
against her forehead and she comes to a sudden halt.

"Well, are you getting on or not?" The shout is obviously
directed at Wenwen since she is the only person left at the stop.
She seems to come to some realization and moves forward a step.
But just as she is about to step into the bus another large
raindrop splashes against her forehead. It runs down the bridge
of her nose. It is raining, just as it had been that evening.

Wenwen checks herself and backs away from the bus. She
hears the sound of the door closing, "chrr ... bang," and the bus
starts off. "Lunatic!" the conductor mutters. This exclamation
sounding through the sensitive microphone seems to rip the
stillness of the night and echo on to the ends of the world.
"Lunatic! Am I a lunatic?" Wenwen asks herself. Now she is a
solitary figure standing on a suddenly silent street pondering
over the necessity of walking home the distance of seven long bus
stops. Wenwen can't help shuddering as the night grows deeper
and the rain falls harder.

She does not feel any real regrets however. A thought, formerly
hazy, now becomes clear. Perhaps he will appear now, wearing
his raincoat, riding his bicycle.... Hadn't he said, "Any time you
are in trouble, for instance, when it's raining and there are no
more buses, someone will be sure to appear and come to your
aid." Having said that, he had gotten on his bicycle and flown off
into the night. The speeding bicycle spokes had left a reflection of
shining whirling circles on the rain-washed road. Who will come
to help this time. His is the only image that comes to mind.

A dense misting rain is falling and making a soft swishing
sound. Wenwen pulls her scarf tighter about her head. Both
hands push deep into her overcoat pockets as she follows the
bus down the road. Two bicycles come up from behind and fly
by. They quickly disappear in the misty sheets of rain. Because of
the rain everyone is rushing home, but she....

How was it that she had been "late for the bus" that time? She remembers. Old Ai had been chatting with her till quite late. Old Ai was Wenwen's workshop supervisor, also a kindly old lady, like a favorite aunt. She liked Wenwen, and Wenwen's mother had great faith in Old Ai. People said Old Ai and Wenwen had been brought together by fate. Old Ai had introduced a "boy-friend" to Wenwen. His name was Yan and he was a university student who had entered school through the exam system that had been instituted with educational reform.

"You two can get to know each other," mother had said to Wenwen. "Why do we have to get to know each other?" Wenwen had asked quietly? After some hesitation her mother had replied, "For love." In an even quieter voice Wenwen had said, "Love is not like that." How can this kind of "introduction" lead to love? What a farce, Wenwen thought to herself bitterly. An "introduction" was something contrived, arranged beforehand, like a race. Both parties come up to the starting line and at the sound of a starting gun they are off and running: meet-get-to- know-each-other-marriage. In the past Wenwen had believed love must be something very beautiful. Her brother had mocked her, "A white cloud floating on the horizon, a red sail gliding on the sea, a mystical prince holding out his hand to you that's your idea, right?!"

Wenwen had neither acknowledged nor refuted her brother's sarcasm. She didn't know if love really was a white cloud or a red sail. But she did know that love was more beautiful, better than those things, whether from out at sea or on the horizon. She had believed that such true feelings really did exist, and were waiting for her. In her heart love was like an unpainted canvas, a soundless song. This was the purest of beauty, a boundless beauty a beauty she could not be without. If she ever lost this feeling, life would be incomplete. Of course, this was how she had felt in the past. Under incessant winds and scorching sun the beauty had faded. Yet, no matter what, the crack of a starting gun could never takes its place. "No, never!" Wenwen shook her head resolutely.

Again her brother had mocked, "A white cloud floating on the horizon, a red sail gliding on the sea. . . ." He had gone on, "But don't you see, as soon as the boat comes into port it will be inspected at Wusongkou, and if its origin is not clear it won't be allowed to dock in Shanghai. If the prince has no residency card then there won't be any grain or cotton ration coupons, no sugar, no soap, no bean products. Wenwen be realistic!" This marine biology major of the class of 1970 had studied his specialty for just one year. Then for four years it was making revolution, then a year working on a farm, and finally, though nobody knows why, he had been assigned to teach music at a high school.... Now, his only recurring worry was whether he would be able to buy enough seafood to show off his culinary skills. This was probably the last sorry remnant of what had once been his passion for the sciences.

"Crazy!" mother had exclaimed in exasperation. Wenwen herself had laughed, but it was a laughter infused with sadness and futility, as if she were laughing at her own past. That Comrade Yan had seemed a self-respecting type. He hadn't come around and made a nuisance of himself pestering Wenwen, and this had given her a good opinion of him. But Old Ai had felt the hesitating stage had lasted too long. After all of three months Wenwen still had not given any indication. That evening at shift change, Old Ai had pulled Wenwen aside and said, "I've watched that boy grow up...." After the elderly lady had told her the young man's life story Wenwen had run out the factory gate to the bus stop, only to see the last bus pull away. And then it had started to rain....

It had started to rain then just as it had this time, drop after drop falling on her forehead, and then it had begun to fall continuously in a fine mist. To Wenwen, the pitter-patter of the rain sounds like people in hushed conversation.

Moisture accumulates on Wenwen's forehead and a bead of water drips down off her brow. She sticks out her tongue and catches the droplet, then continues on her way. Before she knows it she has arrived at another bus stop. Wenwen again asks herself, "Am I a lunatic?" "No!" she quickly replies. "He still might come, when I least expect it, just when I am about to give up hope. Just like that night...."

On that night Wenwen had shouted "Wait, wait!" after the departing bus and had started out in pursuit. She had known that her legs could not match the speed of the bus, but she had run after it anyway. It was all she could do, and people are always reluctant to throw away their last hope. As long as there was still some ray of hope she would run and run, until it had disappeared. A bicycle had passed her by, and even it was falling farther and farther behind the bus. Yet Wenwen had run on and again called out "Wait, wait!" Her shouts had sounded desperate and pitiful in the silent night. The bicycle had turned around. On a deserted street why shouldn't he have thought that the "Wait, wait!" had been for him. The bicycle had come back and stopped before Wenwen. The memories of that night rush back to her now.

"No, no, I didn't mean you." Wenwen waved her hand despondently as she watched the bus' tail-lights disappear in the distance. She involuntarily lifted her head to glance at the sunken face of the dripping heavens.

"I'll give you a lift," the bicyclist said. He wore a raincoat and a rain hat covered half his face, yet she sensed that he was a young man.

"On your bike?" Wenwen's eyes lit up, but only for an instant, for she was immediately on her guard. What was his real motive? She shook her head, "No!"

"It's okay, the traffic police are off duty. If we do run into any, I'll just go like this (he raised his left hand) and you can hop down from the bicycle."

Wenwen liked his misunderstanding of her refusal, and this made her relax a little. Droplets of water fell from her hair as she once more shook her head. It was raining harder now, and she had quite a few bus stops to walk. She couldn't help taking another look at the bicycle.

With his rain hat covering his eyes he had not seen Wenwen's hesitation and urged, "Quick, get on, it's raining harder." It was true, it was raining harder and harder, the soft swishing sound had turned into a roar.

"You're not getting on? Well, I'll be going then," he said blandly and got up onto his bicycle.

"Hey, wait a minute." Wenwen became anxious. If he went there would be only herself on the deserted road. She forgot her fears and ran to the bicycle. She got up on the luggage carrier behind him.

He put his feet to the pedals and the bicycle shot forward.

Wenwen almost fell off and reached forward to steady herself. But she quickly drew her hands back and clutched onto the bicycle frame instead. Suddenly she became nervous. Who is this person? Where was he taking her? Oh, oh, you've been too rash. She called out suddenly, "Where are you going?"

Her shouted question startled him and the bicycle wavered. He slowed down and said, "Follow the bus route, right?"

Right, but he had seemed a bit too quick on the uptake, which increased Wenwen's uneasiness.

"Right?" he turned his head to ask, and the rain hat slid back on his head.

Wenwen nodded without uttering a sound. She had seen his eyes, large, bright and very clear. They were eyes that seemed able to penetrate to the very bottom of everything. Wenwen felt more relaxed, but she still couldn't be at ease with this stranger, even if he did have a pair of honest eyes. Eyes? Hmmph! Wenwen shrugged her shoulders bitterly. What do eyes prove? In the past there had been another nice pair of eyes, but . . . she suddenly sighed.

The young man peddled hard against the wind. With the added burden it looked like he was struggling. He was leaning forward, his broad shoulders were going up and down. Wenwen, sitting behind such shoulders, was protected from the rain. she raised her head and looked at him. Her sense of unease would not go away. Might he have dishonorable intentions? He could very easily turn into a side street or lane. The road was dead quiet, the traffic police had gone, and yet he continued to follow the bus route. He didn't seem to have any inclination to turn into an alley or dark place. They had already passed three bus stops and were passing a mid-road flower bed when he suddenly let go of one handle bar and wiped the water from his face and head. The water inadvertently splashed onto Wenwen's face. She closed her eyes tightly, lowered her head, and laughed at herself for being so suspicious.

"Where do you live?" the young man asked.

Ah ha! Now it starts. Wenwen had become vigilant again. He would go on to ask her name, and then he would say, in typical fashion, shall we make friends? Hmmph! She had heard all this before. The method of that boy had been much more poetic. The first thing he had said was, "I seem to know you from some-where." But later he.... Wenwen closed her eyes somewhat sadly.

"Where is your home? Where should I stop?" the young man asked again. Only then did Wenwen realize that she was not on a bus that would halt at each stop. No matter what, however, she couldn't tell him the address. She only said, "It will be alright if you stop at the third bus stop from here."

The rain slackened but raindrops continued falling. Even though his shoulders had afforded some protection, Wenwen's overcoat had become drenched and water was dripping down off her hair. She could only lower her head, close her eyes and submit to the rain's assault.

"Beautiful!" the young man suddenly exclaimed in a soft voice.

What's beautiful? Wenwen opened her eyes with a start. What was happening? The rainy night had turned into a golden world. Its glow flooded her heart with warmth and gentleness. Was she dreaming?

"Look at the street lamps!" The young man seemed to have heard Wenwen's silent question. So it was the street lamps. On this part of the road they were a golden orange in color. "Do you like it?"

"Who wouldn't like it?" Wenwen answered earnestly.

"Oh, there are many who wouldn't care. Today money is what people are concerned about. Money can buy food and clothes how great! This light, though, can't even be touched and no one can get anything from it. Yet I often wonder what the street would be like without this light." As he said this he looked back at Wenwen.

"And not only the street ...," Wenwen continued his line of thought. Then she discovered the bicycle was stopping and the young man got off. He unbuttoned his raincoat and, before Wenwen knew what was happening, had shaken it out and draped it over her shoulders. Had he seen Wenwen shivering like a drenched cat or had the golden glow softened him? She could not tell.

"I don't need it! I don't need it!" Wenwen raised her hand to push off the raincoat. Trying to decline his offer, with all her reservations gone now, she suddenly felt embarrassed.

"Take it! Take it! I'm in good shape. As soon as any rain falls on me it evaporates. Look, I'm steaming all over!" True, a wisp of steam was rising over his head. "How far from the bus stop do you live?"

With no more hesitation, Wenwen told him the street, the alley, the building, the door number everything. In the warmth of the golden world all precautions had become superfluous.

"Look up ahead," the young man said in a lowered voice, as if he were afraid of disturbing a beautiful dream.

Ahead of them was a sky-blue world. The street lamps on that section of the road were all a light blue in color. "I come this way every day, and I always slow down when I ride through here. And you?"

"I'm always in a crowded bus. I've never noticed." Wenwen answered honestly but could not help feeling a twinge of regret.

"You won't be able to do that again," the young man assured her. The bicycle moved very slowly, as if reluctant to leave. But, after all, it was only one section of the road and the bicycle would have to pass out of it before long. When they left the sky-blue world it suddenly felt much colder, much darker. The night was deeper, quieter, and that conquered sense of wariness and fear crept back into her heart. Fortunately, they soon arrived in front of Wenwen's home. The bicycle came to a gradual halt. Wenwen got off and ran into the portico where she took off the raincoat and handed it back to the young man, saying, "Thanks for its use. Thanks!" She was home and she felt free of anxiety, all light and easy.

The young man put on his raincoat. Even though he was soaked through he was full of vigor. "Thanks for what? If you hadn't run into me, someone else would have done the same for you."

"Really!" he continued earnestly. "When I was working in the countryside, one time I travelled to the commune headquarters to get a work notification form for a transfer to a factory. When I reached the headquarters I discovered that someone else had already taken the position. I furious. On my way back, my bike and I took a nasty spill off of a dike. My leg was broken and I couldn't move. There was no village within ten miles and not a person in sight. So I just closed my eyes and lay there. Suddenly, the ear to the ground heard the sound of approaching footsteps. I wanted to get a look at the person, but my eyes wouldn't open. That person seemed to put some grass on my leg. I guessed it was some medicinal herb because then I was able to struggle to my feet."

"It was a dream," Wenwen interrupted, even though she had been spellbound by his words.

"It was a dream, but not long afterwards a group of children out cutting grass for the pigs really did come by. And they managed to carry me to the commune hospital."

"Really. Anytime you are in trouble, for instance, when it's raining and there are no more buses, someone will be sure to appear and come to your aid." After saying that he got back on his bicycle and disappeared into the distance.

.. Wenwen passes another bus stop and still no one has come. She can't help stopping and looking around. She realizes that she is b ing silly. The young man had probably just been making casual conversation. How could she take it so seriously? What he ha said had been very moving. But Wenwen had lost all faith in life during the past ten years. Was it possible that something of tha. faith had returned, called back by the words of that stranger? And who could tell whether he had told the truth or had made it all up? Wenwen reproaches herself for being once more charmed by nice-sounding words. She should have come to her senses long ago. When he who had been sent to her by the white clouds and red sails had said, "We aren't suited for each other," she should have woken up.

Him! She didn't know if he had come from over the horizon or from the sea. He had stood on a ground strewn with shards of glass. Sunlight shining on the glass had reflected multi-colored rays onto his form. . . .

Those had been the days of "return to classes and make revolution." Wenwen had taken up her long neglected bookbag and happily gone off to school. A night-long fight had just ended on the campus, the windows of the main education building were glassless, like eye-sockets that had lost their eyeballs. Carrying her bookbag, Wenwen had walked slowly over the broken glass toward the school gate.

It was then that she had seen him. He was not wearing a red

armband, but like her was carrying a bookbag. What was he waiting for? Was he waiting for Wenwen? She didn't know. As she walked by him he had turned and walked with her out of the school gate. Suddenly he had spoken:

"I seem to know you from somewhere."

"The same school!" Wenwen had replied indifferently.

"It wasn't at school," he had insisted.

Wenwen had been puzzled and stopped.

"Where was it?" He was trying hard to remember.

Wenwen had become perplexed, and she too had suddenly felt that she had seen him somewhere.

"In a dream." His lips had formed those words. Had he really said that, or had it been her imagination? Anyway, Wenwen had smiled.

They had fallen in love soon after that first meeting and they had found true mutual understanding, not through words, but through each other's eyes. And what a pair of eyes they were! Sincere, deep. There was so much that she could see in them. . . . Now the blank canvas was filled with color. The soundless song had found a melody. Wenwen had put all her heart and soul into this love. She was intoxicated, she forgot everything else. She forgot about her own physical existence, the passage of time. Yet time moved on relentlessly, and class after class of students inevitably graduated. Their turn came too. He had become restless and anxious, and when he finally received notification of a job at a mine he went wild with joy. Wenwen had been happy too, because he wasn't worried anymore.

Then Wenwen received her assignment. She and all her classmates were sent to work in production brigades in the countryside. Because she would be parted from him, she was somewhat sad. But surely faithful true love would make up for this misfortune. Yet he had said, "We are not suited for each other." This was something that Wenwen had never imagined could happen. Love had been crushed by the problems of where you lived and how you made a living. How could love be so fragile? And yet it was true. This was life, real and practical, much more so than white clouds and red sails. Wenwen hadn't even a chance to cry before she had been whisked off on a train going north. The paintings and songs in her heart had all vanished.

Only a barren wasteland had remained. Somehow, at some time, however, that barren wasteland had once again become fertile. Had that moistening spring rain done this?

After that spring shower Wenwen had gone out every evening. She would always first run out onto the balcony and look about. When she worked the daytime shift, before coming into the house, she would pause a few steps off and look around. Was she hoping that out of some shadow or from around some corner he would appear with an earnest, kindly mien, "So, we meet once more?" People today are all so cunning. They pay a price, but only in order to gain much more in return. Those eyes may seem honest and caring, but who could be sure?

But he never appeared. Ten days, twenty, a month, and still no sign of him. Yet she still often went to look down from the balcony. Perhaps it had become a habit. And later some vague sense of expectation merged with it. Why, who knows? Perhaps precisely because he never came again, Wenwen began to recall most vividly their parting, those last few words. . . . As she looked back upon it all now, she no longer remembered her fears and caution. From beginning to end her memories were immersed in the glow of gold and blue light.

* * *

Through the heavy mist Wenwen approaches the fourth bus stop. The rain stops and its soft voices fade away. Occasional drops of water fall from the eaves and splash on the ground. She sighs softly, unwinds her scarf. Then, again, slowly, hope rises in her heart. Maybe he knew that it would not rain heavily today, that it would not last long. Maybe next time, when it really rains, when she would be in real trouble. . . . Even Wenwen herself cannot explain it. This hope, why won't it go away, die? It is only a beautiful fantasy. And yet, how much she believes it. She has placed all her faith in him.

Last Sunday she had told Comrade Yan, on one of his rare visits, "I already have a 'friend'." He had gone away. No sadness or anger. He was very realistic, not vain in the least. As long as there was no pretence on either side, their parting could not be a sorrowful or angry one. As soon as Yan had gone, Wenwen's brother had rushed out of the kitchen where he had been frying fish. "Wenwen, are you crazy? What 'friend'?"

She had insisted quietly, "If I tell you I have one, I have one!"

"Old Ai understands both of your situations. Under such circumstances being introduced to such a 'friend' is very reliable," her mother had urged gently.

"I have one!" Wenwen raised her voice. Again she thought of the golden light and the young man saying, "This light cannot be touched."

"Oh, I know. On the horizon, out at sea. ..."

"You are the one who should go out to sea," Wenwen had cut in angrily. "Didn't you once have dreams too? About the sea? Where are they all now? Where? In your frying pan!"

Her outburst had silenced the brother for a moment. But he soon recovered. "This is life, life! All you have are daydreams!" He put his hands on her shoulders, and pleaded in earnest, "You must not hold up your life for some romantic fantasy. You've already paid the price."

Wenwen had shaken off her brother's hands and turned away. She had pressed her face against the French window that opened onto the balcony, her eyes searching in the shadows under the trees below.

* * *

Several bicycles, carrying with them the sounds of soft music and laughter, approach from behind. Some young men, with a girl on the back of each bicycle, pass by. Perhaps they have just come from a dance. They are far ahead now, only a single strain of music lingers above the otherwise silent street, "Beautiful flowers don't often bloom and good times are hard to come by. ..."

Wenwen shakes her head. Her short wet braids slap against her cheeks. She hadn't noticed when it had started to rain again. Life holds many joys, and certainly the right to dream is one of them. Wenwen didn't want any of the others, just this one. Even though it had brought her pain she still wanted it, insisted on it. If she didn't have her dreams, what would life be ...? Wenwen is also vaguely conscious that she still believes, and always has, that dreams can come true. Just like the golden light glowing up ahead. It looks so vague, indistinct, not touchable, like some far-off vision. And yet it really does exist, bright and shining, turning the solemn black of the night into a beautiful golden glow. And when someone walks by a long shadow is cast. Without dreams, without ideals, without the yearning for human friendship, what would life be like?

Wenwen walks into the warm embrace of the golden glow. She pauses every now and then, her heart full of hope. Will he come? Maybe. He had said, "Anytime you are in trouble, for instance, when it's raining and there are no more buses, someone will be sure to appear and come to your aid."

"Who are you?" Wenwen asks.

"I am who I am," he smiles.

"Are you a dream?"

"Dreams can come true."

The sky-blue world, as if veiled in gauze, now spreads out before her, pure and peaceful. Wenwen walks into it smiling.

The rain, misting down, is again making a low swishing sound. It washes the road clean and bright, lighting up the fresh, sky-blue, murmuring world.

Translated by Michael Day

Life in a Small Courtyard

J ust as we returned from our tour, the new building of the Municipal Song and Dance Ensemble had at last been completed. Meanwhile, the houses in the old, small courtyard near the East Railway Station, which had originally been our headquarters, were now to be used as accommodation for our families. Moreover, it was rumored that the station square was to be enlarged and our small courtyard was just within the limit of those houses marked for demolition. It meant that in the near future the authorities would reallocate us new living quarters. The future looked good.

Within a couple of days, the rehearsal hall, together with the small stage in the courtyard, had been divided into more than ten separate rooms; the building used for storing the sets was also divided into four rooms. Even the kitchen was transformed into two rooms. No reason to turn up your nose at our untidy small courtyard; it allowed some young couples to get married, and had also enabled a number of families of three generations crowded into a single room to separate. As a result, A'ping and I were given a room in the former rehearsal hall. Though it was by no means large, neither was it too small. When the new living quarters were allocated we would be able to get a small flat. Before long, all the rooms in the courtyard, except an eight-square-meter room beside the lavatory, were occupied. Thus, the housing problem of the Municipal Song and Dance Ensemble was, at last, solved. Even more, the two sunniest and biggest office rooms, which could be exchanged later for a suite of three rooms and a kitchen, was now being occupied by Huang Jian, the son of the director of the Cultural Bureau, and his wife Li Xiuwen, who were not members of our troupe.

Originally, these two rooms had been left vacant. Perhaps we all realized that such good rooms could not belong to us. Even if we had occupied them temporarily, we would sooner or later have had to move out. An inconvenience. Wiser to make a more modest choice from the very beginning. As was expected, a week later, Huang Jian and his wife had moved into the two best rooms in our courtyard.

On the first night, Xiuwen forcibly dragged me to her home. I stopped dead in my tracks at the door, unable to recognize our old office room. From the center of its light blue ceiling hung a chandelier. A suite of natural-colored, wood-grain furniture appeared both simple and tasteful. A spring-mattressed bed was covered by a dark green and black rhombus-patterned bedspread. Over its head was a white wall light. Between a pair of small armchairs stood a floor lamp with an apple-green lampshade, casting a soft green circle of light on the floor. It was like a miracle.

The scene reminded me suddenly of the little room in which Xiuwen and I had lived together in the past. There, four beds had been placed side by side. The one nearest the wall had a bed-spread made of handwoven cloth and a rattan suitcase at the side. It was Xiuwen's. Next to hers was mine. We had just been transferred from the countryside with a wage of eighteen yuan per month.

And now, wearing a pair of red thick-soled slippers, Xiuwen gracefully paced up and down the light green room After turning on her large television set, she handed me a cup of milk and a dish of cakes. She had become prettier, almost enchanting. Of course, she had always been attractive. At first, she was a member of our chorus. Later on, due to some problem with her voice, she could no longer sing. The ensemble kept her as an announcer. When she first stood before the microphone, the audience whispered, commenting on her appearance. Huang Jian was one of her ardent admirers. However, Huang Jian's first love had not been Xiuwen but . . . How far my thoughts had drifted! I shook my head.

"Does the milk taste bad?" Xiuwen asked in amazement.

"Oh no, it's fine." I awkwardly tried to gloss over my blunder. "But, I don't really want it. I've just had supper."

"Then, have some fruit?" Picking up a big pear from the fruit tray, she peeled it slowly with a stainless knife and cut it into slices, which she stuck on some toothpicks. She handed them to me.

"Your room's lovely!" I exclaimed sincerely, full of praise. I reached for a second slice of pear. I was not used to this dainty way of eating fruit. In the past, I could have gobbled down four large apples at one go, wher the ensemble distributed fruit bought cheaply from an orchard. Xiuwen could devour even more than I. Now she merely nibbled at a slice.

"Although Huang Jian isn't from Shanghai, he has good taste. Whatever I like, he always tries his best to get for me." Her smile was self-satisfied. "I haven't seen your place yet! A'ping and you are both from Shanghai, so your home must be beautiful!"

"Some home! When we're on tour, our home goes with us."

"That's true. You should try to change your job. Do you want to be a dancer all your life?"

"Of course not. When I'm too old to dance, the troupe will find something else for me to do."

"Then it'll be too late. Look at me, I'm now working as a typist in the Cultural Bureau. It's an easy job. In fact, typists are badly needed in several other places too. Try to find some way to get transferred!"

"Easier said than done!" I sighed, reaching for my fourth slice of pear, and saying to myself, Who can compare with you? The daughter-in-law of the bureau director.

Suddenly the window was pushed open with a bang, as three little heads and six staring eyes emerged above the windowsill. Following their line of vision, I saw on television a fierce fight going on . Turning my head again, I recognized they were Jiang Mai's children. Having graduated from the Provincial Art College in 1967, Jiang Mai had joined us as a trombonist. Some said Jiang Mai had once been a stylish fellow, and there had been a number of young girls madly chasing after him. Carried away by this, he overdid things. His handsome looks quickly faded. All his girl-friends ditched him. When he was thirty, he finally found a young girl worker called Xiao Zhang, who agreed to marry him. Their domestic bliss was brief.. Xiao Zhang insisted on having a daughter. But unfortunately, she gave birth to three sons in succession, and if our leader had not hinted enough is enough, she would surely have given birth to a fourth or fifth! Owing to their tight financial situation, the couple quarreled and grumbled frequently. Though their neighbor for only a week, I was already accustomed to their constant bickering. You can't imagine how they sniped at each another!

Going over to the window, Xiuwen smiled at the three boys and invited them in. The children, however, were not used to such hospitality and shyly disappeared. I remembered how Xiuwen disliked being disturbed. On tour, when some of our colleagues brought their children with them and the kids cried or made a noise at night, Xiuwen would complain bitterly. Now, she had changed completely. How a comfortable life can improve one's tolerance of others!

Huang Jian returned. On seeing me, he halted, seemingly embarrassed, but quickly recovered his composure and went to wash his hands. Why be like that? Let bygones be bygones. Ever since he became friendly with Xiuwen, I had left him alone. But it seemed he still hated me. I often had a laugh over it. But now, I also felt somewhat uneasy. Before swallowing the last slice of pear, I stood up and hastily took my leave.

Passing a room that had originally been used as a dressing room, I heard someone saying, ". . . She's not pretty at all. Granted she has large eyes, yet they're expressionless. She has a high nose, but it's a snub one." The speaker was Ren Jia, wife of Hai Ping. She was well known for her jealousy. Ren Jia was afraid her husband was too handsome and she was too plain. It made her very nervous, and that, in turn, made all of us very nervous too. One of her methods was to attack other girls. At this moment, I didn't know who she was going on about. Xiuwen's eyes were both large and beautiful. As for me, people said that my nose was high, but only A'ping considered that it was a bit retrousse. Was Ren Jia speaking about Xiuwen or me?

As I entered my "Home," I saw A'ping ecstatically practicing conducting before a mirror. He used to talk a lot about music and poetry before our marriage. How I had been fascinated by such unworldly things!

* * *

The next morning, I saw Xiao Ji, a carpenter with the stage design group, squatting at the entrance of the lavatory and brushing his teeth. I was puzzled. It took me three or four minutes to make it out. He must have moved into the small eight-square-meter room. Its door formed a right angle with that of the lavatory. But I had still no idea when he had moved in there. He hadn't made any noise. The stage design group of our ensemble was, as a matter of fact, regarded as the most unimportant section, and its carpenters were practically anonymous. Furthermore, Xiao Ji was, by nature, a simple, taciturn man. Nobody ever took any notice of him.

We were having breakfast when Xiao Ji stepped into our room. As he was a rare visitor, we stood up to welcome him. Smiling shyly, he handed us two packets of sweets. Waving his hand, A'ping said, "No need for that!" Xiao Ji's face turned red. I realized what they meant and immediately took them, saying, "Congratulations!" Xiao Ji turned and left, while A'ping was still saying, "No need for that!" What an ass! Only after I had held them up for several minutes so that he could read the "wedding sweets" printed on them, did he exclaim, "Oh! he's got married!"

"You're such a nitwit!" I scolded.

This irritated him, so he explained, "The change was too sudden. I wasn't prepared for it."

I ignored him, but thought to myself that there was some truth in what he said. We were not prepared at all. There had not been the slightest warning. Xiao Ji always did things quietly. But, who was his bride?

Having finished our meal, we locked our door and went to fetch our bikes. Jiang Mai, Hai Ping and his wife also got theirs. We all glanced simultaneously at Xiao Ji's room. He was just locking the door. Beside him stood a young girl dressed in a purple jacket, with a dark gray scarf round her neck. Her braids were coiled up on top of her head. Her forehead and mouth were both very broad. She wore a pair of spectacles. They came over to us. Xiao Ji gave a nervous smile but the girl was relaxed and accepted our curious glances.

"She seems a very lively girl," Old Jiang was the first to comment.

"Stands like an artist," added A'ping.

"She's got a kind of dignity," concluded Hai Ping. His remarks were usually accurate. I gazed at Ren Jia anxiously. She sneered, "She looks too serious. Not sweet enough." How harsh she was! I wondered whether she was also as exacting with her students.

"Their sweets were the cheap kind, so they can't be well off." Old Jiang was always very sensitive about the question of prices, a result of his being hard up. I looked at him pityingly.

Having reached the ensembles's headquarters, I saw that the leaders were collecting money from everybody to buy presents for Xiao Ji and his bride. But the bridegroom was doing his utmost to stop them, declaring loudly that the reason why he hadn't breathed a word to anyone about his marriage was to save his colleagues spending their money. No one listened to him. It was a tradition that whenever anyone got married, we gave presents. It helped to make us feel like one big family.

I was chosen to give Xiao Ji the present from our group. Soon after supper, I went to his room.

The door was unlocked. I heard the sound of hammering from inside, so I knocked several times. There was no response. I pushed open the door and stepped into the room. Xiao Ji was nailing up a picture; there were already several lying here and there on the floor. The bride was hanging one on the wall. Three walls were already full of them, making the place look quite beautiful. Turning their heads at the same time, the newlyweds greeted me, "Welcome! Sit down, please!"

But the only stool in the room was being stood on by the bride, so I had to sit on the edge of their bed.

Putting down his hammer, Xiao Ji went to make tea for me, while his wife got down from the stool and hurried to bring me a dish of sweets. I looked around the room: only a table beside the bed, a kerosene stove, a pot and some enameled bowls. With a dish of sweets in her hand, the bride came over to me, asking, "Does our room seem very shabby?"

Should I nod or shake my head?

"But, actually, it isn't!" Pointing to the pictures, she went on, "Look, we have magnolias, bamboos, mountains, rivers and the sun ..."

Smiling, I turned to Xiao Ji and scolded him, "Why don't you introduce her to me? I can't just call her 'bride'!"

Before he could open his mouth, his wife said, "Let me introduce myself. I'm Lian Zhu. I just graduated from the fine arts department of the provincial art college. I'm now working as a teacher in the first middle school." She spoke the Beijing dialect with a strong provincial accent.

I then introduced myself, "I'm Songsong, one of the dancers."

"Were you an educated youth from Shanghai?"

I nodded my head. I gazed at her. The more I looked at her, the more I felt Ren Jia's remarks were unfair. In fact, Lian Zhu was very charming. It was just that she rarely smiled.

"I'm from the seaside."

I chuckled, drawn to her more and more. I realized from her accent that she came from the area around the port of Lianyun.

An outburst of noisy quarreling interrupted us. Amazed, Lian Zhu stood up and walked toward the door. Xiao Ji and I followed her. I told her, "You'll get used to it after a week."

Opening the door, I spotted the shadow of someone moving toward us from the darkness and calling my name. It was Xiuwen! I remembered that, although she had been living here for more than a week, she was still curious about each quarrel. She would listen to it, inquire what it was all about and then spread the news.

"Xiao Zhang sent Old Jiang to buy half a pound of meat, but Old Jiang bought a whole pound. Now they're at each other's throats. Listen, it's getting worse. Let's go upstairs and try to patch things up between them!" Her big eyes glistened with excitement. I was immediately aware that what she suggested was not so much aimed at patching things up but at watching the fun. Feeling disgusted, I remarked indifferently, "No need. Let them sort it out themselves." Although they had quarreled for more than six or seven years, even fiercely, they had no wish to divorce.

Lian Zhu agreed. "No couples want outsiders to interfere, Everyone has some self-respect."

Turning her face to the bride, Xiuwen looked her up and down. She urged, "Let's go and have a look at their room." Grabbing me by the hand, she dragged me there.

All of a sudden, her room and furnishings emerged before my eyes. I tried to hold Xiuwen back, but she had already rushed inside and was standing in the center of the almost empty room. She winked at me. Fearing that she might blurt out heaven knows what kind of criticism, I hastened to divert her attention.

"Are you going to watch television tonight?" I asked.

"Television?" She gazed at the bed on which lay two thin, old quilts, replying vaguely, "It's silly to look at television every night."

"What about listening to your cassette tapes?"

"You can't listen to the same music over and over again."

"Where's Huang Jian?" I uttered the name I was unwilling to mention.

"Gone out to have fun," Xiuwen answered unhappily.

As it happened, Huang Jian's voice sounded in the yard, "Xiuwen! Xiuwen!"

"He's come back. Go home quickly!" I pushed her, relieved that she would have to leave. She moved toward the door slowly, saying, "We've nothing to talk about."

Finally she left the room, and the noise of the quarrel in the upstairs room also died away.

Looking up, Lian Zhu inquired in a soft voice, "Do they always quarrel?"

"Yes. They're often short of money."

"Really?" Turning around, she stared at me and then at Xiao Ji. In spite of her thick glasses , I could still see a look of doubt in her eyes. That was natural. Newlyweds only thought about love. Love . . . How had they fallen in love? I couldn't restrain my curiosity and asked them.

The corners of Lian Zhu's mouth moved slightly, until she gave a rare yet moving smile. She gazed at her husband, who smiled back at her. Who would ever have noticed that this silent young carpenter had eyes like deep pools?

"How we fell in love? Where to begin? . . ." Lian Zhu felt embarrassed.

"Say whatever you like," her husband encouraged her.

"Oh, it's very simple," Lian Zhu began at last.

"No, it's very complicated, in fact, " the young man countered.

"We waited and waited. Shortly after we had been transferred here from the countryside, I went to study at college. He had to wait again until my graduation. It was always wait, wait. What about you?" Having nothing more to say, Lian Zhu launched into a counterattack.

"Oh, we're an old married couple now."

"Nonsense! You're the same age as I. Twenty-nine, right?"

"Twenty-eight. It was really nothing special. He just kept pestering me with poems and music."

"And you didn't chase after him?"

"No, of course not!"

"What?" Lian Zhu seemed sorry.

"Didn't you also send him a poem?" Xiao Ji suddenly asked.

"How do you know that?" I cried out.

"Oh, my dear Songsong!" Putting her arms round me, Lian Zhu giggled and soon I did too.

I sat there till after ten o'clock, then happily said good night. As soon as I reached my room, my joy evaporated. A'ping told me that the leader of our ensemble had just telephoned him to say that rehearsals would begin tomorrow and we would go on tour again the following Monday. I refused at once. "I won't go!"

Putting down his pen, A'ping stood up and reached out his hand to console me. I pushed him aside, walking toward the bed. "I won't go! Why should we go again? We only came back two weeks ago! I won't go!" I threw myself facedown on the bed. To go on tour meant packing in a hurry, loading and unloading our luggage, setting cold stages and living together in a big room with many of our colleagues. . . . I was on the verge of tears.

Coming over to me, A'ping embraced me and said comfortingly, "I'll be there to help you. . . . Fill your hot water bottle."

"Is that all you can say?" I yelled angrily.

"What else do you want me to do?"

"I want you to get me transferred to another job. I don't want to dance any longer. I need a stable life, a settled home. I want . . . I want a baby!" The tears ran down my cheeks. Xiuwen's comfortable room appeared before my eyes. Ah, how much I wanted . . .

Upset, A'ping stroked my hair awkwardly.

* * *

To leave on schedule, we had to work overtime. It was already very late at night when we returned home. In silence, we squeezed into the former janitor's room to leave our bicycles. After that, without saying good night to one another, we all hurried to our respective rooms. Most of our colleagues had some hot soup and warm rice ready, whereas A'ping and I ... How I longed for some hot soup! A'ping held my hands tenderly. Though I had worn two pairs of gloves, my hands were still cold. He put them into the pockets of his overcoat. I drew them out at once. I didn't want such tenderness. What I needed badly was a stable family life, not embraces and kisses!

Involuntarily, I stooped in front of Xiuwen's window, through which the apple-green light dimly shone. How cozy to be bathed in such a mild light. What was Xiuwen doing at this moment?

Several voices whispered below the windowsill—Old Jiang's three boys.

"Doesn't Aunty Li like to watch television?" It was Old Jiang's youngest son, only three years old, speaking in a childish treble. "Why doesn't she like to watch television?"

Xiuwen's silhouette could be seen at the window; the soft light made her face even more graceful and charming. I unconsciously touched my own cheeks, but because of the weather and stage makeup, my skin had become rougher.

The door was suddenly pushed open and Huang Jian came out. On seeing me, he smiled unexpectedly. Why did he smile at me? Was it because he no longer hated me? Or was he mocking my refusing him in the past? My heart ached. I wanted to get away, but my feet wouldn't move.

"Let's go," A'ping said, biting his lips. His deep eyes flashed. He looked unwell. I started to move.

As soon as we reached our room, I threw myself on the bed, wanting to lie there forever. But my stomach was rumbling with hunger. A'ping had bought me two stuffed steamed buns from our canteen, but, as I was angry with him, I had refused to even look at them. I hadn't eaten anything for nine hours. I got up from the bed, took a bowl of cold rice and filled it with some hot water. Just as I was about to eat, A'ping snatched it away from me. "Why let yourself get run-down?"

"I'm hungry!" I shouted, stretching out my hand to grab the bowl.

"Don't you see that I've already begun to cook a meal!" Having put aside the bowl, he continued to cut the cabbage.

"I can't wait!" I stamped my feet irritably.

"Have a cookie then." Putting down the knife once more, he handed me a can of cookies.

"They're too dry. I don't want them! I won't eat them!" I pushed away the can. It slipped from his fingers to the floor.

"You just want to pick a quarrel," he said, his lips trembling.

"Who wants to pick a quarrel? I . . ."

"It's you!" he interrupted me roughly. "You . . . you regret you made a wrong decision. If you had married him, you could also have become a wealthy lady and led a comfortable life!"

"You!" I was speechless with rage and shock.

Flushed with fury, he continued, "What were you thinking? I told you clearly I had no money, position or ability. I said you'd suffer if you married me! I warned you, didn't I? I was afraid all along you'd regret it. And as I expected, you do!"

Not knowing why, I suddenly slapped his face. Turning around, I flung myself onto the bed, sobbing. After a time, I fell asleep. When I woke up, I discovered I was lying under my cotton quilt, a hot water bottle at my side. The room was empty. Where was A'ping? Where had he gone so late?

I felt I was suffocating, as if there were a heavy weight on my chest. I was very hurt. How could he say such things to me? I had suffered so much by marrying him, yet he said that I regretted it. If I had taken a lift in Huang Jian's jeep that night, then I would . . . but, instead, I had chosen to hitch a ride on the back of A'ping's bicycle. Why had I done it? I was thinking that he could always play the piano at dancing practice; that he could conduct the orchestra to follow the steps of my solos. I was thinking of the endless stories he told me about Beethoven and Tchaikovsky. Because of this, my parents became angry with me, as did Director Huang of our cultural bureau. . . . Now A'ping said that I . . . Tears again ran down my cheeks. Had I ever regretted it? Did I envy Xiuwen for her good luck? No, I had never envied her. On the contrary, I looked down on her because she was so cheap. When Huang Jian declared his love for her, she immediately accepted him. All the young girls looked at her with disdain.

My watch had stopped. I didn't know what time it was, but I was sure it was very late. There was not the slightest sound in the courtyard. Suddenly the noise of a car engine broke the silence. Huang Jian stepped out from the car. He went out almost every night, leaving Xiuwen alone. How strange when they had such a comfortable room! Why was he unwilling to stay at home and sit and talk with his wife? How we longed to sit carefree at home and chat about things! But we had neither a comfortable room nor the time to talk.

The car headlights were finally switched off. Huang Jian entered his room and silence reigned again. Where was A'ping? Why had I been in such a foul temper? I began to worry about him. Putting on my cotton-padded coat, I quickly got up and opened the door. I hurried along the passage formed by the sets. Almost every room was dark except Xiao Ji's, where a lamp still shone brightly from the window. There were also faint sounds of voices. A pair of young lovers had, of course, a lot of things to talk about.

The gate of the courtyard was lightly pushed open, and a slender figure slipped in. He had come back finally. Unwilling to let A'ping discover that I was waiting for him, I rushed back home.

Just as I got under my quilt, he stepped into the room and came over to the bed. I pretended to be asleep, but my eyelids moved. Then he sat down at the table, holding his head in his hands. The bowl of cold rice and slices of half-cut cabbage remained on the table. So he hadn't eaten his supper. Where had he been?

* * *

It was Sunday, the next day. After breakfast, A'ping went out immediately with some music scores under his arm. I didn't ask him where he was going. I didn't care a fig for him!

It was a fine day without a cloud in the sky. The sun shone warmly, making our small courtyard, which was usually crowded and untidy, appear large and bright. The yard was crisscrossed with clotheslines from which were hanging cotton-padded quilts and mattresses. A group of kids were playing hide-and-seek among them. Old Jiang's three sons were shouting at the tops of their voices. I brought out my trunk to air our clothes in the sunshine. Generally speaking, the climate in the north was very dry, yet, as we had been on tour for two months, our clothes could get musty.

Xiuwen was also busying herself airing their clothes. I saw that they had a lot: overcoats—long, medium and short—of wool or other material. Xiuwen loved dressing elegantly; she never wore trousers that hadn't been well pressed or shoes that were not well shined. In previous years, owing to financial difficulties, she had not been able to indulge herself, but now she could have anything she wanted. All of a sudden, she bent down and started to vomit. I ran over and held her arm. "Are you sick?" I asked. She nodded.

"Does Huang Jian know?" I glanced at their room, but there was no sign of him.

"Yes, he knows. He bought me some medicine."

"Oh." I said no more. It would have been better if he could have kept her company more often.

I left Xiuwen and went back. At this moment, I saw that Lian Zhu was also busy with her clothes. In her trunk, apart from clothes, there were several parcels wrapped up in newspaper.

"What treasures have you hidden there?" I said, pointing at the parcels in the trunk.

"Letters," Lian Zhu answered in all seriousness.

"Letters?" I was at a loss. Picking up one, I saw written on the newspaper: From the municipal ensemble to Sanpu Commune, 1975.

"That year, Xiao Ji had been transferred to work in your ensemble and I was still living and working in Sanpu Commune," explained Lian Zhu.

Another parcel was marked: From the provincial art college to the municipal ensemble, 1977.

"Those were the letters we wrote while I was studying."

One had only "Sanpu,1970" written on it.

"They were the letters we wrote when we were both living in the same village." Smiling for a while, she took the parcel from my hand and laid it in a corner on which the sun shone directly. From her expression, I could guess that she treasured those letters the most.

Counting them, I found there were ten parcels altogether. So they had written to each other for ten years! I exclaimed in surprise, "You were friends for ten years?"

"Yes."

"How was it in those years?"

She straightened her back, and said as if to herself, "Everyday we ate coarse food and worked hard from early morning. But we managed because we had each other."

"It wasn't easy," I sighed.

"Of course there were difficulties. You know the kinds of problems educated youths had when they fell in love."

"Yes, I know."

"If one was transferred to work in the city, the other had to wait. We waited years. At first, I feared I'd be a burden to him. Later on, when I entered college, he feared I'd refuse him." She smiled ironically. "We were always doubting."

Did you ever waver?"

She shook her head slightly. "It wasn't easy, finding each other. We shared good and bad times. It would be unthinkable to start all over again with someone else."

Hearing this, I felt an ache in my heart.

"What if, in the future, well ... when you have some difficulty again, and this difficulty is quite different from ones in the past. Perhaps just an everyday problem, that is to say ..." I muttered, striving to find the right words. "For example, just like Old Jiang and his wife, who quarrel over a few cents. Of course, it's ridiculous, but if you are really short of money then ..."

"Oh, I see," she said, putting one hand on my shoulder and stretching out the other to twist a strand of my hair. She gazed up at the sky. "Material life is also very important to us. I can't be sure that we wouldn't quarrel or grumble over money. Still we can always remember what we went through together. Then I think we can probably manage to get over such problems."

I bent down my head, avoiding her eyes. Like them, A'ping and I had also found each other and faced life's troubles together.

Lian Zhu continued, "It seems ages ago now, but it will always mean something to us because ... because that's love. Without our love, we might have become depressed or lost hope during those years. But how can I preach to you old married couples!

I'm determined to protect our love, to cherish our marriage. But that's not so easy to do."

For us, it was also not so easy. I sighed sadly.

"Why the sigh? Would you like to have lunch with us today?" she inquired, looking at me attentively.

I nodded my head.

The meal was very simple, but I ate quite a lot, probably because I hadn't eaten the night before. I noticed that most of the pictures on the walls had been put into frames. Not every family could possess such riches. With many things to prepare for the coming tour, we parted after lunch.

A'ping still had not come. Where was he? When would he return? I felt miserable because he hadn't eaten for a whole day. I hastened to prepare a meal for him. Having washed some onions, I sliced them and then broke some eggs. I'd cook rice with fried eggs. Before I had finished, Lian Zhu called me to go out with her.

Xiao Ji and Lian Zhu argued over every purchase so it was evening before we finished shopping.

It was already dark and the streetlights lit up either side of the river and shone on its surface. While we were walking slowly along the bank, Lian Zhu remembered her hometown: "How beautiful it was with blue waves, golden sun, shells, sandy beaches and sea gulls. Standing on the shore, I felt I owned that vast world. Our life was so beautiful and we were so deeply in love. So we're not poor at all."

"We're only short of money," Xiao Ji added drily. We all laughed.

Back in our courtyard, the news on the radio reminded us it was already seven o'clock. Xiuwen was washing clothes and waved as soon as she saw us. When we went over to her, she asked Lian Zhu in a low voice, "Did you chat with Hai Ping yesterday?"

"Hai Ping?" Lian Zhu, baffled, looked first at me, then at her.

"That tall man with wavy hair."

"Ah, you mean that handsome one? Yes, we talked a bit while I washed clothes here yesterday."

"Good heavens! He and his wife have just had a fight about it. Didn't you know his wife's very jealous?"

"That's ridiculous!" Xiao Ji said angrily and pulled Lian Zhu away with him.

Opening her mouth awkwardly, Xiuwen didn't know what to do. I felt sorry for her. To smooth things over, I said casually, "So we'll be off again soon. How I envy you!"

She forced a smile. Xiao Ji had embarrassed her. She bent down to pick up the wooden tub, but couldn't lift it. I realized that she was pregnant and asked, "Where's Huang Jian? Why doesn't he give you a hand?"

"He's bought a washing machine for me, but it hasn't been connected yet. It can't be used for the time being."

I helped her carry the tub to her room. Huang Jian had money; he could buy a lot of things, but money can't buy everything. At her door, I put down the tub and was about to leave when she said suddenly, "When you go away I'll feel lonely again."

"Then don't let Huang Jian gad about so much. You must make him stay at home with you."

"We don't seem to have much to say to each other." She had expressed this many times, but now she seemed depressed. I wondered whether she had been upset by the unpleasant scene or whether, because I had only admired her, I hadn't noticed her unhappiness before.

How to comfort her? Huang Jian and she had fallen in love with each other at first sight. Perhaps it had been a bit too easy. They had never experienced any difficulties; their romance had been quite smooth. After a while I said, "No, you won't feel lonely. You have your television set, tape recorder and . . ."

"I'm tired of them," she said, shaking her head.

The gate of the courtyard was suddenly pushed open for a car. Huang Jian threw out a parcel which Xiuwen caught. She quickly unwrapped it and found a new short jacket in the latest style. With a cry of joy, she left me and rushed into her room to try it on. This would keep her amused for the moment. When she grew tired of it, Huang Jian would buy her a new one. But what if he could no longer produce something new, or she tired too quickly of his presents? What would happen then? The apple- green light could not be a substitute for love.

This made me long for A'ping. What was he doing? I went home, but there was no light on and the door was locked. When

I went in I saw the onion slices and bowl of eggs untouched on the table. Where had he gone? I got on my bike and rode along the main street.

Where could I find him? First of all, I went to our new building. Perhaps he was practicing there. But there was no sign of him. Then, I headed for the municipal cultural center, in case he was chatting with his buddies. But it was in darkness. Then I thought of his students. I hurried to their houses but he hadn't been to the first two I called on, so I went to the third one. This was the home of Doctor Zhang, who worked at the municipal hospital. His daughter was taking piano lessons from A'ping. Doctor Zhang told me that A'ping had just left there an hour earlier and that he had already signed a sick-leave certificate for me, which A'ping had taken. I was at a loss to understand. Doctor Zhang said, "He came yesterday evening and said he desperately needed it. This morning he came again to urge me to write it, so I promised to give it to him this evening. I gave it to him because he never asked any favor from me before." So that was it! I left without a word. Racing home, I nearly knocked down some pedestrians. How impatient I was to find A'ping!

Riding over the Huo Ping Bridge, I saw a familiar figure standing under a streetlight. A'ping! The dim light cast a faint shadow on the ground. With both hands, he was holding the railing looking at the river. What was he thinking about? I wanted to call him, but I was too excited to utter a sound. Putting down my bike, I ran over to him.

On hearing my steps, he turned his face, stared at me silently and produced a sheet of paper from his breast pocket. I took it, folded it and slowly tore it into pieces.

"What's wrong with you?" he asked in a daze.

"Nothing." Tears ran down my cheeks.

"What's the matter?" He removed the pieces from my hands.

"If I remain here, how can you manage?" Sobbing, I grabbed the pieces again and threw them into the river.

With his eyes shining brightly, A'ping embraced me tenderly.

"What were you thinking about here?" I asked him in a soft voice.

"I was thinking about how we stood here the first time. Do you still remember? It was precisely here that I said, 'I love you!' I'd been in agony for ages, afraid that you'd reject me. It was clear that you could lead a more comfortable life if . . ."

I covered his mouth with my hand, but he took it away and continued, "But you said you loved me and told me, 'I only want you. I want no one else but you!'"

* * *

It was time to set off again. The leader of our ensemble decided to arrange for the bus to pass by our courtyard. Early in the morning, we gathered together in the yard to wait for its arrival and say good-bye to our families.

The parting conversation between Old Jiang and his wife was filled as usual with calculations.

"Mail me twenty yuan next month."

"I'll send you thirty."

"Nobody asked you to send so much," snapped his wife, ignoring her husband's kindness.

"You'd better pay more attention to your meals during the tour."

"I'll mail you thirty."

"No, I need only twenty."

I couldn't refrain from laughing. They still loved each other. They were only short of money.

Ren Jia and Hai Ping stood face-to-face. Ren Jia fixed her eyes full of worry and fear on Hai Ping. Hai Ping said something to her, which I couldn't hear distinctly, probably to set her mind at ease. To tell the truth, apart from his being handsome, there was nothing to give her cause to doubt him. It was not easy for Hai Ping to endure the jealousy of his plain, narrow- minded wife. If he didn't love her, then why did he suffer so? Yet she was too anxious to keep his love to herself. She simply wouldn't share even a tiny bit.

Xiao Ji and Lian Zhu hadn't appeared yet, and the cause was obvious. They had so often been apart before and now they were to be separated again. Xiao Ji was unable to find himself a comfortable job. How long would they have to write letters to each other?

All of a sudden, I felt very happy. At least A'ping and I were always together. I turned to look at A'ping. He held my hands tightly; as usual they were as cold as ice. He put my hands into his deep overcoat pocket. It was very warm because he had put a hot water bottle in it. What a silly, dear fellow!

The bus arrived. After we had all stowed our luggage on the racks and sat down, I noticed the apple-green light was still shining in Xiuwen's home, pale in the dawn. Huang Jian was gazing at me from the window. Before he could do anything, I smiled at him.

The bus was carefully driven out of the gate. Our small courtyard was not so poor after all.

Translated by Hu Zhihui

The Stage, a Miniature World

There was no telling when the Yellow River had flowed across here; after all, it was long, long ago.

There was no telling when the Yellow River had stopped flowing across here; after all, it was long, long ago, and it left behind a dry river bed.

Though dry, it was still a river. When the rainy season set in, the water in the river was very clear. It wound through a small, dusty, loess-filled town adding a watery charm.

The river was spanned by small plank bridges, which were then replaced by concrete ones. Gradually they were widened and strengthened. The earth banks were renovated section by section and built higher and higher. They were tarred and divided into pavements and a road for vehicles. Along the river, lampposts were erected with lights like flower petals, and a green railing enclosed shrubs and flowers. There was a bus stop here, called River-bank Road.

People never called it Riverbank Road, but nicknamed it Yellow Riverbank. Once, when a new bus conductor called out Riverbank Road, passengers softly grumbled, "Come off it!"

Near the riverbank there was a building, with a board on one side of the gate bearing the words "The Huaihai Region Cultural Troupe." The troupe, though not very big, had a dance group, a chorus, a drum song and dulcimer ballad group, orchestra, stagehands, janitors, cooks, men who boiled water and swept the floor, accountants, secretaries, a director, several deputy directors and, in particular, a man who, though not a director, had the final say on everything.

Whenever the troupe started on or came back from a tour, there were always trucks parked in the open space in front of the building. Neighbors and passersby could see a tall, sturdy man with a ruddy face standing in the highest part of the courtyard. When he said "Let's begin," everyone under him complied. If he said "Stop," they would have a breather. Then someone would ask him, "Do we fix the lights or the scenery first?" He would reply firmly, "First fix the lights." His manner was impressive. After the trucks were loaded or unloaded, he would go over to a thin old man who was smoking and watching the scene, say a few words to him and then the old man would nod thoughtfully. This was all outsiders could see.

Insiders knew that the old man was in fact the director, and the tall man with a ruddy face was nothing more than an ordinary member named Fukui.

When the director decided to go on tour, the route would be determined by Fukui. If the director wanted new recruits for the troupe, it was Fukui who would be in charge of the examination and investigation of their backgrounds. If he wanted to prepare a new turn, Fukui would make the choice. If he wanted to call a meeting, Fukui would whistle and assemble the troupe. If he wanted to criticize someone, Fukui would summon the miscreant. In short, Fukui carried out whatever policy the director put forward. The latter trusted the former and the former was indispensable to the latter, because he was resourceful and energetic.

As the troupe had recently been going through a bad period, the director called cadres and activists to a meeting to hear their opinions and suggestions. Unexpectedly, however, the meeting was wrapped in a shroud of pessimism and despondency— they had nothing but complaints.

"We're finished!" Jiming, the bandmaster, was in despair and poured cold water on everyone present. "It's the eighties, but we're stuck in the fifties. It's not like the Cultural Revolution, when we could put on nothing but eight model revolutionary operas and a Tibetan dance and still pack them in. Today, there are dubbed films, traditional operas, symphonies, and light music. What have we got? We can't go on like this."

Brighter members of the troupe realized that in a roundabout way he was saying that they couldn't simply continue in the old ways and that they must find a solution. But the director impatiently interrupted, "What'll we do then? Do you want us to disband the troupe?"

If you're thinking of disbanding it then the earlier the better. Don't let's waste time. We're old; it doesn't matter so much to us as it does to young people." Though Jiming looked quite sharp, his conversation was rather muddled.

"What? Do you think that I assembled you here to discuss how to disband the troupe?" the director flared up.

"I don't think that our prospects are so bad," said Fukui . "Our troupe has its good points: drum songs and dulcimer ballads are full of local color. We should keep them. We don't have to follow the fashion. Let others use light music and electronic instruments. I don't approve of these fads. They're old bourgeois stuff. Too vulgar!"

Jiming snickered, but he would never argue with Fukui.

Fukui hated his snicker. He knew it was contemptuous. Jiming, who had graduated from a music conservatory, looked down upon him, an acrobat. Thinking of this, Fukui flushed crimson.

"Anyway we don't want that stuff. Light music and oriental dances will never have my approval. Let's stick to our own style."

Jiming snickered again.

The director frowned; he also disliked Jiming. From his years of experience in various troupes and companies, he knew that some of Jiming's opinions were accurate, but he'd rather support Fukui.

"Don't laugh!" he said to Jiming. "You're entitled to your views, but I think there's some sense in what Fukui says."

"Of course," answered Jiming, who was so keen on defeating his rival that he forgot what he'd come here for. Before the meeting he'd been bursting with suggestions, but they had to wait until after his complaints. Like a great actor preparing to go on stage, he had to create an atmosphere.

"Go on, Fukui."

"I think, we can let Chen Yuying do an additional ballad with dulcimer accompaniment. We can revive the 1976 handkerchief dance. That dance has some kick in it. Besides, let's add some fiddles and suona trumpets to the orchestra; they've got something...."

Jiming snorted and cast a furtive glance at the director: a lot your assistant knows!

The director was furious. Though he knew Fukui's suggestion wasn't very good, he adopted it anyway.

Fukui looked at Jiming with hatred. Arrogant bastard, he thought. You're no more than a graduate student. I'd like to have it out with you.

* * *

Rehearsal time. Fukui was responsible for everything: fixing the time, mustering the performers, sweeping the floor, writing a program and putting it up backstage.

On seeing the program, Jiming bawled, "Immediately after a female solo there's a dance. There's no time for the orchestra to get into the pit. Who devised the program? He's got no common sense at all."

Fukui was, in fact, glad to have advice or suggestions. The more they shouted for him and the more questions they asked him, the more important he felt. But they ought to be polite. He ignored Jiming's noisy outburst.

The solo ended. The orchestra had to cross backstage and struggle into their places in the pit. It took them about seven or eight minutes to get settled.

The director frowned.

Fukui ran to the pit and barked, "Can't you make it snappy? Come on, do it once more!"

The members of the orchestra growled, "Who planned the program? Let him try it."

If the two items had been switched, this question could have been very easily solved. But since it was Jiming who had concluded that the maker of the program was an idiot, Fukui insisted that it was practicable and made sense.

"What do you mean there's not enough time for you to get down to the pit? There's plenty of time."

"Sure, there's plenty of time if we jump straight off the stage."

"How about your trying it?"

School-leavers and graduates had never had a very high opinion of Fukui the acrobat.

Sensitive to their contempt, Fukui waved his arms in a huff saying,"If you say you can't do it, then let's give up the whole thing!" With this he went to the director. "Jiming won't do it."

"Why not?"

"I don't know."

"Without him the earth doesn't rotate, does it?"

"Of course it does. How about playing a record instead of using the orchestra?"

"Well, do as you think fit."

And so a record took the place of the orchestra.

The record had been made by a song and dance ensemble, the creators of this dance, whose instrumental performance was definitely superior to theirs. But the dancers sulked and their moodiness was infectious. As the dancers fell out of step with the music, the audience began to sense the mood of depression. Despite this, the director said complacently, "Marvelous, isn't it?"

"Of course!" Fukui chimed in.

Jiming snickered again.

From that day on, they dispensed with the orchestra at rehearsals. Jiming was left with nothing to do. Though miserable, he looked quite cheerful, as if he had gained an advantage, and laughed all day.

In the orchestra, there was a man named Wan Youyi who had been a drummer and who was virtually the conductor. Later, the orchestra appointed another to take his place, so all he had to do was beat the drum and strike bells. The principal percussion instruments, kettledrum, military drum and the like, had been assigned to some young people from conservatories and art institutes. Seeing them happily play and blow their instruments often made him feel lonely.

Now that the orchestra was also left idle, he became busy.

After roll call every morning , he didn't leave as early as before, but ran upstairs and downstairs to watch the dancers doing their exercises, the chorus training their voices, or he sat down to read a newspaper.

When he met Fukui, he said, "It's too bad having nothing to do all day."

But his words brought no response.

"Just because Jiming's thrown up his job, we've been left idle." Fukui looked at him and said, "The troupe can keep going, even without an orchestra."

"What I mean is that the orchestra could perform without him," Wan Youyi suggested tentatively.

"Of course!"

After a pause, Wan Youyi went on, "A friend of mine gave me two bottles of good wine. I feel lonely drinking by myself, so would you honor me with a visit and drink with me?"

After a moment's thought, Fukui replied, "Fine."

Fukui was fond of the bottle. The moment he lifted a glass, he looked on the world as his friend. If someone wanted to make friends with him, he only needed to drink with him. The moment he'd become a friend, Fukui would take him into his confidence. If you were honest and generous, Fukui would stick up for you any time you needed his help. Furthermore, he never kept his advantages all to himself but shared them with his friends. In his opinion, there was no point in drinking alone.

Soon Fukui and Wan Youyi became bosom pals.

And before long, Wan Youyi was promoted to be deputy conductor. When Jiming snickered again, Wan said to the director, "If you trust me, let me have a try at conducting the orchestra."

"Be confident. I'm sure it'll be a success," said the director.

"Of course it will!" agreed Fukui.

Wan was much more active than Jiming. In meetings he'd never grumbled but often put forward the sort of suggestions Fukui hoped for.

"Chen Yuying's ballad with the dulcimer accompaniment should be longer, I think. Sitting in the stalls, I heard two old ladies applaud. But the dress she's wearing is dowdy; it should be brighter."

Soon Chen Yuying's performance became longer, and a long red skirt was wrapped around her waist. Her bosom was covered with gold and silver spangles, dazzling under the spotlights. Her fellow performers standing in the wings shook their heads and muttered. Jiming laughed again. Fukui sat bolt upright on a box in the wings and heartily enjoyed every line she sang.

There was a young man in the orchestra who nicknamed Chen "S" because when she walked, she wriggled like a snake. Fukui had enrolled her and two comedians six months earlier. When they arrived, the orchestra was short of a bassoonist, three dancers were pregnant and a carpenter had replaced an electrician, who had gone to study at a university. Once, the carpenter narrowly escaped electrocuting himself. Everyone clamored for new recruits. The troupe was short of money, and income was falling. They should have been trying to reduce staff numbers, not get new people. Hearing that Fukui had recruited three people for the troupe, the others rushed into the hall to find a young woman coquettishly singing and playing a dulcimer. After they had patiently sat through her performance, the two comedians chattered and jabbered for a long time. Fukui roared with laughter while the others put on forced smiles.

"Perhaps they've been dragged here from the riverbank," someone remarked caustically.

There was a group of street performers on the riverbank, most of them old men earning their daily bread by singing ballads to the accompaniment of clappers. The stories they told were invariably about Wu Song flirting with Pan Jinlian[1] or Yue Fei[2] having an affair with a girl. Though vulgar, the street singers drew bigger audiences than the cultural troupe.

The three performers were formally hired without delay. The ballad singer, Chen, who came from a county town, even brought her two children along.

The newcomers and Fukui paid frequent visits to one another as if they were sworn brothers, and strangers often assumed that they were from one family. Weren't there many family troupes and companies touring in the towns and villages? In Fukui's opinion, that sort of troupe was good, and easy to keep together.

Though the troupe was in difficult circumstances, the variety show group was reinforced and gained both new recruits and new instruments. But the orchestra couldn't even afford to buy a

---

[1] An adulterated version of a story taken from *Outlaws of the Marsh*.
[2] A famous historical figure.

jazz drum, and the stagehands failed to get new scenery. They growled in protest then grumbled aloud. The director grew worried, thinking everyone was slacking except Fukui, who was the sole support of the troupe.

The director had considerable experience and knew that the variety show group was losing its sense of proportion and that they were increasingly vulgar. Despite this, he still supported Fukui, because the latter was the only one in the whole troupe who did not oppose him but remained loyal. Surrounded as he was by intellectuals, he believed that only those who came from worker and peasant families were pure, enthusiastic and full of drive. Although he'd been engaged in cultural work for several decades and was considered an intellectual, he knew his own type well and was determined not to be contaminated by them.

* * *

They staged their show.

For the first three performances, only sixty per cent of the tickets were sold.

After the show, some of the audience complained as they left: "There wasn't a single exciting item the whole evening."

Looking at the playbills pasted on walls, one said in disgust, "Hmm, they're going from bad to worse."

The following evening, a lot of people lined up at the theater gate to return their tickets.

From the third day on, the ticket office began to sell the remaining tickets at half-price every afternoon, lowering the price from forty cents to twenty.

Outside the theater everything was quiet, but inside it was lively. Hot altercations occurred every day.

One item in the program was a symphony produced by Jiming. As he had been helped by some of his friends in the course of rehearsals, he asked the director for some tickets to invite them to see the show.

"Fukui's in charge of tickets. Ask him."

He had no choice but to approach Fukui. "Give me eight front row tickets." He was as tough and arrogant with him as if Fukui owed him a big favor. His attitude implied that tickets didn't belong to Fukui, but to everyone in the troupe. Naturally he wanted his share.

But Fukui considered the tickets his own property and was also very fussy about the way he was approached. "There are none." His attitude, no less tough and arrogant than that of Jiming, embodied his principle of life: If you treat me well, I'll treat you better. If you treat me badly, I'll give you a worse time.

"I saw you give some to Chen Yuying a moment ago."

"A moment ago's a moment ago. Now's now."

"Don't you try to push me around, you dirty dog!" Jiming cursed.

"Who's a dog? Don't swear at me!" Fukui exploded.

They went quarreling all the way to the director, who was irritated, but asked, "What's the matter?"

"Ask him!" Jiming was reluctant to speak first.

"I gave Chen Yuying some tickets, because when I transferred her here I had to lean on quite a lot of people. I had to give them some complimentary tickets for all they'd done for me."

"Naturally, anything for Chen Yuying," Jiming laughed.

The director didn't like his tone. "Just say what you've got to say."

"All I want is for you to treat us all equally." He strayed from the point again.

"In any case, I have no spare tickets. I couldn't give you any for love or money. There're plenty at the ticket office. You can get as many as you want, but you must pay for them," Fukui said bluntly. The director liked this sort of character: simple and straightforward. They caused him, the boss, no headaches.

That was only a squabble. They caused worse to come.

One day when a ballad singer was giving a performance, the orchestra sat in the pit, giggling at her even though there was nothing funny in her act. During a comic turn, they heard great sighs instead of laughter. As the theater was half empty, their giggles and groans were clearly audible. No sooner had the curtain fallen than the ballad group turned on the orchestra and started a quarrel.

What happened backstage was much more exciting than the performance.

Confronted with an atmosphere of hopelessness and an increasingly disruptive troupe, the director resolved to leave. He requested a transfer, saying that he was too old for the job, though he was only fifty-eight. He said his health was poor and he had a liver problem, so he couldn't carry on with this vagrant life, with the troupe constantly moving from place to place. In short, he couldn't stand it any longer.

After careful consideration, the cultural bureau granted his request.

The director felt as if he'd been relieved of a burden. When the decision was declared, however, he suddenly felt a little miserable because the people about him were irrepressibly cheerful and didn't try to dissuade him from leaving. That evening Fukui came to invite him to a farewell dinner. He was too moved to utter a word, thinking that Fukui still had some affection for him. Tears welled up in his eyes at the thought.

After three glasses of wine, tears flowed down Fukui's cheeks. A tall, strong man, he sobbed like a child.

"I know you think highly of me," he said as he toasted the director. "I'll never forget; even my children and grand- children ..."

Unable to hold back his tears any longer, the director said ruefully, "I've let you down, Fukui. When the question of your application for Party membership came up, I said I thought you had a peasant mentality. And you weren't allowed to join. I hope you won't bear a grudge."

"No, never, Director. You'll come to understand me some day. Because I've been mixed up with those people, you can't easily tell who's good or bad. It's entirely my fault that I'm not a credit to you, nor worthy of your support."

"Do your job well, Fukui. When I return to the bureau, I'll never forget you and I'll bear you in mind."

Wine was useful: it stirred the blood. No wonder Fukui was fond of it.

A new director arrived. He was forty-five or so, full of revolutionary enthusiasm, and had been in the army for many years.

He was determined to overhaul and consolidate the cultural troupe. He followed the Party principle of relying on the broad masses and encouraged them to take part in meetings. He then declared that they should stop rehearsals and performances for two weeks to air their views and discuss problems. They should have no fear of speaking out; it would not be held against them.

If anyone had a problem, he would see them, either in his office or at home. He lived in flat 302, No.3, at the Yellow River Housing Estate. He was a forthright speaker and, though unrefined, his language was straightforward and understandable. His powerful speech was accentuated by resolute, hard gestures.

After a week, the new director had jotted down half a notebook of complaints, all leveled at Fukui.

"Whoever flatters him is promoted, whoever opposes him gets stamped on."

"He's completely uncultured. He knows nothing about the arts and he's ruining the troupe."

"When we were hard up, he got a number of unnecessary new recruits. Apparently they'd invited him for a drink."

"He's created a little clique to attack us."

"He never forgets an injury."

In short, the embarrassing position of the troupe was entirely due to Fukui. If they got rid of him, it might possibly prosper.

The only way out appeared to be for the new director to get Fukui transferred.

He, however, had his doubts. "How come he plays such a crucial role?"

"He has power!" one activist told him. "He may not be the director, but he has the final say in everything."

"How did he get it? Wasn't he just an acrobat before?"

"The old director trusted him and allowed him to do whatever he liked."

"Why did he trust only him?" the new director asked again.

"He toadied to him." someone replied.

"And he often invited him for food and drink."

"But he is competent . . .," said a less stern observer.

"What can he do?" Jiming angrily interrupted. "He can help load and unload a truck. So can any laborer."

"Right!" the other chorused.

Though the new director was still puzzled as to how Fukui could have played such an important role, he made up his mind to get rid of him. He believed firmly in the purification of the revolutionary ranks.

* * *

The news that Fukui was to be transferred traveled fast, and everybody was delighted. But Fukui, thunderstruck, threw himself down on his bed and lay under his quilt all day. He ate nothing, but he drank. Almost no one took any notice of him except Wan Youyi and Chen Yuying, who sometimes dropped in to console him. For their part, they felt uneasy and had a premonition that something bad would happen to them. Why did they feel like this? They hardly dared think about it, but they vaguely sensed that at this juncture they had better keep away from Fukui. Before long, no one came to see him; he was left lying in bed all day. The wine he drank was hot; the tears he shed were bitter. Through the window came the distant sound of singing, laughing and the sharp notes of a violin from the orchestra, which made him feel even more miserable.

It was time for the troupe to set out. This year's quota was two hundred and fifty performances. Though the year was almost ended, they had only completed a third. After purification of the ranks the troupe should have been in fighting form.

The new director set up a temporary work group, including Jiming, to plan the tour.

The route was charted by the work group, After much effort they arranged a contract with a theater and fixed the date. Days passed. The starting date was approaching. As the arrangements took shape, they grew increasingly complicated, but they had to keep going though the details bored them to death.

First of all, the whole troupe of performers had to be transported to their destination— a theater in a city 150 miles away. Every one of them had his own luggage. In addition, the railway station near by was only a small one and a terminus. They wondered if they could get themselves and their luggage on board during a four-minute stop. As far as they could remember, they would have to get onto the platform much earlier than the other passengers and four or five carriages would be specially reserved for them. But they did not know they'd got this priority treatment in the past. All they could do now was gaze at one another in speechless despair.

"Fukui made all the arrangements before," someone said, breaking the silence.

The new director wrote a letter of introduction, affixed an official chop to it, then told a man to deliver it to the railway station and negotiate. Soon the man came back saying, "It's no good. They say they have to abide by the regulations."

The new director was dumbfounded. There's no other way, he thought. Everyone has a ticket so they must be able to get on the train. When it arrives, they'll have to charge on and I'll bring up the rear. If necessary, they'll have to jump on. Or we can work out a military maneuver in advance.

The second problem was how to transport the sets, props, lamps, musical instruments and music stands to the theater. Armed with a letter impressed with a chop, the new director went personally to the station to negotiate. Of course there were freight cars, and they could send their luggage the next day. But no one knew when the freight cars would be coupled onto a locomotive.

"When is the latest date they'll be moved?" the new director asked.

"The end of the year."

He caught his breath before going on, "And the earliest?"

"The earliest? In about a fortnight."

He turned and made for home, walking in a daze.

Summer had not yet arrived, but it was hot for May, and hot weather made people lazy and unwilling to exert themselves. The lazier they felt, the more they remembered the many things they still had to do: Even if there are freight cars, how do we get the sets and props and luggage to the freight yard? If we get them loaded onto the freight cars, how will we get them unloaded and transported to the theater? All those trunks and bags'll wear us out! The whole work group silently sat there, too exhausted at the prospect to say a word.

"Has anyone got any friends working at the railway station?" the new director asked.

Pulling themselves together with an effort, they gazed at him.

"Even a friend of a friend would do," the new director suggested.

"Jiming," someone said, "weren't you at college with someone who's got a relative working at the railway station?"

Jiming brushed the suggestion aside and replied quickly , "No, nothing doing. I hardly know him."

"You could call on him a few times to renew the acquaintance," the new director suggested.

"No, sorry. That man's not much good; he's a bit of a hypocrite. I don't want to have anything to do with him."

"If you won't, I'll take your place. Could you introduce him to me?"

"Sorry, no. Anyway it's his wife who works at the station, and she's got no power at all, so it's useless to ask her for help," he explained, trying to wriggle out of an embarrassing position.

What he'd said was true but it was not the main reason. The main reason was that he disliked asking a favor of anybody. If anybody helps you, he thought, you have to express your gratitude. Even if you don't, if he asks you for help later, you are honor-bound to give it. The need to repay kindnesses was a real nuisance. He insisted on remaining aloof from this particular transaction.

When they were at their wits' end, they thought of Fukui.

"At least Fukui could manage this sort of thing." They finally acknowledged that Fukui was irreplaceable.

"He is still drawing pay from the troupe," Jiming said . "He's supposed to carry on working until he leaves."

After careful consideration, the new director had no alternative but to brace himself and go to Fukui to seek his help.

Though he was still lying on his bed, Fukui got up when he saw the new director walk in.

"Have you any complaints to make, Comrade Fukui? Please don't keep them to yourself." The new director knew that he had to take the initiative.

"No, I have none, Director," Fukui replied in a low voice . "I'm only angry with those who played dirty tricks. . . ."

"Do you think their complaints were unjustified?"

"Overhead is heaven, under my feet is the earth and in between are my parents. All of them are watching me. Honestly, I have a clear conscience. I've sweated so much for the troupe I think I could fill the Yellow River." As he spoke, he looked as if he were going to cry.

"Please don't upset yourself." The new director poured him a cup of water.

"When we'd finished our performances in the south one year, we couldn't get hold of a truck. I let them go home by train; then

I and eight helpers got the sets, props and the luggage to the railway station on carts and loaded them into freight cars. It was snowing and the ground was icy. We slipped at every step, pushing and lugging those carts along. But now ..."

"Ah ..." The new Director didn't know what to say and was rather moved himself.

"I know I've got my shortcomings. I'm a bit too simple to deal with that crafty lot and I didn't really try to get on with them. I accept some of their criticism, but personal attacks from those lay-abouts—never!"

"We all have to look objectively at any criticism, but as your leader, I hope I'm not biased and I'm sure you'll be treated fairly."

"I believe you, Director."

"I hope you cheer up. Now, we are facing some problems...." The new director felt ashamed to talk about it, but finally, with considerable hemming and hawing, he told him the truth.

"I am honored by your faith in me, sir," Fukui said simply. "For your sake, sir, I'll find a way round it."

"Not for my sake, but for the troupe's."

"I understand."

Fukui got up.

He found a solution.

The cultural troupe set off on tour.

* * *

As they got off the train they saw Fukui leading a dozen carts toward them. After their luggage was loaded, they strolled out of the exits swinging their arms. Walking down the street, they found it bright with playbills. At the gate of the theater, a pudgy manager smilingly greeted them and ushered them into a clean backyard, in which there was a row of houses with red-tiled roofs. On each door four names were written. When they opened the doors, the sharp but fresh smell of disinfectant greeted them. Their beds were covered with straw mats, and the floor was spread with dry earth. After they had made their beds and washed their faces, the bell in the kitchen rang announcing a meal. After their train ride, they weren't tired out and they weren't starved. All was well!

After a break, a whistle sounded summoning them to fall in and go to the station to unload the freight cars. The trucks waiting at the gate drew a crowd of children. Loading and unloading, fixing lights and sets were all directed and marshalled by Fukui and everyone was in his proper place. Fukui was not a man who solely gave orders; he also worked the hardest. On his bare shoulders he carried a trunk weighing about a hundred pounds, his muscles twitching under the strain. Beads of sweat dripped down his tanned skin, which glistened in the sunlight.

"Fukui can really get things done," the new director exclaimed, seeing him bustling up and down the stage.

"He can't leave!" he decided. But should he withdraw his report to the bureau requesting Fukui's transfer?

"If he stays, will he have a bad effect on the troupe?" He turned the question over in his mind.

"Director!" He was unaware that Fukui had come up to him . "The sets are in place. After the electricians try out the lights this evening, everything's ready. Will you allow them some overtime pay?"

"Of course. 'To each according to his work,' " he replied. He'd studied political economy in the army.

"And now would you please give them a little talk?" Fukui suggested.

"Talk? About what?"

"The performances start tomorrow evening. They need a reminder about discipline."

The director had no idea about the rules of discipline for a cultural troupe though he was familiar with the army's "three rules and eight points for attention."

"Get up at seven every morning, roll call at eight, then rehearse. They do nothing in the afternoon." Fukui explained.

Fully briefed, the director repeated the rules to the whole troupe.

In the evening, the new director sat in the dark theater, curious to watch the lighting rehearsal. Suddenly the stage was flooded with swaying multicolored beams of light, which thrilled and dazzled him. Under the lamplight, a man walked back and forth and clambered up and down. Sometimes he stood in the light and cast a gigantic shadow on the stage.

All of a sudden, the new director made up his mind that he had to keep Fukui in the troupe, because he needed him, because he was helpful. However, he would never let himself be controlled by him like the former director. He must impose discipline upon himself: Don't be deceived by his flattery. Don't drink his wine. Then he relaxed.

The program they were going to put on this time had been endorsed by the temporary work group and the new director. Several new items were included: a Spanish dance, a Japanese fishermen's dance, a female solo, an instrumental ensemble and songs from films. Besides, they had borrowed a new idea from somewhere—a school-leaver would play an electric guitar. When the guitar was played and its humming, vibrant sound reverberated in the theater, the audience went wild. Young people couldn't contain their excitement and from time to time sang along with the music. Both the guitarist and the audience were ecstatic. It was a thrill because they'd never heard the instrument before. Soon, audiences would be sick of it and would return to the haunting and moving sound of their own traditional instruments and folk songs. Soon, too, it might be possible to adapt some of the better aspects of foreign music. For the moment, quite a few people were concerned about "thrills."

"Director, what are they cheering for?" Fukui was indignant. "Young hooligans!"

In the theater were a number of young rascals with long hair sitting there stamping their feet and whistling, making an outlandish uproar.

"What can we do?" The new director didn't like them either.

"We can't keep on worshipping everything foreign. We have our own things."

"You're right!" Fukui had exactly expressed his own feeling. He simply could not get used to the noise. But he was modest and, as a newcomer unfamiliar with the profession, had taken the cultural troupe, theater and audience as he found them, assuming this was simply how they were. Now, however, he looked fondly at Fukui, feeling that he'd found a sympathetic friend.

"Chen Yuying's ballad singing with a dulcimer has a national flavor," Fukui continued, pressing his point.

"But they say it's crude," the new Director said doubtfully.

"And just who are they?" Fukui was angry again. "Some people in our troupe insist that the moon in foreign countries is rounder than it is in China. To them, everything Chinese is worthless rubbish!"

"Well, I agree with you." The director reflected for a while before going on. "What about having her put on a show for me tomorrow? Then I can decide."

The new director was very pleased to hear her sing, as she came from his home village and her dialect was familiar to him. But the acting and jokes that punctuated her singing were so vulgar he could feel goose bumps all down his back. Nevertheless, he suppressed his reaction, still thinking that cultural troupes, the theater and national cultural forms should be taken as they were found. So he did not object.

Some people saw national culture, backwardness and conservative ideas as the same thing and praised them extravagantly. Others also regarded them as the same thing but were equally strong in their opposition.

On hearing that Chen Yuying's ballad singing would replace the instrumental ensemble, Jiming was hardly able to stop himself from swearing, as he bawled at the new director, "Do you understand art or not? You simply can't distinguish between good and bad, highbrow and lowbrow, can you?"

The new director was furious at his attitude, but then Jiming stopped shouting and began to chuckle, and the director realized that though Jiming was an intolerable character, he was very passionate about his work.

"There's no need to shout. Of course you know what's what, but you should learn a little modesty."

"I don't want to work here any more."

"Do you think I can be bullied by threats of resignation?" the new director said, losing his temper. At the same time, he remembered that even when Fukui had been severely criticized, he hadn't refused to help. In the course of working here, he had gradually come to understand the troupe, and knew that he did not need men who did nothing, but did need those who could do solid work. And Fukui was the ablest of them all.

After the tour, the cultural troupe came home. The first thing the new director did was go to the bureau and withdraw his report. There they told him they had not accepted his dismissal of Fukui.

Fukui continued to work in the troupe.

He joined the temporary work group.

In meetings, he often made speeches, but Jiming did no more than snicker.

* * *

Gradually, the new director allowed Fukui a free hand in his work, and gave him more and more responsibility. But he often warned himself, don't be deceived by his flattery. Don't drink his wine.

In fact, Fukui didn't flatter him or invite him to drink. Only once when there was fried chicken in the canteen, he, Wan Youyi and a couple of others bought some with a few other dishes to go with their wine. Seeing the new director coming with a dish and a bowl of rice in his hand, they invited him to join them, but he declined. Another time, when the new director saw Fukui drinking with the retired director, he couldn't help feeling doubtful. What Jiming and others had told him did not seem totally accurate, and Fukui was not necessarily intending to make use of a retired boss. Certainly, the retired director was in no position to help him. The invitation must be an innocent one, he thought. As the new director's doubts gradually faded, he felt a growing antipathy for those who had complained to him.

Fukui worked conscientiously so as not to let down the new director. For his part, the director entrusted him with important tasks.

When summer came, it rained every day. Water filled the dry riverbed to the brim, then overflowed its banks and flooded most of the town. A number of people in the troupe lived in a low- lying area. Some of their houses had been neglected for years and were in a dangerous state. Fukui felt it his duty to help them through the disaster. The troupe sent over twenty strong, young men to help the families move or repair their houses and drain the water away. Meanwhile they vacated a few offices to lodge some of them. Fukui was in charge of all this.

Some of the houses that were allotted to the homeless were large, some small; some of them were good, some bad; some faced north, some south. But they were quite satisfied with any form of shelter from the rain and wind so no one quibbled about the accommodation offered to them. It was only after they'd settled in, relaxed and had time to look about that they noticed striking distinctions: Those who had complained about Fukui were in old and shabby rooms facing north. The four members of Jiming's family were in the smallest and worst rooms, far from running water but close to the lavatory. Those who were considered to be Fukui's friends were all placed in sunlit and spacious houses facing south. Wan Youyi and Chen Yuying were allotted two of the vacated offices. The distinctions once more embodied Fukui's principle: If you treat me well, I'll treat you better. If you treat me badly, I'll treat you worse.

Jiming went to ask the new director. "Why are we treated unequally?"

"During a crisis you can't afford to be too fussy about accommodations. See for yourself where Fukui is staying."

It turned out that he was sleeping in the corridor.

Jiming could do nothing but sulk.

The new director was angry with him for his selfishness.

The work of repairing the houses and draining the water was also organized by Fukui. As his house was last on the list, no one could find fault with his work.

The rain stopped, the floodwater receded and the sun shone brightly. Trees and grass took on a fresh green look. The new director was in high spirits and said to Fukui, "Have you ever thought of applying for Party membership?"

"Only when I'm daydreaming," Fukui flushed red.

"Why don't you make an application, then?"

"I'm not qualified."

"Whether you are qualified or not will be decided by higher authorities. But you really should apply!"

The next day, Fukui handed in his application.

The third day, word spread through the troupe.

"Fukui's made an application,."

"Yes, he's applying for Party membership."

Jiming sneered again with a rather mysterious look.

It was as if Fukui had committed every possible scandalous error.

The new director flared up. He associated this sort of gossip with people who had a prejudice against the Party and those who looked down on Fukui. Striking his chest, he said to himself,

I insist on recommending him for Party membership!

Fukui was admitted into the Party.

He worked more vigorously and more people came over to his side.

His attitude toward the ordinary workers was unchanged. He still ate and drank with them but retained his principles. He would not tolerate disharmony and insisted on high moral standards.

The new director was very pleased that he'd recruited such a good Party member. He made another report to the bureau in which he recommended Fukui for a higher rank.

The new director encouraged quite a number of activists, and he turned to them when there were problems in the troupe. He no longer relied on the temporary work group, because the members always grumbled and poured cold water on his ideas. He could not stand those pessimists. Boldness and confidence were essential in making revolution. Pessimism would not do. The work group disbanded itself as it had completed its historic mission.

At the end of the year, they had not yet fulfilled the quota—two hundred and fifty performances—so they had to go on performing.

The first day, they sold sixty per cent of the tickets.

On the second day, there was half a streetful of people lining up at the gate of the theater to return their tickets.

At one o'clock every afternoon, the ticket office began to sell the remaining tickets at half-price.

Outside the theater everything grew quiet.

Inside it grew livelier day by day, as squabbles and quarrels arose again. And the quarreling backstage was more exciting than the performance on stage.

One day, an odd-jobman daringly patted the new director on the shoulder and said, "Well, mate, your troupe hasn't made much progress lately. I don't think it's got much of a future."

"What the hell do you know about it? Nowadays every cultural troupe in the country has its difficulties. We've almost been supplanted by foreign films, martial arts films and light music. But the fact that we can stick to traditional forms shows that we've achieved a political victory. Social contradictions are bound to be reflected in our troupe. Ideology's very complicated ...," the new director expounded at length. After all, he thought, these disagreements are part of life in a cultural troupe, or anywhere in the theatrical world.

Translated by Song Shouquan

The Base of the Wall

There used to be a wall here.

Lane 499 was on one side of the wall; Lane 501, also known as the Garden of Health and Joy, was on the other.

In 1958, during the Great Leap forward, the wall was dismantled for iron smelting. This brought Lane 499 and the Garden of Health and Joy into view of each other.

The wall was dismantled, but the base of the wall remained.

More than a decade has gone by, but the base still lies entrenched here. It sticks up out of the ground an inch high, and if you are running and not careful it can trip you.

* * *

The Garden of Health and Joy:

This is a lane with only ten houses. Ten families lived here, each with a little garden surrounded by an iron fence and gate.

A university biology professor lived at No. 1. His specialty was the study of human life. He used to say that a single life was like a whole world in itself. His wife had killed herself during the "Smash the 'Four Olds' Campaign," and for the simplest of reasons. The rebels wanted her to take off her pointed leather shoes, and when she refused they had slapped her face. That slap made her lose the desire to live. The couple had two daughters. The older one was grown-up and studying in university; the younger was only thirteen and named Duxing.

No. 2 belonged to an old doctor. He had studied abroad, was a highly skilled practitioner, and had run a private clinic before Liberation. His house was not the same as the others, having been remodeled. There was a reception window just inside the door. After Liberation, the government assigned him to continue running the clinic, but he had asked on his own initiative to work in a public hospital. He had a wife, one son, a daughter-in-law, and a grandson. The grandson was Duxing's schoolmate, a thirteen-year-old named Chongchong.

A big capitalist lived at No. 3. Previously, only the legitimate wife of this factory boss had lived here, with their son, Fanping. But not long after the movement started, his two concubines and their families were driven over here to live with them. Each of them had a child, a girl named Fanxin and a boy named Fanzheng.

No. 4 was the home of a musician. His children had all grown up and become musicians themselves. Only his youngest daughter, Didi, was left. She wasn't old enough yet to sign up for the exam to enter the conservatory high school but she could already play well pieces from Paganini and other famous composers. The sound of music always floated from their house. In spring this music, mingling with the fragrance of lilacs and peach trees, sounded as if a fresh bubbling brook was flowing through the lane. Later, their house was raided and the piano and violin taken away. Only silence remained.

At No. 5 was the owner of a cotton mill. . . .

At No. 6 a famous film actor. . . .

At No. 7, a professor. . . .

At No. 8. . . .

It was very peaceful here, for neither adults nor children were in the habit of loitering in the lane, and although only a wall separated them, neighbors were as unknown to one another as if they had lived at opposite ends of the earth. When they met in passing, they would exchange a slight smile at most, but never stopped to chat. Nor was there any contact among the children here, even though they all studied at the same special elementary school nearby. They did yearn to stay out in the lane for a while and play with the children next door, or to run freely out of the lane and down to the little corner store to buy something really junky to eat. But this was against the rules; the grown-ups considered it ill-bred. As a consequence, the children could only sit silently within their spacious living rooms or pretty bedrooms and try to imagine what the coarse, crowded, yet fascinating world outside was like. Of course, once they grew up, they might disdain such yearnings, and never leave their living rooms and bedrooms again.

But before Duxing and her generation could grow up or scorn their yearnings, their desires were realized in an unexpected way.

The Cultural Revolution began.

Smashing the "Four Olds," house raids, driving off servants, sealing off houses, carting away furniture ... a storm raged through. The parents became so exhausted they could no longer watch over their children closely. Now the children were needed to carry a basket and cross the road to buy vegetables at the market or to go to the grocery for oil, salt, soy sauce, or vinegar. Sometimes, they went to pawn a bundle of old clothes at a second-hand shop. But even these days of hardship that had suddenly fallen upon them offered their rewards. Now the children had a great deal of freedom. They could make friends, go outside, stand in the lane, look about them, gaze down the road, observe Lane 499 over by the wall base, and peer at the outside world with apprehensive eyes.

But the world was a disappointment. The shop windows were a monotonous red; the passersby were dressed in monotonous blue, brown, and gray; and Lane 499 was so, so ...

Lane 499.

Here's what Lane 499 was like.

Here there were twenty houses, with seventy families living in them. Every building had a flat terrace off the third floor, and every terrace had a tar paper shack built on it to make more living space.

At No. 1, on the first floor, lived a man who worked at a candy factory, with a family of six: his mother, himself, his wife, and three sons. The eldest son had settled in Xinjiang to "support the frontier." Son number two was a leader of the Red Guards at his high school. He wore a red arm band a foot wide and had a three-inch army belt around his waist. He swaggered in and out with his head held high and his chest stuck out, a figure of incomparable power. He had travelled throughout China "making revolutionary contacts." The youngest boy was a thirteen-year- old named A'nian. He idolized and envied his second older brother. Unfortunately, he was only in the eighth grade, and elementary schools had not been allowed to carry out the Great Cultural Revolution, so he could only "make revolution" in the lane. Luckily for him, there were quite a few capitalists, revisionists, and "counterrevolutionaries" in Lane 501 next door, so there was plenty of "opportunity for a hero to display his talents."

On the second floor, in a little room under the terrace, lived a mother and son. A widow known as "the Ningbo Lady," she was on the Neighborhood Committee, and Lane 501 was under her jurisdiction, so she was the one person from Lane 499 who had had some contact with Lane 501. Her son had been a very ambitious and hard-working boy who always stayed at home studying and didn't have much to do with people. In fact, in some ways he had a touch of Lane 501 about him and perhaps he had wanted to join the world of Lane 501 some day. He was an excellent student, at the top of his class at Shanghai High School. Of course, just getting into Shanghai High School was as good as having one foot in the door of a university. Besides, he was an honors' student! Then the Cultural Revolution broke out; he couldn't understand it and went out of his mind. He wore a thick padded jacket even on the hottest days of summer and repeated over and over, "Fudan University! Fudan! Fudan!" Eventually people turned the pronunciation around a little and called him Fulan, which meant "Rotten." Now, Rotten didn't hit people or yell at them; in fact, he was even more docile and obedient than before, even to younger kids like A'nian. As a result, A'nian often set him to scaring Duxing and the others from Lane 501, and Rotten was very effective.

On the third floor lived a couple who worked at a poultry yard. The husband was the quiet type. But if he didn't say much, once he did open his mouth, every other word was a foul one. As for the wife, she couldn't stop talking. You name it, she had something to say about it.

At No. 2, a woman and her children lived on the first floor. She was an attendant in a hotel. Her husband had died, and rumor had it that her children had more than just one daddy. The birth of her youngest daughter, Aqin, was a particularly dubious case since the husband had been dead over a year when she arrived. The more the rumors got around, the more dubious seemed the background of the children. It wasn't just that none of them looked the same, but they were all such a handful. Especially Aqin. She was certainly pretty and bright, but rather ... Well, at her age, to be sticking her chest out like that and always up to something with the boys.

On the second floor lived a street sweeper and his family.

In the attic was a newlywed couple. The husband was a good poker player and would play all night once he got started.

A half-blind old grandmother lived at No. 3. Her son had died and her daughter-in-law remarried, leaving her with three grandsons as pigheaded as they were ugly. The oldest and the second had both gone off to make revolution, taking even their bedding down to General Headquarters and leaving the third boy, Sanzi, at home. This one was a flunk-out, still in the eighth grade with A'nian and Aqin even though he was already fifteen.

At No. 4 lived a barber's family.

A waiter's family....

At No. 5 there was a member of a comedy troupe who could speak every kind of dialect. Often when people were enjoying the cool of a summer evening he would put on a song-and-dance routine for everyone, bringing happiness to this cramped and run-down alley.

At No. 6 ...

At No. 7 ...

Here it was all noise and confusion. There was a row or two every day, but once a fight was over, that was that. Nobody held a grudge or kept track of the lesson they'd been taught. Anyway, everyone was packed in so tight that making up was as unavoidable as fighting. And so it went, an endless cycle of fighting and making up and then fighting again. The children all went to a locally run grade school. They made themselves at home in the lane after classes, since in many families there were grown-ups on the night shift who had to sleep, and usually each family possessed only one room.

The alley was very cramped for so many people. And yet, had it been even more crowded, they would never have thought of crossing the wall base into spacious lane 501. They stood on the base sometimes and looked toward it in wonderment. It was an unknown and mysterious world. All the doors there were kept tightly shut, as though no one lived inside. Yet it was obvious that people did. Listen! The music is so pretty, nothing like the song-and-dance routine. Look! The door has opened and out they come: young, old, middle-aged, children. They are dressed so neatly—how pretty! And they have a special way of walking. Even though that old guy has a hunched back, you feel that he is easier on the eyes than your average hunchback. The Ningbo Lady says that all the floors in their houses have carpets and they've got refrigerators and televisions and everything. How lucky! How special they are! How nice it would be to go over and take a look. But there always seems to be something barring the way and keeping people from getting any closer.

At last, an opportunity had come. They could not only walk over there, they could force those heads down, heads that had always been held up so high, they could even kick the people in the back of the knee and make them kneel, push them around. It turns out those people are perfectly ordinary—their necks can bow, their legs bend, and as for their skin, it can bleed too. Well! Very interesting! Their doors are thrown wide open and the refrigerators, televisions, pianos, all carted off. How many things they've got! They've got everything! Why? But we have nothing! Not even a definite bed of our own. OK, OK, take it all away and make everybody the same! That's Communism! And yet there is still a little difference. Yes, there's still a little difference.

Well, anyway, no matter what, we've crossed the wall base, and here we are in the Garden of Health and Joy. How spacious it is here, how clean and tidy! Now this belongs to us. Those ladies and gentlemen won't be able to look down on us anymore. It's time we put down their fancy airs.

* * *

The Garden of Health and Joy:

Turbulent as it was, the world still constantly tempted them to stick their heads out and watch it all wide-eyed. It was so dull and depressing at home that you sometimes felt suffocated. They were lonely and longing for contact—Duxing, Chongchong, Fanping, Fanxin, Fanzheng, Didi. They became acquainted and started seeing a lot of one another. Together they shopped, and washed vegetables and rice in the alleyway. In the evening they deserted the grown-ups to gather quietly in one of their kitchens. There were no lights here at night anymore; the grown- ups wouldn't allow it. Apparently showing a light would just be asking for trouble. If you absolutely had to turn on a light, you had to draw the thick curtains first. What games could they play in a pitch-black kitchen? They told stories.

They would each tell one story, taking turns. Didi told stories about music, Beethoven's "Moonlight Sonata," Strauss' "Vienna Woods," Berlioz's "Symphony Fantastique." Chongchong's stories were all based on things he had heard about life overseas. His family had a lot of relatives living abroad, and his stories usually centered around a few drifters. But the capitalist society in his stories was a far cry from the one their teacher told them about.

Fanping's stories were all true, things he had heard from his dad. He was the eldest son and the favorite. His father treated him like a grown-up and told him about everything. His mom didn't know as much as he did. He was already sixteen and in the 11th grade, but because of his "bad background" he didn't qualify to join the movement, so he hung around the house all day playing with his younger brother and sister. His stories were about tough, ambitious men: how they landed in Shanghai with a bedroll on their backs, started as apprentices, made more and more money, and ended up as big bosses. Fanxin's stories were true too, things she had picked up from hearing her mother gossiping with her friends. They were all about the various complications arising out of love affairs. Fanzheng was pretty tongue-tied and got very nervous when it came his turn. Then Fanping would get his half-brother off the hook by saying, "Just have him bark like a dog." Sometimes it was "meow like a cat."

Duxing's stories were very strange. They were about things that could never actually happen in the real world, such as a girl waiting for a ship with red sails to arrive from across the sea bearing a handsome prince, or about a fisherman who told the sea, "I love you," and then was drowned by the jealous ocean on his wedding night. They all liked to hear her tell them, for her stories carried them off to a wonderful land, far, far away from real life, and much more beautiful. In such troubling times, it was a pleasure to take these magic trips. But Fanping didn't think so at all, and always listened with a scornful air as Duxing told them. Even with all the lights off, so it was so dark you couldn't see your own hand in front of your face, let alone make out the look on someone else's face, they were all aware of his attitude, since he laughed where he shouldn't have laughed, sighed where he shouldn't have sighed, and gasped where there was no reason for surprise. He said that Duxing was a "lunatic explaining her dreams." Since he was the only high school student among them, the youngsters generally went along with what he said. But there was one instance when they rebelled. This was when he suggested that they should all sneak out quietly one by one while Duxing was telling her story and leave her talking to herself in the dark. No one would agree to this. Chongchong even got mad and told Duxing.

"There's something about them that I really don't care for."

"I don't either," said Duxing.

"My father says that no matter how much money their parents have, they still don't have any culture."

"No, they don't."

"Let's not hang around with them anymore."

"Not be with them?"

"No, just us, and Didi, that's all."

"That's not enough people. It'll be lonely."

"Don't you like peace and quiet better?"

"I used to. Now I like more people around," Duxing said softly. "When there are lots of people I'm not afraid."

Chongchong said nothing.

"Chongchong?"

"Yes?"

"Can ... can I discuss something with you?"

"Sure!"

"My dad, well, lately he's been criticized some more. I'm afraid they'll come and raid our house again."

"So?"

"I'd like to leave my diaries and stamp collection at your place. Can you keep them hidden for me?"

"Me? I'll go home and ask my grandad, OK?"

"Ask your grandad?" Duxing was disappointed. "Forget it."

But Chongchong wasn't about to forget it. "Then I won't ask my granddad; I'll just ask my mother, OK?"

"Forget it!" said Duxing.

Chongchong didn't persist, and the two of them fell silent.

Just then Didi came out and called to Duxing, "Can you go shopping with me?"

"Sure."

"Chongchong, how about coming with us. If there are more of us, the people from Lane 499 won't go too far."

"OK."

As the three of them walked toward the lane, Fanzheng approached, panting. He was quite tubby, and already out of breath after just a few yards. "Me, too, me too! I'll come with you, too."

As they turned from the passage into the alleyway, they saw some kids standing on the wall base between 499 and 501, just hanging around with nothing to do. But as soon as these kids saw the four of them come out, they began to perk up, and a shout was heard: "Here come the little swells!"

Didi gripped Duxing's hand, Chongchong's face flushed, and they all quickened their pace in unspoken accord.

"Little Swells! Bastards!" And after the shouting came a shower of dirt. The noise and clouds of dust followed them.

Duxing's heart began to pound with anger and fear, and her face flushed a deep red. But she kept her self-control with all her might and held on to Didi to keep her from running. She slowed their pace and said quietly, "Don't run, they'd like nothing better than to see us running away." Their outward composure irritated the kids from 499 all the more, and this led eventually to the throwing of pieces of brick and gravel. A piece of brick flew past and then a resolutely aimed stone hit Fanzheng in the back with a thud. He bore the pain without looking back and just kept on walking calmly along as if he hadn't a care in the world. At this point someone shrieked from behind them, "Rotten! Charge!"

Didi couldn't take it anymore. With a frightened wail she wrenched free of Duxing's hand, dashed forward, and was in the street in a flash. Duxing cried out, "A bus! Look out! A bus!" Didi miraculously managed to dodge the bus and ran across to the sidewalk on the other side. Chongchong bolted across too, and Fanzheng, after a moment's hesitation, finally took to his fat little heels. Duxing ran a few steps despite herself and then a handful of dirt poured down the back of her neck. She stopped and turned around furiously. Rotten was standing there in front of her in his thick padded coat, with a handful of dirt, leering at her with a silly grin and mumbling, "Fudan University, Fudan U., Down with . . .!"

"Rotten! Charge! Charge!" A boy's voice was yapping as if to a dog. Rotten took a tentative step forward, but when he saw that Duxing was standing her ground, he stopped in his tracks, still giggling, "Fudan U., Fudan University's the best!"

"Rot—" The boy shouted one syllable, then broke off abruptly. Lane 499:

A'nian's flailing fists fell. Rotten, hearing no new orders, looked back in confusion toward the others, and then suddenly turned and fled.

"Rotten, are you scared of a little girl?" asked Sanzi.

"Not very promising to be scared of little girls; Rotten will never find a wife." Aqin giggled. She liked hanging out with the boys. They couldn't shake her no matter where they went.

Rotten looked at them and burst out with some kind of gobbledegook in a foreign language. Nobody could make out a word of it and they all howled with laughter.

The girl turned and walked away.

The doors in Lane 501 were all shut tight; not a soul was in sight. They fell silent for a while, and, briefly, even felt rather let down. But they didn't stay that way very long. A'nian suggested they go to one of the houses in 501 and make a phone call for fun. It didn't matter which one; anyway, they all had phones, and once you knocked on the door they wouldn't dare not let you in.

They charged off across the wall base and started pounding at the closest iron gate, the one at No. 1. Someone came to open the door at once, a white-haired old man. According to the big character poster over the door, this old man was a "reactionary academic authority." They remembered how many books had been carted off from his house during the house raids: several truck loads. And there had been lots and lots of childrens' books among them, colored ones, as pretty as could be. A'nian remembered the time when he had wanted to subscribe to a kids' magazine and his mother wouldn't let him because they couldn't afford it. His blood boiled: What right did this old man have, what right did any of the people in this lane have, to be so loaded? When they raided No. 3, there was enough knitting wool alone to cover two double beds; at No. 2 they had gold and silver! But A'nian and them—they had only pickles to eat day after day! It was so unfair!

A'nian stuck his thumbs in his belt and yelled, "We're coming in to make a phone call! Come on, come on, make way! A good dog doesn't get underfoot!"

"My boy, you ought to show more respect for people," said the old man with quiet dignity.

"You aren't a person, you're a cow ghost and snake spirit!" shouted A'nian.

"Down with reactionary academic authorities!"

"Thinking of overturning your verdict? No way!"

The old man said no more, but looked at them silently. His eyes were very bright, with an inexplicable glow that had something very fierce about it. A'nian murmured to himself, see if you scare me, you old goat!

The old man stepped aside silently and they swarmed in. The room, which had once been called the living room, now had several beds packed into it, just as at A'nian's but it was still a lot better than A'nian's house. The bedsteads were carved and there was a phone on the pale green wall. They rushed over to it and snatched the receiver, which, after a round of scuffling, ended up in A'nian's hand. He put it to his ear and listened. There was just a buzzing noise inside. He was a little bit taken aback, and whispered, "Who are we calling?"

They all looked at one another in dismay. Now what? After a moment, Sanzi said, "I've got a number; it's a guy in my class.

They run a corner store and have a public phone. The number is 575580."

"You sure?" A'nian asked doubtfully.

"Sure, I'm sure! When you say it in Shanghai dialect, it sounds like 'Wife Ol' Nun! Once a Bun, Once a Bun!'"

They all laughed.

"OK, we'll call them, order them to close their store; no more exploitation!" A'nian made up his mind and then dialed the "Wife Ol' Nun" number.

There was an answer at the other end. A'nian flushed with excitement and said in a shaky voice, "Hello! Is this the corner store?"

"Let me listen!" the others were begging.

"You're hogging it!" Sanzi was ready to take action.

"A'nian, let me listen a little, OK?" Aqin laid a hand on him, and he glared fiercely at her.

Countless hands reached toward him, and he had to raise his arms to fend them of. He shouted into the phone, "Socialism is here, you know that? You can't exploit people, got that? . . ." He started to make a speech, but just as he was getting warmed up, the receiver was suddenly snatched away by a hand smelling of face cream. A'nian's eyes bulged. "Give it back!"

"Let me listen for a while!" Aqin put the receiver behind her back .

A'nian twisted her arm as hard as he could. She wouldn't let go, but went on struggling and giggling, apparently getting a big kick out of the fight and trying her best to make it last. But she was no match for A'nian, and the receiver was finally snatched back. But they had already hung up at the other end. A'nian shook the receiver a few times, turned, and walked away, followed by the rest of them.

The old man was standing silently apart and moved aside to let them pass. When A'nian got to the door, he turned around again to give him a look, but his glance fell instead on a black- edged photograph on the wall of a very beautiful woman. A'nian recognized her: she was the one who killed herself after getting her face slapped. He couldn't see what was so special about having your face slapped; to go off and die for that was beyond him. If A'nian considered all the slaps he'd swallowed going back as far as he could remember, he'd never come up with a total. When his dad got tanked and blew his top, he handed them out left and right. When his mom was worn to a frazzle—Whap! The day before yesterday he had snuck a few of the leaflets his brother had brought home and sent them flying from the top of a big building nearby. He had gotten quite a shellacking from his brother, and, of course, he had hit back as best he could. These people really couldn't take it, they were just stinking intellectuals! They weren't the same as regular people.

No, not the same at all. Those four little swells just now were really something. Their clothes were very ordinary, just dark blue shirts, but there was still something fancy, or foreign, even capitalist about them. Mind you, the two girls weren't even as well dressed as Aqin! I mean, Aqin's got fluffy bangs and two loose pigtails tied with fancy black bows. But those two, they had short hair lying flat on their heads and bare foreheads. And yet, the more you looked at them, they . . . well, you couldn't quite put your finger on it. Weird! And besides, the way they walked was different too. Even now, when Rotten sent them flying, they still didn't seem upset or embarrassed. And the girl who didn't run, she was the strangest of all. Even Rotten could tell that. He just turned tail and came running back. A'nian ransacked all the vocabulary at his command to come up with a description of that girl's manner. Just as he was letting his imagination go, there the girl was, watching coldly as A'nian and his gang came out of the iron gate of her garden. A'nian stopped despite himself and glanced at her. She looked right back at him without a trace of fear. "Stuck-up!" The word suddenly came to A'nian.

* * *

Lane 501:
Duxing looked bravely at the bully. She felt weak and frightened, but she refused to run away. Her father had often told her, "A human being cannot be humiliated, nor can he lightly submit."

Her father was in biology and specialized in the study of human life. According to him, human beings had already existed on earth for three billion years. That meant that every life had traveled a distance of three billion years down to the present.

Human beings were something precious and should have self-respect.

Even as Duxing watched the gang walk farther away, her misgivings were growing more and more intense. She closed the gate, drew the bolt, and walked over to a corner of the garden. She lifted a cracked flower pot, sighed with relief, and hurriedly replaced it.

For the past few days, her father had been "struggled against and criticized" at school. When he got home, he told her and her sister, "They may come back for another house raid. If you have any diaries or letters, or whatever, you'd better get rid of them before they get us in trouble."

Duxing was really worried. The last time their house was raided, she had managed to save her stamp albums and diaries by hiding them in a hole dug under this flower pot. But she still felt uneasy. Once, when Didi's house was raided, they had dug up the entire garden to a depth of three feet. It was too dangerous here. The stamp albums were ones that her mother had begun to keep as a girl. After Duxing had gotten old enough, her mother had passed them on to her. The diaries Duxing had kept since the second grade. They were a record of the days when her mother was with them. She couldn't bear to burn them, but still less could she bear to let them fall into the hands of the Rebels. She would have to move them somewhere else, to some secure place.

But where could she find a secure place? She had thought of Chongchong's house first. It had only been raided once, during the "Four Olds" Campaign. According to her sister, his grandfather was a well-known democratic figure, without any political background, so compared to their place it was somewhat safer. Besides, she liked Chongchong best of all her friends. He was bright, sensible, knowledgeable, and very nice to her. She was surprised to find him so fainthearted that he had to ask permission from grown-ups. Duxing was sure that the grown-ups in his family would not allow him to do something like this. Who wasn't looking for some peace and quiet these days? Duxing didn't blame him. She sighed softly. Then Fanzheng occurred to her; she liked Fanzheng best of the three in his family . . . She had heard him say once that he had a secret place. After they had moved in, their house had been raided again by Red Guards from Beijing. He had hidden some articles made of gold there, and they had escaped detection. Yes, she would try asking him.

Once Duxing had made up her mind, she stood up, walked out the back gate, and went to No. 3 to look for Fanzheng.

But there was such a racket coming from No. 3 that Duxing took fright for a moment, thinking that people had come to make trouble again. But as soon as she calmed down and listened, she realized that it was something else. It was Fanping's mother, Fanxin's mother, and Fanzheng's mother having a quarrel, and a loud one at that—they seemed to have not the slightest fear of attracting attention and bringing on the Red Guards.

Duxing hesitated for a moment and then called several times, "Fanzheng!" Then she stopped. It didn't seem proper to be bothering people at a time like this, so she turned around to leave. Then an upstairs window opened and Fanzheng's chubby face appeared, looking flustered and anxious. "Did you call me?"

Duxing nodded. "You're busy; I'll go."

"No, I'll come right down." Fanzheng's head vanished inside and after a moment the door opened. As soon as he came out he exclaimed with a frown, "What a pain. They're fighting again."

Duxing said nothing. She didn't like inquiring about such things, but Fanzheng went on, preoccupied with his own concerns.

"Fanxin's mother cooked a pot of rice, but somebody poured in a whole lot of salt, so it was so salty it made your mouth hurt. She said it was Fanping, and they started shouting. My mother thought she'd play the peacemaker by cooking another pot for them, but then Fanxin's mother turned around and said that I put the salt in."

"What's the point of all this?" Duxing objected gently.

"Really, there isn't any, none at all! Fanping's mother insists that Fanxin's mother and mine want to kill her so that they can get all the property for themselves."

Duxing looked up in surprise, "Are they still fighting over such things in times like these?"

"It's beyond me. What property is left now? Everything has been confiscated."

Duxing didn't know what to say, so she fell silent.

"Why were you looking for me?" Fanzheng suddenly remembered to ask.

"Well, my . . . lately my father has been, you know, I have a few things I'd like to . . . kind of leave here with you. Didn't you say you had a good place?"

Fanzheng frowned again. "The past few days things have been very tense at our house. We hear there's a group of Red Guards coming to Shanghai from Beijing, especially to raid the houses of capitalists. My mother has poured out all our ink. They like to pour ink on your bed sheets."

Duxing knew that he was making excuses and couldn't help feeling disappointed. She just said, "Forget it. I'll think of something else." Then she turned and went home.

That evening, Duxing stayed up after her father had gone to sleep behind the screen in their room, and her sister was also asleep. The more she thought about it, the more it seemed that the gang of bullies breaking in that afternoon hadn't been a coincidence. It was definitely a sign of something. Perhaps her father's school had been in touch with the Neighborhood Committee and asked them to increase their surveillance. Otherwise, why should all those people have forced their way in on one of her father's rare Sundays at home? Duxing was very frightened. She tiptoed out into the garden, lifted the cracked flower pot, and clutched the bundle of things in her arms. Her mother—if only her mother were still with her—she wouldn't need to treasure these things so. Why did you have to die? Father told us not to blame you. People cannot be humiliated; they should protect their dignity with their lives. Why are those people so savage, so cruel? How can they be? According to father, humanity has already travelled for three billion years, and yet they are still so savage. I hate them, that gang of little thugs from Lane 499; how mean they are, how disgusting, always picking on us. But I won't die, I'll fight them!

Mother, dearest mother! I will keep the things you left me, and the memories, safe and sound, I will! But where will they be safe? Where can I be sure of them? She was beside herself with anxiety.

Say! She suddenly recalled the row of holly bushes in the lane. Could she dig a hole inside the hedge? Yes, yes! She could!

They'd certainly be safe there. The holly bushes could keep them secret. Duxing had no time to waste on reflection; she picked up her things, opened the gate, and walked outside.

The lane was pitch-black, without a glimmer of light or the slightest sound. It was already past ten o'clock and there wasn't a hint of anyone in the lane. She peered carefully toward Lane 499, but it was pitch-black there too, and perfectly still. She dashed over to the holly hedge and started to dig.

Suddenly a hand reached out from behind her and seized the bundle. Duxing gasped and turned around to find a dusky face visible in the moonlight, its smirk revealing two rows of yellow, crooked teeth.

"Aha! Burying secret documents!"

Duxing started and leapt toward him, grabbing his collar with all her might, but she was shaken off.

Lane 499:

"Hey! So this is it!" A'nian opened up a stamp album, gaping with delight.

"Wow!"

"Fantastic!"

"Really something!"

He turned one page after another, using up the entire stock of superlatives at his disposal. He had never collected these things. He had collected cigarette cards; they were lots of fun, color pictures of all kinds of heroes, like Guan Yu, Yue Fei and Sun Erniang. But compared to these stamps, they didn't amount to much. They were really crude, but these were beautiful! They were just like paintings, so fine and neat. The colors were so pretty, really nice! A'nian didn't dare actually touch them. After he had looked through the first album, he ran out to the sink and washed his hands, soaping them twice, before carefully picking up the second album, and then the third.... There were five in all. He spread out his arms and leaned over them like an old hen brooding on her eggs. He was excited and happy; his heart was pounding. They're all mine now, fantastic! Really something! First-rate! Wow! After a while, he remembered the other two things, two notebooks filled with tiny script. He leafed through them casually, and then gave a start. Written on one of the pages were the words "Mother died today because someone slapped her face!"

A'nian's heart skipped a beat. He put the stamp albums aside for the moment and read on anxiously.

". . . Sister says that Mother was too fragile, but Father says it wasn't fragility, but that she protected her dignity with her life; and what value does life have without dignity?

"Mother had never been humiliated like this; she had never been treated with anything but respect. Her students, her colleagues, Father, Sister, me, we all respected and loved her. And she respected others. Even the old worker from the housing office who came to fix the plumbing, she always shook his hand and poured him some tea, even if he never drank it. Mother said that people ought to show respect to one another . . .

"But those people insisted that she take off her shoes right on the street. How could she? Even on the hottest days of summer, Mother always dressed neatly. She said, a human being should look like one. Don't those people understand such things?

"Mother . . ."

The reminiscences broke off here, and the rest of the page was blank. He turned the page, but it was blank too. A'nian turned back, entranced by the diary.

"Today was my thirteenth birthday. As soon as I opened my eyes this morning, I found a pretty package beside my pillow, a birthday present from Father and Mother. I could hardly wait to open it . . ."

Click! The light went out and darkness fell. A'nian yelled frantically, "Hey! The light! The light!"

"What about the light, you zombie! How're we going to pay for it all?!" His mother grumbled, half asleep.

"Brat! It's midnight! What do you need it for?"

A'nian gritted his teeth in anger, but all he could do was gather up the things, feeling around for them in the dark. Inside, he was still wondering what that girl had actually gotten for her birthday present. A'nian had also had thirteen birthdays, but he had never gotten any presents. All of a sudden he longed to get a present, yet at the same time realizing that he probably never would. His mother and father provided him with food, clothing and other necessities, but it would never occur to them to give him anything for his birthday, especially not in such a marvelous way: quietly leaving it by his pillow at night.

A'nian turned over and folded his arms behind his head. That girl's family must be interesting, they were so polite to one another. From what the diary said, it was their respect for one another. They paid a lot of attention to that "respect" business. A'nian couldn't help thinking of his own family. In all fairness, he had to admit that although his mother and father took good care of them, they had no conception of "respect." No, none whatever! A'nian sighed.

The next morning, after breakfast, his father and mother went to work, and his older brother went off to school to take part in the movement. A'nian closed the door and fastened the latch. He opened up the plastic-covered bundle, opened the diary, and singlemindedly began to read. He didn't like reading. It seemed to him that the stuff in books was just put in there by some writer to fool people. But this diary was something real; he didn't believe that pale girl had what it took to write a book. This was real, and new to him, a life he had never experienced, life in Lane 501. This was the kind of life that went on in the peace and spaciousness of Lane 501, behind the roomy parlors, the pianos and refrigerators, a kind of life that intrigued him no end.

"The whole family decided to have a big party to celebrate Mother's and Father's twentieth anniversary. I decided to make dessert all by myself. But I ended up making a complete mess of it. I not only spoiled a lot of butter and flour, but it tasted awful, and on top of that I cracked the cut glass bowl in the oven. I was so upset I started to cry. But Mother and Father comforted me and said they were very happy because I meant well ..."

If this had happened to A'nian, he would have gotten a beating for sure—see if they cared whether he "meant well" or not.

"Father is smoking again. He quit a month ago, but I found him hiding in the bathroom and smoking today, and we all criticized him. Sister said that it showed a lack of willpower, and he agreed."

Children and grown-ups were quite equal in this family. Not like at A'nian's. If he ever dared talk back he'd end up on the losing end of it. What grown-ups said was always right. A'nian suddenly felt very sad and depressed. He realized that his life was lacking something.

"Sister is trying to qualify for the Youth League. She says she is going to hand everything over to the organization and lay her heart bare without reserve. She is going to let the League branch secretary read her diaries. But Mother says that is quite unnecessary. She says that everyone has a corner in her heart in which to keep a few personal secrets, a museum for the spirit that need not be opened up to everyone. I think Mother is right. I am only thirteen, but I have so many secrets, so very many . . ."

"A'nian! A'nian!" Bang, bang, bang! Sanzi was knocking on the door.

"What do you want?" A'nian asked angrily, as though waking from a dream.

"Come play checkers, four-sided free-for-all!"

"No!"

"What are you up to?"

"None of your business!"

"Let me come in and see!"

"No!"

Bang, bang, bang! Sanzi started knocking again.

"Piss off!" A'nian bellowed, flying into a rage.

"If you ask me, you've gone nuts, just like Rotten!" Sanzi left in a huff.

A'nian hadn't even found his place again when there was another noise at the door. This time it was a light tapping, like a chicken pecking at grain. A'nian was afraid it might be someone come to see his parents and got up at once to answer the door.

There in the doorway stood Aqin. A'nian tried to slam the door shut, but not in time. She had already squeezed halfway through.

"What are you up to?"

"Nothing!"

"Aren't you going to play checkers? Four-sided free-for- all."

"No!"

"What's this?" She picked up the nicely bound red diary curiously.

"Don't touch that!" A'nian grabbed Aqin's hand and yanked it so hard that she lost her balance.

But Aqin didn't get mad, and just went on giggling, "Say! So mean? Why aren't you coming outside today?"

"Did I ask you to butt in? Did I?" A'nian was fed up with her. He grabbed her arm, pushed her out roughly, and latched the door again.

Must be lunch time! Not a bit of peace and quiet anywhere! What's all this about places for keeping precious secrets? A museum for the spirit? Shit! The stuff in those people's heads was so complicated, and there was so much of it, and it was so ... so wonderful! In Lane 499, everything was public and right out in the open. Everybody knew everyone else's business and there was no hiding anything from anyone. Like the last time Sanzi squeezed Aqin's cheek, first thing you knew, everybody and his brother were in on it. You were even inevitably forced to come out with what you only thought to yourself.

"A'nian! Hu Weinian!" More noise outside, and enough to wake the dead.

Fortunately, they didn't have any secrets at all, or anything precious to keep. But A'nian did now; he had the five stamp albums and the two diary volumes, and there seemed to be more than just these. He had to find a place to hide them; just sticking them under the covers wasn't going to work for very long. A'nian thought for a moment, then pushed the bed aside, pried up a loose floorboard, and put everything under it, wrapped in the plastic.

"Hu Weinian! A notice!"

"You want to wake the dead?" A'nian stuck his head out the window and then stopped short despite himself. There was a postman standing in the alley, actually holding a piece of paper and looking right up at him.

"Hu Weinian! A notice!"

A'nian tore outside and accepted the notice. Hey! It was a notice of admission to high school. He was assigned to Municipal No. 2 High School. That was a key school! He hadn't passed any exam for it, though. Now the general policy was to assign by district. From now on, there wouldn't be any difference between key schools and ordinary ones; they would all be equal. Sanzi, Aqin, and Mao Er were all going to Municipal No. 2.

* * *

Lane 501:

Duxing, Chongchong, Didi, Fanxin, and Fanzheng all got notices, and they were all going to Municipal No. 2. Before the Great Cultural Revolution, it took a score of at least 180 to get into this school. They were all overjoyed, but their spirits fell after they heard that all the tough kids from Lane 499 were also assigned to No. 2.

And after three days at school, their spirits fell still lower, practically out of sight. There was no change in their lives at all, nor was school at all interesting. Besides, they were constantly running into the people from Lane 499, and that was tough. As soon as they entered the school gate each morning, they had to undergo a strict examination.

"Got your badge on?"

"Got your 'little red book' and 'Three Essays'?"

This was called "checking the five gots." If you were missing even one of these five treasures, the badge, the 'little red book' or whatever, you had to go home and get it. The students entrusted with this inspection work were all children of proper class status, from poor families. The people from Lane 499 all took on this responsibility, and wore red arm bands on their sleeves. Just as soon as they saw anyone from Lane 501, they would immediately raise their voices and look very stern. They were terribly demanding as well. Once, when Didi wore a white plastic badge on a white shirt, Yu Aqin, her pigtails tied up like two little clubs, insisted that she go home and change it, saying it looked as if she didn't have a badge on at all, which defeated the purpose of "warmly loving Chairman Mao."

One day Duxing was stopped by the same girl, and only then did she realize that she had forgotten to pin on her badge when she changed jackets that morning. For the past few days, her father had had to go to work every day even though his heart was troubling him. She and her sister were both beside themselves with anxiety. Now, she just stood there blankly, not knowing what to do.

"Don't just stand there like a dummy; run back and get it!" roared Yu Aqin ferociously.

Duxing looked at her coldly, then turned and left. As she came to the corner, she suddenly heard footsteps rushing up behind her.

"I'll give you a badge."

She turned around, and it was that boy from Lane 499. They weren't in the same class, so she didn't know his name. But she knew that he was the one who had grabbed her things that night. She knew very well how inhumanly cruel those people were. You couldn't get their sympathy even if you got down on your knees and begged them. And she was certainly not going to beg him. Her mother's mementoes were gone, but her mother remained in her heart, in its most precious corner, where no one could snatch her away.

He held his hand out to her, with a huge badge in it the size of a saucer.

She looked at him coldly, then turned and walked away, without uttering a word. When she had gone a few paces, she heard him mutter, "OK for you!" Duxing wanted very much to turn around and take a look, but she wouldn't permit herself to. She hated him, because he hated her. And why did he hate her? She had never done him any wrong; they didn't know each other at all. And yet his hatred of her ran so deep; he was sorry he couldn't run her whole family out of Lane 501. She just couldn't understand it. How could anyone be happy when there was so much hatred in life?

Father's illness was entirely due to his unhappiness. It was his heart: it had grown too heavy having to bear all his joys and anger, happiness and grief. And so it simply got sick.

Fanxin had told her there had been yellow croakers at the market for the past few days, very fresh and very cheap, too. But you had to get up early for it, the earlier the better! Duxing wanted to buy some. Her father didn't feel like eating. He took only a little bit at each meal. It was all because the food wasn't tasty. Vegetables really were scarce at this season, and her older sister wasn't much of a cook. Duxing couldn't cook either, but she was responsible for the shopping. She decided that she would buy some yellow croaker. She thought of talking with Chongchong and the others about going together the next morning. More people meant greater strength, and they wouldn't have to be afraid of those bullies shoving them around. Whenever those kids from 499 saw them going shopping, they got a glint in their eyes, as if waiting to rejoice in some disaster to befall them. Besides, they were always cutting in front and crowding them out of line. She detested them, but at the same time she dared not provoke them. It was a little better if you had more people; they could keep your spirits up, if nothing else. If Chongchong and the others went, there would be more people, but, by the same token, wouldn't there be less fish? No, better not ask them. Duxing would sneak out by herself, leave at three in the morning and be first in line. Nobody could butt in front then.

It was absolutely pitch-black out. The wind blew like the scraping of a sharp knife against her cheeks as Duxing walked down the deserted avenue, but she was perfectly happy. She would definitely be first in line, no doubt about it. Look, there isn't a single soul out on the street. Up ahead at the market there is no one, only a dim yellow light. But as she drew nearer, she broke into a run despite herself, as though afraid someone might come up from behind her. She made it to the fish counter in a single dash, and there really was no one there. But she could see a line of bricks, broken baskets, and stools strung out in front of the counter. From recent experiences, she knew that these stood for people; they were people's tokens. She sighed and took her place honestly at the end of this strange line, lined up behind a tile. At least there were only a few "people" in front of her, only fifteen souls. She calmed down and began to watch the tightly closed shutters over the counter. Hmm, there was a slit of light showing, and people talking inside. Had the yellow croakers come?

People started arriving: a woman, who lined up behind Duxing, then a man who took his place in front of her. The tile had served its purpose and was kicked aside. As the sky began to get a little light, more and more people came, forming a long, long, and somehow very crude line, with Duxing squeezed tight against the man in front, so that no one could cut in front.

Now the sky was bright, and the air above the market echoed with the din of voices. But Duxing heard nothing, fixing her eyes on the shutters ahead of her as they opened slowly. An old man announced, "There isn't much fish, so those in back don't need to wait!"

Well, Duxing could be said to be near the front, but she began to feel uneasy. Besides, she could feel a turbulent force pushing its way up from behind her. Then she saw that the gang from 499 had come, a big bunch, both boys and girls. They charged ahead, forcing their way past everyone else. The line was disrupted at once and broke up. People were shoving each other and yelling, their baskets held up in the air. Duxing instinctively fell back a step, but a boy's voice just behind her said, "Push forward, or you won't be able to buy any."

Duxing tried, but she couldn't budge. She saw the shopping basket on the boy's head swim past her like a fish. The gang from 499 were all right in front of the counter, and she couldn't help admiring them. Those people were very strong, and they relied on their strength, but Duxing could only rely on order. Now that this age of disorder was upon them, she was left without any recourse.

With a shout, the crowd broke up. There was nothing left on the counter but a few fish scales; the fish were gone. Duxing stood there woodenly for a moment, then turned and started to walk back, only to meet again the kids from 499, all smiles.

"Hey! Did you get some yellow croaker?"

"Got one empty basket!"

Duxing looked at them blankly and kept on walking. They fell silent somehow, as though they had taken pity on her. Suddenly, a boy stepped forward, blocking her way. He held up a fish and tossed it into her basket. After that, a girl tossed another one in, and another, and then the tall boy tossed in a small one. Duxing was terror-struck, and it took a moment before she understood. She looked up, her eyes sweeping coldly over them once. Then she turned over her basket, spilling all the fish out, and walked away.

Lane 499:

"Who does she think she is!"

"We'll show her a thing or two!"

"Sanzi, what are you doing taking a big one; only the little one is yours!"

"Bull! The big one is mine."

"I saw it plain as could be. The big one is A'nian's; he led off giving them to her."

"Hey, A'nian! Here's your fish! Don't just stand there like a dummy!"

A'nian stood silently watching Duxing (he already knew that her name was Duxing; what a funny name!). She was far away now. Why was her look so cold, so full of hatred and disdain? She despised A'nian, despised him, and now A'nian was admitting that she had every right to. He had read all of Duxing's diaries and he was ashamed, ashamed of himself and even more of his father and mother.

That evening, the head teacher of A'nian's class came to visit. His mother wasn't home, only his father, who was just having himself a fine old time, sitting with one foot up on a bench digging the dirt out from between his toes and nursing a liquor bottle.

"Dad, my teacher is here," called A'nian, feeling very awkward for some reason.

"Oh." His father turned to look at the teacher and nodded, still rubbing the crack between his toes with one hand. "Have a seat!"

The teacher sat down and, perhaps without meaning anything by it at all, looked at his dad's raised foot. A'nian blushed.

But his dad was quite nonchalant, noisily sipping his liquor and chomping on his peanuts.

A'nian's face went red and white by turns. He wished for all the world that he could hide his head in a hole somewhere. He wasn't the sort of student to be respectful to his teachers. At school he treated them with the same arrogance as the other students. But this time . . .

After the teacher left, A'nian blew up at his father. "That was really disgusting! My teacher comes, and you go right on picking your feet!"

"Your teacher's got no feet?"

"A grown-up, and you don't understand more manners than that!"

"Here's for teaching your old man lessons!" the father shouted, giving his son a hard slap.

A'nian swept the cup and plate off the table while his father stared dumbfounded.

A'nian started to cry, hurt as he had never been before. This was the first time in his life he had felt humiliated by a slap. He was so upset he bit his pillow and tore a hole in it. His father jeered at him, "Where did you pick this up? Cranky blockhead!" The next day, everyone in the lane knew about A'nian. Now they all laughed at him for being a "cranky blockhead." For the first time in his life A'nian felt alone.

"Hey, A'nian!" Rotten was giggling in the doorway.

A'nian gave him a look and turned away without saying a word.

"They say you're just like me now, passed the exam for Fudan U.," Rotten said, laughing.

"Get lost!"

"It's good to go to school! To get an education! I'm going to register tomorrow, at Fudan, Fudan U.!"

A'nian turned again to look at Rotten. Suddenly he realized that this lunatic was capable of saying something sensible once in a while. "Get an education and then what?"

"If you're educated, people respect you." For the moment Rotten seemed to be completely rational.

"If you're educated, you know how to respect other people," A'nian added gravely.

"Yes! Yes!" Rotten started to skip for joy. He came over and tugged at A'nian. "Go to Fudan, let's go!"

"Don't get all worked up!" A'nian pushed him away, and Rotten walked away downcast.

The sound of the song-and-dance act floated up from downstairs. A'nian was sunk in gloom. All of a sudden he wanted to write something; how about a diary! What could he write it in? You couldn't find anything like a proper notebook in their house. He crawled under the bed and pulled out Duxing's diaries. The last half of one of them was blank; why not write it there?

He started to write. "Today I'm very upset and depressed. I keep thinking about that Duxing. She hates me so much and it's all my fault. I've treated her terribly; why did I have to be so mean to her? Was it just because they have nice food and clothes and houses? That's pretty low; no good at all! They are highly educated. But now she despises me! We're next door neighbors; why have we never had anything to do with each other before? If we had, there wouldn't be all this hating!"

It took him a long time just to write these few lines. Lots of the words were spelt wrong, and besides, he felt that he hadn't expressed himself clearly. He felt a profound sense of regret and heaved a sigh. What did she do every day? He wanted to go see. He'd go tonight!

Why was Lane 501 so dark at night? Why didn't they turn on any lights? And there wasn't a sound either. Wait, yes there was, in the kitchen of No. 3. It was pitch-black in there too, but someone was talking—a girl's voice.

"The daughter of the sea was willing to give up her three hundred-year lifespan to become a human being and have a human soul. The witch of the sea said, 'Fool! If you want to be a human being, you'll have to give up your fish's tail and grow two legs. It's very painful.' The little mermaid said, 'I can bear it.' The witch said, 'Once you've turned into a human being, you can't change back. And if you do not win the prince's love you will turn into sea spray!' 'I'm willing.' 'I won't help you change unless you give me your tongue.' 'I'm willing.' . . . ."

A'nian was spellbound. He had never heard such a story. Why was the little mermaid so anxious to become a human being? Was it that great or happy to be a human being?

"When the prince was about to be married, the witch gave the mermaid a knife. If she stabbed the prince in the heart before sunrise, she could turn back into a fish and return to the sea. Otherwise, she would turn into sea spray. But the little mermaid threw the knife far away into the sea. She wouldn't hurt the prince and so she turned into spray. . . ."

A'nian wanted to cry; his heart had melted. He looked up and gazed into the pitch-black lane, his heart brimming with a feeling of mystery and peace that he had never known before. This was Lane 501!

Lane 501:

The peace and calm here were short-lived.

After dark, the gate of No. 1 was violently thrown open. The other nine doors remained tightly shut, without a ray of light or the slightest noise, as though they wished only to sink below the ground, to be forgotten by the world and left in peace.

The door of No. 1 stood wide open, and a light was brought out to iluminate the place. A loudspeaker of deafening volume was set up. The gateway was filled with people, all of whom had walked over from Lane 499 to take part in an on-the-spot criticism meeting.

Duxing was coming home from a fellow student's house. As soon as she entered the lane, her heart skipped a beat. What was happening? So many people surrounding the entrance, such a bright light! Her heart began to pound, and she broke into a run. But just as she did, her arm was grabbed by a strong hand. Before she could scream, another hand covered her mouth, an earthy-smelling hand that stopped her breath. She struggled with all her might, but the hands swung her around and pulled her away in a different direction. They ran terribly fast, so fast that she stumbled over the wall base, but she was dragged up before she could fall down.

They ran up several stairs, down a musty hallway smelling of greasy smoke, and through a door. Once Duxing was released, she got her footing to run away, but the door was closed and there he was leaning against it, gasping for breath and looking at her with a nervous grin that revealed yellow, crooked teeth. Yes; this was Lane 499.

Lane 499:

As he looked at her, Duxing backed up a step and demanded, "What do you want?"

A'nian wiped the sweat from his face with a grimy hand and stammered, "My name is A'nian. Don't ... don't hate me!"

Duxing bit her lip, walked toward the door, and reached for the latch.

"No! You can't go back. At your house ..."

Duxing stopped and looked at him, hatred masking the fear in her gaze.

A'nian could scarcely go on. "At your house, there's trouble at your house; you can't go back. I've been waiting for you in the lane all this time, 'cause I was scared for you."

Duxing stared at him.

"I'm on your side, honest!"

Duxing sneered.

A'nian stood there, wondering how he would ever make her believe him. He raged at himself for having been so mean. He was silent for a while, and then he suddenly looked up, strode over to the bed, crawled under it, and pulled up the floorboard.

"Look!"

Duxing looked doubtfully down at the hole in the floor.

"I didn't spoil them at all," he stammered, "I only wrote on a few blank pages; I've been keeping a diary."

Duxing's legs gave way; she knelt on the floor, took the package up in her arms, and began to cry. Great tears dropped onto the floor, one after another. A'nian's nose twitched; he didn't know what he could do to make her feel better, so he just said over and over, "I'm giving them back to you; I'm giving them back to you."

Still sobbing, Duxing suddenly clutched his hand. She wanted to say something, but she couldn't find the words. A'nian was astonished, and blushed to the roots of his hair. He felt so awkward, so sad, filled with agony and yet so utterly, utterly happy. It was true, he was happy! So happy he trembled for joy.

Suddenly there was a big noise, someone knocked on the door and yelled, "Brat! What are you up to? Open up!"

"My dad!" A'nian's face fell. He didn't know how his rough and ill-tempered dad would treat Duxing, and he was even more afraid of how his dad might embarrass him in front of such a young lady.

"Killing yourself? Open up!"

Bang, bang, bang, bang, bang!

"The kid has hung himself in there!"

"Is someone inside?" His banging had brought the neighbors out.

"The kid is dead!" His dad was beside himself.

"Now there mustn't be a real accident here!" More and more of the neighbors were gathering around. It would have been easier to try to jump over the moon than to try to do the tiniest thing here without everybody finding out.

A'nian and Duxing were paralyzed. They stood hand-in-hand, unable to move a muscle.

The pounding on the door stopped. Instead there was the quiet creaking of metal scraping on wood. They were prying it open!

The door opened and people poured in like floodwater through a broken dike, only to come to a stupefied halt.

Silence.

"A girl."

"Looks like that old guy's daughter."

"How did she sneak in here?"

Aqin chimed right in too. "Yes, yes, her name is Duxing. Why haven't you gone home? The Rebels are looking for you. They want you to come clean . . ."

A'nian's dad shouted her down. "You just back off a little; this isn't any of your business."

Aqin looked at him in astonishment. She moved hesitantly to one side, but she couldn't bear to leave.

"Dad," A'nian's brother spoke up, "We should send her back; she has to show the Rebels where she stands."

"Cut the crap!" His dad glared at him.

"You can't cover up for the children of cow ghosts and snake spirits; I'm going to report."

Whap! Brother caught one on the ear. His dad turned and said to the crowd, "I'll handle this myself; I don't need your help. But anyone goes shooting off his mouth, he'll answer to me!"

No one said anything. Rotten's mother made her way out first, very quietly, and the others followed after, with Aqin dragging her feet and looking behind her all the way out, in blank amazement.

A'nian's dad came over to Duxing and said, "Don't be afraid; I'll go out and have a look. You can go back after those people have left." Then he turned and walked out, closing the door as he went.

Duxing was shaking all over, but she gradually calmed down as she watched this gruff and husky man leave and began to feel a certain sense of safety. She stopped crying, raised her head, and looked around the room, asking quietly, "This is your house?"

"Yes. It's awfully run-down." A'nian felt very awkward. "We're very poor."

"No, your house is nice." Duxing meant it. She felt a kind of warmth here. Of course it was poor and cramped. Lane 501, where she lived, was more spacious and comfortable than this, even after being raided and sealed. With each family having its own house, there was no occasion for friction with the neighbors; peace and harmony could be maintained. But this meant people were cut off from one another. They understood mutual respect, but the respect did not necessarily lead to warmth. Yes, in Lane 501 people kept their distance from one another.

"A'nian! Come here a minute!" His dad was back.

Father and son went out, closing the door behind them.

Although they lowered their voices as much as possible, they were still perfectly audible to Duxing.

"Brat, how come you're mixed up with her?"

"She lives in Lane 501, right by our place!" answered A'nian, not without a certain slyness.

His old man didn't say anything for a while, and then asked, "You know her dad's a cow ghost and snake spirit?"

"Yes," muttered A'nian, "but people can't be so cruel to each other. They're human beings, after all!"

His old man was silent for a while before answering, "Sounds like you're catching on, little rascal."

It was the middle of the night before things quieted down at No. 1, Lane 501, and A'nian took Duxing home. Nobody breathed a word of what had happened. Even A'nian was amazed to find that the residents of Lane 499 could actually keep a secret. Nevertheless, many days later, Aqin spread the rumor that A'nian was sweet on a young lady from Lane 501. A'nian offered no explanation. He didn't pay any attention to Aqin and Aqin didn't pay any attention to him. She had been accepted into a little theatrical troupe and now strutted in and out of Lane 499 dressed in khaki fatigues with a real waistline, swinging her short pigtails around, chest and behind stuck out, as though the whole place were beneath her notice.

After this, a change seemed to take place between Lanes 499 and 501. It is hard to describe. Between the grown-ups nothing seemed to change, but when the youngsters met, they nodded and smiled, and sometimes they paused to chat. To their surprise, both sides had discovered that barriers were created by a lack of contact. Why should they be arrogant and harbor prejudice against the other? Since they lived on the same street, why couldn't they stop when they met and get to know one another a little, exchange a few words, even if it were no more than a simple hello? Maybe then the barriers and hatred would disappear. Perhaps even understanding and friendship could grow.

Two years later, they all graduated. The assignment plan was thoroughly "red." They were all sent out to the countryside to "make revolution." Whether they were from Lane 501 or Lane 499, off they went in little groups, to Jiangxi, to Anhui, to Yunnan, to

Heilongjiang, all over the vast world. In that world there were no wall bases.

Epilogue

By the time the ten years of catastrophe were over, the youngsters had become adults in their twenties, and, by and large, had already found their places.

Lane 501:

Chongchong got back to Shanghai on grounds of illness in 1973 and went right to work in a neighborhood production unit. After the fall of the Gang of Four and the thaw in Sino-American relations, he went to live with an aunt in America who had no children of her own and came into his inheritance.

In 1974, while she was assigned to a farming village, Didi applied to music school, but when she was rejected for failing the "political check," she killed herself. She didn't leave any suicide note— just smashed her beloved violin.

Fanping graduated with the class of 1966 and was assigned to work earlier than the others. He used to be at a state farm in the suburbs of Shanghai, but not long ago he was transferred back to be a worker in a state-run factory. Countless girls are after him because a great deal of money was returned to his father, and the children all got quite a lot, him most of all.

Fanzheng came back to Shanghai because of illness and works in a production unit. He isn't hard up for money either.

Fanxin was transferred to a provincially run factory in the first batch of workers recruited back from Anhui. She is now married to a wealthy, if none too young, overseas Chinese and lives the life of a contented housewife in Shanghai without any further need for wages or a residence permit.

Duxing passed an entrance examination for university in 1977. Her father had hoped she would continue in his profession and study biology. But she wanted to study social economy. Life is full of mystery and wonder, but it is also very practical. If people are to have a good life in this world, they need the most rational social forms and organizational structures. She is now fascinated with this realm of study that is more practically related to real life.

In Lane 501, the sealed-off rooms have been reopened, the belongings that luckily managed to survive have been restored, the sequestered salaries have been made up, and the confiscated savings returned. The lilacs once again spread their fragrance, and the peace and tidiness of bygone days have been recovered. The melodically flowing sound of a piano is heard once again. And the iron gates are once again tightly shut.

Lane 499:

Most of the kids here came back to Shanghai via the replacement route, to take up their parents' occupations: in barber shops, restaurants, condiment shops, sanitation units, and so forth.

Sanzi had no one to replace, so he settled down in a little out-of-the-way town in Anhui. He's got two kids already and speaks nothing but Anhui dialect. He doesn't come back to Shanghai much, partly because money is a problem, partly because he doesn't much feel like it.

Aqin went right on hanging out with the boys. In Jiangxi she got mixed up with one shady bunch after another, and in pretty questionable ways. It's said that she was held there for re-education a few times. Eventually she ended up somehow or other getting married to a local man and produced a baby boy before nine months had passed.

A'nian's older brother was arrested after the fall of the Gang of Four. He had stomped on an old school principal at a struggle meeting during the Cultural Revolution and broken two of his ribs. The old man had died afterwards, so he was sentenced to do seven years at Tilan Bridge.

As for A'nian, he passed the entrance examination for a university Chinese department in 1977. He regularly publishes essays and short poems about human nature and humanism in the school magazine, and some of his poems are regularly copied into diaries by romantic girls. His father doesn't understand these poems and essays, but he has a great deal of respect for his son, and is proud as punch that he has become so educated.

Lane 499 is just as cramped and rough as ever. There are more children in the lane now and so it is even more crowded and noisy than before. But no matter how tightly they are packed in, they never go to Lane 501 anymore to play or make trouble.

The base of the wall is still there, entrenched. Almost an inch high, it sticks up from the ground in stubborn silence.

Translated by Daniel Bryant

Between Themselves

B icycles sounding their bells shuttled in and out of the lane, a two-way lane used as a thoroughfare. It was lined with smart modern houses, but at one end people had built many shacks. None of these had gas installed, so firewood crackled and smoke belched as they lit their stoves. A boy seated in front of one smoky stove was eating pot stickers. First he ate the pastry, keeping back the meat stuffing. He put those pitifully small meatballs in the bottom of a large bowl, then ate them one by one.

"Did you never eat meat in your last life?" swore Grandad. Grandad was eating a big bowl of thick gruel.'

The boy chomped the meat stuffing.

"That child chomps like a pig," said Granny, across the way. She was lighting her stove, her tattered fan wafting up wreaths of black smoke.

"I've not stinted him of meat. The wretch must have starved to death in his last life!" Grandad angrily rapped his chopsticks on the back of the boy's head.

Ducking, the boy chomped more loudly.

"Damn it! The meat stuffing in these dumplings has shrunk to a piddling speck." Grandad picked one up from his grandson's bowl, then dropped it back in disgust.'

A woman on a small-wheeled bike rode out from the lane and shot through the smoke. He spat at her, his gob of spittle landing on her back carrier. He was expert in spitting far and accurately.

Soon all the meat stuffing was gone. The boy got up, put his satchel on his head and raced off. In his hurry he trod on Granny's foot. She screeched, "Are you blind, young devil!"

Grandad chimed in, "Drop dead, you wretch!"

By now the boy was out of sight. His school was just around the corner, close enough for him to run home in the ten minutes' break to gobble a ball of cold rice.

Satchel on his head, he dashed forward as he made a hooting noise with his mouth, like an automobile horn. He trod on someone's heel so that his shoe came off, knocked over a child, fell over himself, got up again, rubbed his knees, and sprinted on. When he reached the school gate two of his classmates stopped him to see if he had brought a handkerchief. He produced one, grimy and black but neatly folded. After some hesitation they let him pass, as it undoubtedly was a handkerchief.

Having run this blockade, he dashed on, knocking right into someone else who staggered without falling over. Shouts went up near by.

"Wang Qiangxin's bumped into Teacher Zhang. Bumped into a teacher!"

He pulled up.

Still stunned, Teacher Zhang turned to smile at him. "Never mind, it wasn't deliberate."

At that, as if reprieved, he ran on.

"Wang Qiangxin, say 'Sorry.' Hurry up and say 'Sorry'!" shouted the children behind him.

Teacher Zhang stood steady to adjust his glasses and straighten the books in his hands, then went on his way.

"Good morning, Teacher Zhang!" two girls greeted him.

"Good morning," he answered rather awkwardly.

"Good morning, Teacher Zhang."

"Good morning."

He nodded repeatedly all the way to the staff room. When the bell rang, footsteps thudded and pandemonium broke loose, then the playground quieted down. With a sigh of relief he produced from his bag an unwrapped loaf he had bought in the grain shop, poured himself some boiled water, and started to eat. His class wasn't till the second period.

"Your breakfast?" a colleague asked.

"That's right," he answered, gulping down a mouthful.

"You really rough it," remarked another colleague.

"Hmm," he mumbled, his mouth full.

"Thick gruel makes the best breakfast, I think," someone else commented.

"Hmm." He gave up eating, wrapped the remaining half of his loaf in a piece of paper, and put it back in his bag.

The sun lit up the level playground where the gym teacher was drawing lines with white chalk. These lines and the white stripes on his track suit gleamed in the sunlight. A sparrow was hopping along. From one classroom came the sound of children reciting a lesson in unison. They were dragging it out, knowing it by heart.

* * *

The bell rang. Pandemonium. Children poured out from every classroom, converged in the playground, then surged out of the school gate.

Picking up his books and box of chalk Teacher Zhang went back to the staff room where Teacher Tao, the teacher in charge of Form Four, was lecturing Wang Qiangxin.

"Stand here and think seriously about your behavior in class today." With that she went off to the canteen with her bowl and chopsticks. Wang Qiangxin, left in front of her desk, kept shifting from his left foot to his right, from his right foot to his left. He scratched himself, sticking his hand up his back beneath his jacket or down his collar to scratch. He couldn't keep still for a second.

Zhang opened his drawer and took out his bowl. As he passed Wang Qiangxin he heard the boy's stomach rumble. He stopped and lowered his head to ask, "Are you hungry?"

Wang Qiangxin said nothing, and simply grinned at him.

"Were you rowdy again in class?"

The boy smiled and said nothing, hanging his head sheepishly.

"Can't you keep quiet?"

The boy smiled awkwardly, fidgeting all the time.

Zhang went back to get the half loaf of bread from his bag and offered it to the boy.

Wang Qiangxin eyed it as if afraid to take it, but finally he took it. He bit off big mouthfuls and chomped them, looking vigilantly around.

A wizened, bent old man stumped in, his shoulders hunched helplessly forward, his arms unwillingly thrust up behind, as if doing an exercise to radio music.

"So the young devil's been kept in again!"

"You must be his grandfather," the teacher guessed.

"What's the young devil done this time?"

"Own up, Wang Qiangxin," said Zhang.

"In our Chinese class I fidgeted and talked," he mumbled with crumbs on his cheeks, his head tucked in defensively.

"Damn you!" The old man slapped his head.

Zhang had grabbed the old man's hand in dismay. But the old fellow, proving stronger than the teacher, pulled his hand up so that they both hit the boy.

"This won't do. This is no way to treat him."

Having worked off steam with a few whacks, the old fellow told the teacher, "All right, now that I've whacked him, let him go home for his meal."

That put Zhang on the spot. This wasn't for him to decide. He wished he had left before to keep out of trouble.

"If he makes a row again, Teacher, you must beat him. You can beat him to death and I won't hold it against you."

"What an idea! It's better to reason with him."

"Well, I'll take the young devil back; you teachers are very busy."

"Go along," was all Zhang could say.

The old man dragged his grandson off. Zhang picked up his bowl and chopsticks and left the staff room. At the door of the canteen he met Teacher Tao. He passed her, then decided to turn back and tell her, "Wang Qiangxin's grandfather has taken him home."

"Taken him home?" Her bulging, myopic eyes stared through her glasses.

"That's right." He hung his head guiltily.

"You gave permission?"

"His grandfather came. . . ."

"I wanted to talk to his grandfather."

"I ..."

"Fine, so you came to his rescue. You're playing the hero— I don't want to play the villain. I wash my hands of him. You take him over." She went off in a huff.

With a sigh of exasperation, he stomped out of the canteen, his appetite gone.

Meanwhile Wang Qiangxin was wolfing down his meal. Granny, across the way, looked up from the basin of clothes she was washing and saw the boy eating, and heard him chomping away.

"Isn't it disgusting the way that child eats," she said to her neighbor, Maomei, who was sitting on a stool knitting.

"His face is disgusting too," agreed Maomei. "His ears are too small and his eyebrows and the corners of his mouth turn down as if he were crying."

"That's right. That child cried nonstop from the day he was born. Cried his mother to death. Then, strange to say, he stopped crying."

"Doesn't even cry when his grandad beats him up."

Wang Qiangxin was full now. He put down his bowl. Lifting the lid from the wok, he scooped out some rice crust and munched it.

* * *

Bikes passed in both directions, their bells ringing. Cars came and went, their horns honking.

Teacher Zhang rushed to the bus holding a pancake and fritter, and managed to squeeze onto a bus. The door shut, catching the back of his jacket.

"Comrade, my jacket's caught in the door." he said.

"Please buy tickets or show your monthly ticket," the conductor called over the microphone, drowning his voice.

He kept quiet. At least his bottom hadn't been pinched.

"If you're not getting off, comrade, let's change places," suggested a woman, squeezing up to him.

He tried to move forward but failed, his jacket caught fast. He apologized, "I'll get down first at the next stop."

The woman moved onto the step above him, her white neck just opposite his face. Her wide-open collar showed an angora sweater, and under the round, woolly collar of this lurked a sparkling golden necklace. His heart palpitating, he turned his head to avoid staring at her.

There was a sudden commotion. One of the passengers had lost a purse.

"Hand it over at once, whoever took it!" yelled the conductor. "Otherwise we'll drive to the police station."

"Give it back quick! Give it back quick! We don't want to be late to work!" other passengers shouted.

"Look on the floor, everyone, to see if a wallet's been dropped."

They jostled one another, looking on the floor.

His heart beating faster than ever, he broke into a sweat and his face turned pale. He forced a smile, a most inappropriate smile. The glance the woman threw at him made his heart contract. Sweat trickled down his neck.

"It's all right, I've found it," someone called out, stooping to pick up the purse. The others pressed forward.

"Look and see if anything's missing."

Nothing was missing.

He relaxed. The woman glanced curiously at him again. The door opened and he nearly fell out. She got off the bus and looked closely at him again before going off.

Reaching school, he saw Wang Qiangxin at the gate. He called, "Wang Qiangxin, I've something to say to you."

The boy stopped and started scratching himself, first reaching under his collar then up his back.

"Can't you keep quiet in class?"

The boy said nothing, smiling cryptically.

"Do you have to make such a noise?"

Still smiling, he sniffed hard, as if to sniff everything up into his head.

"Yesterday when I let you go home for lunch, your teacher was angry with me." Zhang had to tell him this frankly.

He looked up as if puzzled.

"If you go on misbehaving, you'll make it awkward for me." This said, Zhang casually stroked the boy's head and went on.

Someone in the staff room told him, "The head wants to see you. Wants you at once."

"The head wants me?" His heart missed a beat. Forgetting to put down his things, he hurried to the head's office.

"Ah, Teacher Zhang, please take a seat." This politeness reassured him to some extent.

"Did you want me for something, Head?" He perched on the edge of the seat.

The head opened a drawer and took out a sheet of stiff paper, which he handed to him. "First read that."

It was an official letter from the unit in which his father had worked twenty years ago, stating clearly in black and white that his father, who had been labeled a Rightist in 1957, had now been cleared. He stared blankly at this document, unable to work up any sense of elation. To him, his father was a stranger who had long ago left home and died of edema on a farm in Yancheng. His father's colleagues had told him, "Your old man was quite different from you. If he'd been like you he wouldn't have got into trouble." And from his childhood onward, in school, in the street, wherever he went, people pointed at him behind his back and said, "His old man ..."

"His old man ..."

"His old man ..."

"Congratulations." The head, who doubled as Party secretary, sprang up to shake his hand. Zhang hastily stood up but staggered, not standing firm till the head had sat down again. "We're going to remove from your dossier all the material on your father. I hope you'll buck up and work hard, without letting this weigh on your mind."

"Of course, that's ancient history now," he replied.

"It's past and done with; let's look ahead," the head urged.

He went back to the staff room to pour a cup of tea. Not till he sat down did he realize that his underclothes were all wet. The bell rang, followed by what sounded like the galloping of a cavalry. In a flash, the empty playground was full of children. Girls skipped over ropes or rubber-band chains, boys dashed here and there helter-skelter. Teacher Tao came in, her face grim. His heart thumped; he stopped drinking tea. Without so much as looking at him, she went straight to her desk and sat down without a word. Not daring to question her, he watched from a distance as he sipped his tea. When he finished he got up to go to the toilet. Seeing Wang Qiangxin dashing about, his head covered with sweat, he called him to a halt.

"Wang Qiangxin, did you make a row again in class?"

"No!" The boy looked up in surprise, the droop of his eyebrows more obvious.

"Teacher Tao is angry," he whispered.

"Not with me. She praised me in class."

"What did she say?" Zhang suspected that the boy had mistaken sarcasm for praise.

"Teacher Tao pointed at me and told Zhang Ming, 'Even he's kept quiet, but you're making a row.'" He was spluttering, gulping back spittle, his front and back teeth, above and below, so jagged that his mouth seemed full of teeth. He looked so ludicrous one couldn't help but pity him.

* * *

Zhang overslept. As soon as he opened his eyes he saw from his old-fashioned chiming clock that it was already seven. Having no time to buy breakfast, he ran to catch his bus. When he reached the school, it was empty. He asked the janitor why and discovered that it was only half past six—his clock was a good hour fast. As he put his things in the staff room, he felt a sudden craving for dumpling soup, so he hurried to a small restaurant next to the school. It was crowded with customers, some concentrating on eating, some bored with waiting, and these inevitably stared at him. He stood at a loss in the doorway, not wanting to shove his way in or to withdraw. Tentatively taking a few awkward steps in search of an empty seat, he felt more eyes on him, so he beat a hasty retreat.

A few more steps took him to a stall selling pancakes and fritters, where two fair-sized lines had formed, one to buy bamboo counters, the other to exchange these for fritters. As was only right, he went to the back of the line for counters and took from his wallet some small change and grain tickets.

"Teacher Zhang!" someone called.

Looking up, he saw Wang Qiangxin in the line, two counters clutched in one hand and one chopstick in the other to pick up fritters! He had nearly reached the wok.

"Teacher Zhang, get your counters, quick."

Zhang nodded at him with a smile, though knowing that this was easier said than done.

Wang Qiangxin, standing in the line, clamped his chopstick

between his lips then rotated it so that it rattled against his teeth.

"Take the chopstick out of your mouth, Wang Qiangxin, or it'll hurt your throat, " Zhang felt constrained to warn him.

The boy did as told, repeating, "But your counters, quick, Teacher Zhang."

There were still three people ahead of Zhang in the line.

Wang Qiangxin reached the stall. He slowly handed his counters to the girl selling fritters, but didn't reach out to take them, just staring at the specks of oil on them.

"Take them, quick!" the girl urged.

"Too hot," He said, procrastinating.

"Not after all this time," snapped someone behind.

"I'm small, afraid of hot things," he replied brashly, then called to Zhang again, "Hurry up!"

"You can't buy for other people," those behind objected, squeezing him out of the line. Only then did Zhang realize why the boy had been stalling. He said with feeling, "I'll take my turn; there aren't too many people."

"Have one of mine, Teacher Zhang, I'll line up again."

"No, no."

Wang Qiangxin thrust a fritter at him, smearing his jacket with oil. Zhang had to take it and wrap it in a pancake. Walking off, he turned back and saw the boy lining up again while eating. His method was to bite one end of the fritter and hold it in his mouth, pulling it farther in after each bite. The fritter disappeared slowly, as if swallowed whole.

During the break the door of the staff room burst open and two girls helped in a third, who was crying. A group of boys behind marched Wang Qiangxin straight up to Teacher Tao's desk. These boys had pushed over the girl, then fallen on top of her. Now she couldn't raise her arm, which was badly hurt. Teacher Tao had no time to investigate. Instead she took the girl straight to the hospital, coming back at noon to announce that her arm had been broken, the bone splintered.

After school that afternoon, Teacher Tao called those boys to the staff room to find out what had happened. Since Wang Qiangxin was one of them and Zhang suspected that he was involved, he sat somewhat apart to listen intently.

"Why did you knock her over?"

"We didn't mean to."

"Why were you pushing and shoving?"

"Just for fun."

"What fun is there in that? Was it a game? Who started it?" Tao's voice was stern.

"Wang Xin shoved me." Zhang Ming was the first informer.

"Zhu Yan shoved me." said Wang Xin.

"Feng Gang shoved me," said Zhu Yan.

"Luo Hong shoved me," said Feng Gang.

"Meng Xiaofeng shoved me," said Luo Hong.

"Wang Qiangxin shoved me," said Meng Xiaofeng.

"Zhang Ming shoved me,"said Wang Qiangxin.

So they had come full circle. Teacher Tao had to laugh.

"But who started it?" This was as impossible to find out as what first put the earth into orbit. So the hospital expenses had to be divided among them. Teacher Tao paid one share as she was in charge of that class and responsible for it.

"Go home and tell your parents, understand? When the time comes I'll give you the receipts to take back and show them. Off you go!"

Once outside the staff room the boys raced off, slinging their satchels about and teasing one another.

Zhang followed them out and stopped Wang Qiangxin.

"So you've landed in trouble again. You had me on tenter-hooks."

The boy grinned, very thick-skinned.

"Can't you stop making trouble?"

He just smiled.

"Your grandad will wallop you again."

Still he smiled.

"Can you pay the medical fees?"

That wiped the smile off his face.

"Shall I help you explain to your grandad?"

"No use. Anyway we can't pay."

"Why not?"

"Yesterday he went to ask my dad for money, but Dad gave him very little. Grandad came back cursing."

"How can your dad act that way?"

"His wife's a terror. And he's in a bad position, so he has to do as she says." This was said most phlegmatically.

"What a know-it-all you are!" Zhang frowned.

"What's strange about that?" He smiled enigmatically.

"If you really haven't the money, I'll pay your share for you."

"Honestly?" His drooping eyebrows went up incredulously.

"Honestly. As long as you 're told, and stop making trouble."

"All right." Agreeing readily, he started off, as if afraid the teacher might change his mind. He turned back abruptly to say, "Want to eat mutton hot pot, Teacher?"

"Why ask?"

"I can queue up for the tally for you. I often go in the morning for a tally, then make forty cents by selling it in the afternoon to someone who couldn't get one. I won't charge you anything."

"Living on my own I don't eat mutton hot pot," said Zhang.

* * *

After school Wang Qiangxin's grandad tugged him back there by one ear, and in the other hand held a pole for hanging up clothes. The boy, his head on one side, took short, rapid steps to keep up with the old man. He knew that if he struggled it would be the worse for him. The old man, who knew Teacher Zhang, went straight up to him.

"Teacher, help me beat this young devil. With one foot in the grave I can't beat him hard; you must help me." He bawled this out, panting. All the teachers in the staff room turned to stare.

"What's happened? Do take a seat." Zhang felt embarrassed.

"I'm at my last gasp, can't move. When I told him to wash the rice, the young devil refused. Dashed off with me chasing behind. I'll do him in!" He struck out with the pole. The boy jumped over it as if jumping over a skip rope.

"Come here, Wang Qiangxin," ordered Zhang. "Hurry up and apologize to your grandad. Say you're sorry."

"Sorry," muttered the boy, inching forward.

"What farting use is it to say sorry? Help me wallop him, Teacher. I won't hold it against you if you kill him." The old man thrust his pole into Zhang's hand. Zhang took it, not knowing what to do with it.

"All right then, Grandad, he's acknowledged his mistake. Wang Qiangxin, say 'I was wrong.'" Zhang's voice rang out as if he were pleased with himself.

"I was wrong," the boy droned, like a mosquito.

"See, he's owned up honestly. Let him off this time. If he does it again I promise to help you teach him a good lesson." At last he saw the old man and boy out and came back for his things. A colleague said, "Wang Qiangxin seems to listen to you, Old Zhang."

"Oh no," he disclaimed.

"He behaves like your son."

"Oh no." Despite these modest rejoinders, he felt pleased. On leaving the school it occurred to him to call on the boy's grandad since he was ill. He went for a stroll, bought a bottle of royal jelly tonic, then headed for their lane.

Wang Qiangxin, holding a big bowl of noodles, had squeezed into a neighbor's doorway to watch a fight. Zhang called the boy out and went into his home with him.

Their place was a wooden shack built against the brick wall of a house. The old man was eating noodles too, with pickles. In the boy's bowl, apart from pickles, was chopped pork.

"Wang Qiangxin, why can't you show your grandfather more respect? He's so good to you," Zhang felt touched.

"For some sin in my last life, I owe him a debt I can never pay off in this one," replied the boy.

That shocked Zhang into silence.

Another row had started outside. Unable to sit still, the boy sprang up and rushed out.

"That damned little devil lost his mother when he was three. I've brought him up. I've no money, but I'm better than a stepmother. Only I'm afraid I'm not long for this world."

"That's no way to talk, Mr Wang, you're still hale and hearty."

"Once I close my eyes and pop off, he'll have a thin time."

"It won't be so bad; everybody will help out."

The old fellow, glancing sideways at Zhang, grunted, "Some time back I started saving up for him. With money there's no need to be afraid."

"Not necessarily."

"I've muddled along all my life on the Shanghai Bund, thirty years in the old society and thirty years in the new. I've come to see that men are like fish, money like water. A fish out of water is done for."

Zhang had to keep silent. He knew the old man was wrong, but couldn't think how to refute him. If he thought of a good refutation he'd still have to find the right metaphor for it.

When the row outside stopped, Wang Qiangxin came back to announce, "Our group leader has come."

"I must go." Zhang stood up.

"See your teacher off."

The boy followed Zhang out. A small crowd had gathered around the opposite gate.

"What's the quarrel about?"

"Maomei and her brother keep squabbling. He blames her for not having a job. But that's not her fault."

"No, that's not her fault," agreed Zhang.

They walked to the main road together.

"Now go back."

"Doesn't matter." He walked on with the teacher.

"You must behave better in class, Wang Qiangxin, eh?'

"Hmm."

"And outside school too, eh?"

"Hmm."

They walked for a stretch in silence.

"Why don't you get married, Teacher Zhang?"

"Eh!" Zhang turned to look at him in surprise.

"Has no one introduced you to anyone?"

Zhang's cheeks burned; he was speechless.

"Actually, you ought to marry Maomei."

"What's that!" Zhang was staggered. His head reeled.

"Actually Maomei's not bad except that she has no work. And her bottom's too big."

"How can you talk like that!" His face turned as red as a lantern.

"Why not? Have I said anything wrong?" The boy sounded surprised and looked with concern at his teacher.

"Aren't you too small to meddle with such matters?"

"It's you I'm thinking of. Though Maomei has no job, she's young. You wouldn't lose out."

"You mind your own business."

"I'm thinking of Maomei too."

"She doesn't want you butting in either. Just mind your own business."

They walked another stretch in silence.

"Wang Qiangxin, you really must behave better in school, eh?"

"Hmm."

"And out of school too, eh?"

"Hmm."

The streetlights cast their shadows on the ground one long, one short.

* * *

When school ended, the gym teacher took Wang Qiangxin to Teacher Zhang and said, "Teach this boy a lesson. He kicked up such a rumpus in my class that he spoiled it for everyone."

"Wang Qiangxin, what have you been up to this time?"

The boy said nothing and just smiled.

The gym teacher went on, "When it was time to line up, he wouldn't stand up straight but flopped this way and that. Leaned against a classmate or flopped onto the ground, as if all his bones were broken."

"Is that right, Wang Qiangxin?" asked Zhang.

He smiled and said nothing.

"See, this boy won't sit properly or stand properly. Won't listen to anyone, except you, Teacher Zhang."

Wang Qiangxin, indeed, wasn't standing properly. One of his legs was straight, the other bent, one of his shoulders was higher than the other; his neck and head were askew, his eyebrows crooked and his eyes screwed up.

"Wang Qiangxin, stand properly," snapped Zhang.

The boy shifted to the other foot, still with one leg straight, the other bent, one shoulder higher than the other. He had simply switched around.

"Wang Qiangxin, don't you know how to stand?" asked Zhang patiently.

He shook his head; whether stubbornly or sheepishly wasn't clear.

"Is the boy going through some physiological phase that he's so hard to cope with?" said the gym teacher.

"Stand properly, Wang Qiangxin." Zhang was losing patience.

Still the boy slouched, squinting at him as if playing a game with him.

"Wang Qiangxin, stand properly." Zhang was really angry.

"I won't."he had the impudence to say.

Zhang raised his hand and slapped his face.

Everyone was flabbergasted. The gym teacher grabbed Zhang's arm. "You mustn't beat a schoolchild, Teacher Zhang."

The boy suddenly started bawling, "You hit me, you hit me. Bugger you!"

Zhang stared in a daze at Wang Qiangxin, his mind a blank. It struck him that the character for "sob"[1] with its two "mouths" was a perfect picture of sobbing.

The boy walked sobbing to the door and no one stopped him. They watched him leave the staff room, then turned their heads to look at Teacher Zhang.

Zhang was thinking distractedly of that character "sob."

Before long an old man in the posture of a setting-up exercise came in and bore down on Zhang.

"Bugger you, you hit my grandson! How can teachers hit school children? This is the new society. You're not a teacher in an old style private school, able to cuss and beat kids whenever you please. Bugger you!"

The other teachers managed to stop the old man from butting Zhang's chest. Zhang, sweating and dazed, could only bow with clasped hands.

"I'm going to find your boss, your headmaster!" yelled the old man.

"I'll go with you." Zhang had found his tongue at last.

They went together to the headmaster's office. There, Zhang apologized to the old man before the head.

The next day, Zhang went to Teacher Tao's Fourth Form and apologized to Wang Qiangxin before the whole class.

The third day, in a meeting of the staff trade union, he made a self-examination and accepted the criticism of his colleagues.

The fourth day, Zhang called on the head in his home to relinquish the promotion for which he was due.

The fifth day, the head withdrew a report to the Education Bureau recommending outstanding teachers.

The sixth day was Sunday.

The seventh day was Monday.

[1] Chinese character 哭

The eighth day was Tuesday.

The ninth day, when Zhang was going from his classroom to the staff room, Wang Qiangxin rushed up, his head sweating, his red scarf back to front as if he were wearing a bib. Three or four meters from the teacher he stopped abruptly.

Zhang stopped too.

Wang Qiangxin looked at him.

Zhang looked at the boy.

Neither said a word.

Zhang turned and walked off.

Wang Qiangxin veered and walked off.

Both were rather flurried.

Translated by Gladys Yang

Lapse of Time

1

The clock in the next room chimed four times. Ouyang Duanli opened her eyes in the darkness, not daring to go back to sleep. But it was so nice and warm under the comforter that even lingering there another minute was a welcome thought. She was prolonging the inevitable for as long as possible. Someone's rear door opened, then slammed loudly against the Spalding lock—bang! That was followed by the urgent sounds of someone running down the lane. Duanli gritted her teeth and sat up in bed, pushing the comforter down past her feet, as though forcing herself to resist the temptation of the warmth it offered. A blast of cold air made her shiver. She quickly threw on a sweater and a padded jacket, then some wool long-johns, which were so soft and fluffy she had trouble pulling them on. Five minutes later her neck was bundled up in a long black scarf as she opened the rear door, basket in hand, then slammed it shut behind her and rushed off into the morning, leaving a trail of hollow-sounding footsteps in her wake.

The sky was pitch black. Streetlights shivered in the freezing mist. A few bicycles whizzed past, pedestrians in groups of twos and threes scurried along, a tram bus drove by. Duanli quickly wrapped her scarf around her face until only her eyes showed, just like a typical northern matron. The wind was like a dagger. It sliced through her pants and her woolen long-johns so easily she might as well have been wearing summer pants. Common wisdom has it that cold enters from the feet, that when your legs feel frozen you shiver from head to toe. I ought to make a pair of padded pants, she was thinking. It never occurred to her that Shanghai could have such bitter north winds. Since she'd never gotten up, let alone gone outside, this early, she'd just assumed it couldn't be all that bad. Sometimes, when Auntie Abao had returned from the market without any fresh food, she'd complained, "Couldn't you have gotten up a little earlier?" But Auntie Abao was gone, and now it was her turn to get up early. She sighed.

After crossing the street, she caught up to an old woman with a market basket in her hand, then was overtaken by two girls. Women emerged from the houses facing the street, one after another, cradling their bamboo baskets and yawning as they closed the doors behind them and headed toward the marketplace, keeping their hands warm in their coat sleeves. The legions of morning shoppers swelled. A turn at the intersection, and there was the marketplace, straight ahead. The pale light of the streetlights was like a heavy, turbid pall of mist enshrouding the throngs of people out on the street. The ground was wet and sticky, as though there had just been a rainfall; vegetable peels and fish scales dotted the area. The din was deafening. Everyone was talking, but no one could hear anything that was being said. A motorized cart threaded its way across the street, forcing the crowd to part before it. A cluster of women and children in front of the fish stall began to push and shout and squabble, until a minor riot seemed inevitable. Duanli quickly moved as far away from the scene as possible. Spots like this were the exclusive turf of wild kids and amahs who made their living buying food for other people. Encroachment by anyone else was unthinkable. They seemed to have an unwritten pact of mutual protection. If you got up very early to buy fresh food or some particular desirable item, somehow managing to be third in line, or even second, as soon as the stall was opened, before you knew it you were standing behind seventeen or eighteen people. Even if the only thing in front of you was a brick at your feet, you'd still wind up behind all those people. By crowding in and out and verifying one another's spot in line, these people formed an impenetrable line of defense.

Duanli wedged in among the crowds, despite her misgivings. But no matter how she figured things in her head, she couldn't decide how to spend the eighty cents budgeted for the day's food. Her father-in-law's fixed interest from the state and his salary had both been terminated, and the family had been allocated a total living allowance of twelve yuan per person, not counting the eldest son, Duanli's husband Wenyao, who was employed. He had, of course, reached the age where he should be self-supporting, but unfortunately, he had never pondered what it took to raise a family. Taking his college-graduate salary of sixty yuan, he had married early and fathered two daughters and a son, leaving Duanli at home to take care of the house. Upon graduation from college, she'd been assigned to the Gansu countryside, but refused to go, unconcerned about the resultant loss of income. Who could have dreamt that things would turn out like this? Sixty yuan a month, out of which she had to feed, clothe and house a family of five.

Sixty yuan. After paying for coal, water and electricity, kitchen needs like salt, soy sauce, oil and vinegar, and buying the necessary soap, toilet paper, and toothpaste, every bit of the money left over was earmarked for food—a mere eighty fen a day. And the less food there was to go around, the more gluttonous the children—all three of them—seemed to get. She used to have to force them to come to the table, but now even five-year-old Mimi could manage a bowl and a half of rice at one sitting. On those occasions when she placed shredded pork and greens on the table, six greedy little eyes blinked in amazement, and in no time at all every scrap of pork had disappeared. Duanli came to a hard decision: she'd spend a whole yuan on meat, which she'd cook up with some dried vegetables. That would satisfy their hunger for today; tomorrow they'd go vegetarian.

Having made her decision, she nudged her way up to the meat stall. There weren't many people lined up there, no more than ten or so. As she stood at the end of the line, she carefully surveyed the meat on the counter, settling on a sinewy piece that had some meat and a little fat. Two of the customers ahead of her were attracted to the same piece, buying about two fifths of it when their turns came. Don't sell it all! Her heart skipped a beat. Another customer bought a portion of the same piece, until all that remained was a sliver about the thickness of three fingers. Fortunately, it was Duanli's turn, but she was so nervous and excited that she lost her voice for a moment.

"Which piece do you want? Come on, hurry up!" The young peddler impatiently scraped a small metal bar noisily against the edge of his knife. The people behind Duanli began to shove.

"This sinewy piece here. One yuan's worth!" Fearful that the people behind her might push her aside, she held on to the greasy cutting board with both hands.

The young peddler picked up the meat, flung it down on the cutting board in front of him and sliced off a piece, which he threw onto the scale. "One yuan, twenty fen!"

"I only asked for one yuan's worth," she said apologetically.

"It's only twenty fen more; don't make a stink about it, okay?"

"I'd appreciate it if you'd trim off the extra. I only want one yuan's worth." Duanli's face was red.

"You're sure hard to please. Well, if you don't want it, someone else will!"

"Here, I'll take it, young man," a man behind her said, thrusting his basket up to the counter. Duanli panicked.

"I want it; it's mine!" She snatched it up, took out her purse and counted out one yuan, twenty fen, which she handed over to the young man.

It was good meat, there was no denying it, but she'd spent all of today's and half of tomorrow's food money for it. Say, why not spread it out over two days? The thought eased her anxieties. She walked over and stopped in front of the egg stall. That's what I need, some eggs. Braised meat and eggs is always a favorite. And the children's nutrition is important, especially Lailai, who's growing like a weed. I can't neglect him. She picked out half a *jin* of eggs—forty-four fen. But now, even if she spread her purchases out over two days, she was still four fen over her budget. So what! I'll worry about that two days from now. Heaving a long sigh, she turned and walked out of the marketplace.

The streets, jammed with pedestrians in a hurry and filled with the din of an unbroken file of bicycles whose riders seemed to be vying for supremacy of the road, were bathed in bright morning sunlight. Children on their way to school, book bags flung over their shoulders, chewed on rice balls or flatcakes or oil fritters as they walked. Reminded by the sight of Duoduo and Lailai at home, Duanli quickened her pace.

Wenyao and the children had already gotten out of bed. Good for Duoduo! She hadn't forgotten to light the charcoal brazier and start the rice porridge. The family was sitting around the table eating breakfast.

"Mama, did you get some oil fritters?" Lailai asked her.

"No, but I bought some pork, so tonight we'll have braised pork and eggs," Duanli said comfortingly.

Lailai hooted his approval and turned back to his bowl of rice porridge and salted vegetables, which he finished off without complaint. Duoduo, on the other hand, pouted, listlessly putting kernels of rice into her mouth as though she were counting pearls. She was the most spoiled of all the children, maybe because she was the eldest and had enjoyed a more carefree life than the others. It was proving harder for her to adapt to the family's current hard times than for her younger brother and baby sister.

"Don't forget to take some of this over to Mother and Father," Wenyao said as he shoveled the last few kernels of rice into his mouth, then stood up and walked out.

"All right," she replied, hiding the anxiety in her heart.

"Where's my folder of quotations from Chairman Mao?" Duoduo shouted anxiously, with a stomp of her foot.

"Find it yourself!" Duanli said, trying to keep her anger in check.

She had just thrown a towel around her shoulders and was brushing her hair. She hated to even think about having spent half the morning at the marketplace with her hair such a mess.

"Mimi, you've gone and taken my things again. They won't even let me into school without my folder of quotations!"

Duanli was forced to put down her brush and help her daughter look for the folder. Mimi tagged along behind them. Although she was the youngest, she was the cleverest. The missing folder turned up in the bedding.

"I didn't put it there," Mimi quickly leapt to her own defense.

"If it wasn't you, who was it, then—me?" Duoduo shot a look at her sister, then hastily examined the quotations inside to make sure the "Three Essays" by the Chairman were intact, for this was their textbook. Children had begun going to assigned middle schools at the end of the previous year. God knows what they were studying, but the discipline was very strict, and punctuality—both coming and going—was demanded. Duoduo, who came from a bad class background, had to be even more careful in her behavior than the others.

"Duoduo, talk only when you have to at school. Do you hear me?" Duanli instructed her daughter. "Let the others say what they want. I don't want you joining in or talking back. Do you hear me?"

"I know!" Duoduo replied on her way downstairs. She was such a headstrong child, not someone to let herself be bullied, that Duanli worried more about her than about the others.

"Mama, I'm leaving," Lailai said as he too headed down the stairs. He was still in grade school, an honest boy who usually managed to stay clear of trouble.

With the children gone, Duanli could start brushing her hair again. Her thick black hair, which had once been very long, looked like the velvet down of a black swan whenever she had it permed. Whether it fell to her shoulders or was done up in a bun, it still looked beautiful and luxurious. She'd never considered the time spent on her hair to be wasted. But then during one of the Red Guard searches of the house, she'd been given exactly twelve hours to cut her hair. So she'd cut it. Remarkably, it hadn't brought her the anguish she'd expected. At a time when all of one's worldly possessions were in jeopardy, who could fret over a few strands of hair? She wished only for peace, praying that everything would come to a quick and happy conclusion. The only difference now was that she avoided spending much time in front of her mirror, not wanting to dwell on the way she looked. She hurriedly brushed her hair, then brushed her teeth, washed her face. . . . Whatever she did it was a rush job, and a perfunctory one. In the past she'd lived her life the way she'd enjoy a buttery dried plum: she'd take a dainty bite and savor it as long as she could before taking another. Every minute was filled with flavor, filled with enjoyment. Now she lived her life the way she'd finished off that bowlful of cold rice porridge a moment ago, gulping down one mouthful after another, never stopping to taste what she was eating, concerned only with filling her belly and getting through this particular meal as quickly as possible—getting through this day, this month, this year, this very lifetime as quickly as possible. There were many thoughts she dared not think, for they always led to tears.

"Mama, can I go downstairs and play by the back door?" Mimi asked.

"Be a good little girl and stay in the house with me. After I boil the eggs you can help me peel them." It was a request, not an order. She didn't want Mimi to have anything to do with the neighbor kids, because if anything happened, Mimi would be the one to suffer. Even worse, some unreasonable adult might join in.

Instead of wheedling, Mimi just sighed with a hint of melancholy. How could a child so young know about sighing? She left her mother's side and walked over to the window, where she rested her head on her hands and gazed outside.

Duanli washed the dishes, swept the floor, and cleaned up the room, then washed off the piece of meat and put it into an earthenware pot to stew in soy sauce. She put the eggs into a pot on the brazier to boil.

"Mama," Mimi called from the window, "Fu Zhigao is on his way over to see Little Auntie again."

"Oh," was all Duanli said. Fu Zhigao was a schoolmate of Wenyao's kid sister Wenying, two classes ahead of her. This young man, who bore a striking resemblance to the movie character Fu Zhigao, came from a class background that was as bad as theirs. He, like Wenying, was ineligible to join the Red Guards, because his father ran a private clinic. Since he did little but hang around the house, the two of them had begun spending time together.

"They're going out together," Mimi continued the report. "Fu Zhigao's walking in front, Little Auntie's bringing up the rear."

"Mimi, come over here and peel the eggs for me!"

"Oh boy!" Mimi ran over as fast as her legs would carry her, thrilled to have something to do.

The aroma of the meat stewing in the earthenware pot was tantalizing. But the slices of meat had shrunk in size. Duanli stared at them with alarm, wondering if there was anything she could do to keep them from shrinking any further.

"Hello, Sister-in-Law." Wenguang walked over to the sink with a bowl and a pair of chopsticks in his hand. He turned on the faucet, rinsed the utensils and put them into the cupboard.

"Do you call that washing them?" Duanli said malignantly. As she observed his lazy, slovenly manner, she wondered what had happened to the revolutionary fervor that had once driven him to make a clean break with Father.

"They weren't greasy," he explained in a conciliatory tone as he turned and walked out of the kitchen, pausing just long enough to pat Mimi on the head as he went by. Mimi, who was concentrating on the egg in her hand, took no notice. She gently tapped it a couple of times, then carefully peeled away the shell with her tiny fingers, almost as though she were afraid of hurting it. She was looking very solemn.

Duanli made three shallow cuts on the glossy peeled eggs before putting them into the pot of stew meat, explaining to Mimi, who was standing alongside watching her every move, "That lets the flavor in."

"I just know they're going to be delicious as all get out, Mama!"

Duanli felt a momentary sadness; this is the kind of coarse fare they eat in farm villages. No one in the family would have eaten food like this in days past. If they'd prepared even a small bowlful back then, no matter how well cooked it was, there would have been no takers. Just the sight of it would have disgusted her. But now, surprisingly, she was won over by the fragrance.

When the meat was cooked, it, plus the dried vegetables and eggs, nearly filled the earthenware pot. Duanli picked out the nicest plate she had, then covered it with a layer of dried vegetables, over which she ladled several chunks of meat and an egg. She took it into the adjoining room. Up until recently, the whole family had eaten together, but once Father-in-law's income was terminated, his wife decided that they should eat separately, and so that's what they did.

"Duanli, you folks eat first; give it to Lailai," her mother-in-law said politely.

"It's really nothing, Mother. Let Father try it out." Duanli put the plate down, turned on her heel and left the room. Making a big deal out of a little plate of food like this was more than she could take.

Her plan to spread the food out over two days was defeated by noon. She first divided the food in the earthenware pot with chopsticks, barely enough for three meals—about one shallow bowlful per meal. Now, how was that going to feed five hungry mouths? Regaining her decisiveness, she filled the bowl to the top. If we're going to eat we're going to eat enough! We'll worry about tomorrow when it comes.

The period after lunch was always the most relaxing time of their day. Duanli sighed comfortably, then opened the closet to dig out some old clothes she could take apart and use the material to make a pair of lined pants. She found two pairs of pants, which would do nicely for the lining, and one of Mimi's old padded jackets, from which she could take the cotton filling. Now that she had the material she needed, she sat down and set to work. The first task was to take apart the old clothes, which was more difficult than sewing the new, and far more boring: the sort of job you couldn't rush. Wenying, her young sister-in-law, entered the room while she was working. Though not very pretty, Wenying had a certain tranquil look about her that people found attractive. The two women had not gotten along very well at the beginning, often arguing over trivial matters. If Wenying saw Duanli making some new clothes, she'd complain to her mother; if Duanli noticed that Wenying was wearing something new, she'd take out her anger on her husband. But now that their home had been systematically ransacked, there was nothing left to fight over. Then, too, since Wenying's school was shut down and she had nothing to do, she regularly came into her sister-in-law's room to pass the time, and relations between the two of them had gradually improved.

"What's that you're taking apart, Sister-in-Law?"

"Just some old clothes. I'm going to make a pair of padded pants."

"Are you going to take this one apart, too? Here, let me help." Wenying picked up a pair of small scissors and started in. "Regular padded pants are too bulky. You ought to use some of that silk cotton."

"They took every last ounce of silk cotton we had—and it was all Big Red brand! They even took our silk cotton jackets. They put it all downstairs, then sealed off the place. The only thing they didn't take was your elder brother's camel's hair jacket."

"Couldn't you just wear an extra pair of thick wool leggings? Padded pants aren't very flattering!"

"What difference does it make to an old housewife like me if they're unflattering. Why should I care?" Duanli laughed, only half in jest.

"Nonsense! You show your age less than anyone, Sister-in-Law. But back then you sure were beautiful. I'll never forget how you looked on your wedding day."

"Really?"

"Really. You were wearing a silver-gray suit, with a dark red rose pinned to your collar. Your hair came down over your shoulders and your eyes twinkled like stars, all black and shiny. I was only five then, but even I was dazzled."

"Really?" Duanli smiled wistfully.

"As far as I'm concerned, you look good no matter how you make yourself up. I remember the time your mother passed away, and how, even though you did your hair up in braids to show you were in mourning for a parent, surprisingly, you were as pretty as ever."

"What's so surprising about that? It's easy to be pretty when you're young." The last thing Duanli wanted to hear was talk that would lead her into reliving her youth; the more she heard such talk the shabbier she felt by comparison now, and if she felt any worse she might not find the courage to go on. "This is the happiest time of your life, a stage when life is truly beautiful."

"But all we're allowed to wear are grays, blues, and dark greens, and our hair can't come below our ears, just like country girls," Wenying sighed.

"You can still look good, even with that, and there'll always be someone who will love you," she said to console her sister-in-law.

"But . . ."

"Is that fellow student of yours interested in you? He seems to be stopping by pretty regularly."

"There you go with that nonsense again, Sister-in-Law!" Wenying blushed all the way down to her neck.

"I mean it. You're already seventeen, you know!"

"I never even think about things like that! I want to go to school."

"What good does wishful thinking do? Besides, even if you do get into school, then what? I'm a college graduate and still only a housewife."

"That was your choice. But it won't be mine!"

"That sounds good, but what if you were assigned somewhere else, would you go? For me that would be out of the question. I'd rather stay in Shanghai and eat rice porridge and turnips than be assigned somewhere else where I could eat meat."

"I've heard there's a quota on graduates being assigned out of the area," Wenying said with a worried look.

"Duanli," her mother-in-law called out as she entered the room, a frightened, disturbed look on her face, "there's a crowd of people downstairs wearing red armbands, and they're all from Father's work unit."

"Really?" The two sisters-in-law tensed immediately, and Wenying turned as pale as a ghost. Duanli got up, walked over and closed the door. Composing herself with difficulty, she tried to calm her mother-in-law. "Now don't worry. At worst it's a house search, and we have nothing left for them to take."

"I'm just worried that they're here to pester us with a bunch of questions that we have to answer, but can never answer to their satisfaction. It'll just mean more trouble for your father-in-law."

"Keep quiet," Wenying alerted them in a hushed voice and with fear in her eyes. She was easily spooked, nearly neurotic. After every house search she ran a high fever. "Keep quiet. Maybe if they think there's no one upstairs they won't even come up to take a look."

The three women didn't say another word, staying right where they were and holding their breath. They heard the people moving around downstairs, making sounds as if they were taking things apart and opening doors. "Hey!" one of them shouted, "a couple of you guys give me a hand over here—ummph!" They sounded like furniture movers.

The three women didn't know how long they'd been standing there when suddenly the door flew open, causing them to quake with fright. Someone walked into the room—it was Lailai. They breathed a sigh of relief. The old woman rubbed her chest to calm her pounding heart.

"How did you get up here?" Duanli asked anxiously, as though the child had crossed an invisible barrier separating the downstairs from the upstairs.

"I walked," Lailai answered ingenuously.

"Didn't those people downstairs say anything to you?"

"No. They were too busy moving things around and putting them on a truck outside. Even Little Auntie's piano."

"Let 'em have it! I don't want anything except for them to stay away from here," Wenying remarked wearily.

No one said a word for a while. They heard the front door being closed and locked, then the truck's engine starting. The truck drove away.

"Mama, I'm hungry," Lailai complained. He was eleven years old and growing like a weed. Always hungry, he could eat anywhere, anytime.

"Go make yourself a bowl of rice porridge," Duanli said to him, sensing at once a disapproving look on his grandmother's face. "Here," she said, changing her tune, "here's some money."

Lailai rushed over excitedly, took the ten-fen note from his mother, and smoothed it out before tucking it between the pages of his book. Then he sat down in his chair and continued doing his homework; since he wasn't qualified to be a Red Guard, he had to quietly keep working at his lessons. As the eldest grandson, he was the apple of his grandmother's eye.

Duoduo came home before long. As Duanli chatted with her sister-in-law and mother-in-law, she half-listened to Lailai as he smugly told his elder sister, "Mama gave me ten fen."

"Well, aren't you the one!" Duoduo shot back sarcastically.

Instinctively moving to patch things up, Lailai snuggled up to his sister and whispered something in her ear that softened her mood immediately. That pleased Duanli, for whenever the children fought in front of their grandmother, she was always blamed.

"None of you will ever know how much work it took your father to put this family on its feet," the old woman grumbled. "He came to Shanghai with nothing but a bedroll to learn the ins and outs of commerce. He suffered more than you'll ever know before he managed to open the factory."

"All by exploiting other people," Wenying cut in impatiently.

"What do you mean, exploiting other people? You're starting to sound like Wenguang. Everything I had from my dowry went into that factory, and the money flowed out of there like water."

"Let's not talk about this, okay? If anyone overhears us, there'll be trouble to pay."

"Wenying, there's no reason to talk like that," Duanli chided her young sister-in-law. "Mother, if there's something troubling you, go ahead and get it off your chest. It can't hurt as long as it stays in the family."

"Mama," Duoduo shouted, "we're going to play outside. We'll be back in a little while." Taking Mimi by the hand, Duoduo fell in behind Lailai, who was already heading downstairs.

"Don't stay out there long!" Duanli said to them. "And keep your mouths shut if anyone talks to you."

"We know!" Duoduo answered as the three of them flew down the stairs.

They didn't return till dinnertime, looks of sheer contentment on their faces and the glisten of oil on their lips— there were still traces of curry powder in the corner of Mimi's mouth.

"What have you been eating?"

"Beef soup, Mama," Mimi joyfully proclaimed.

That gave Duanli a start. How could they have afforded beef soup with only ten fen among them? She couldn't believe her ears. "Don't you lie to me."

"Honest, Mama, we each had a bowl of beef soup," Lailai confirmed his sister's statement, gaining increased satisfaction from the worried look on his mother's face.

"How much did it cost?"

"Three fen a bowl. We had one fen left over, so we used it to weigh Mimi. She weighs thirty seven *jin*!"

"Where'd you find a place that cheap?" Duanli was more surprised than ever. "On Huaihai Road?"

"No. It's down a lane, on a tiny little street, a little shop called the Red Guard Cooperative Canteen."

"How did you kids find a place like that?" This was the first Duanli had heard of it. The only restaurants she knew were the

Red House Western Restaurant, Xinya Cantonese Restaurant, Meilongzhen, and places like that.

"We just started walking, keeping our eyes open as we went along. Sister said she wanted us to get our money's worth."

"Duoduo!" Duanli shouted. "How sanitary was the place? I don't want you getting sick."

"If it wasn't sanitary, why were there so many people eating there?" Duoduo argued.

"We sure got our money's worth, didn't we, Sister?" Mimi said. "The guy across from us paid twenty fen for his bowl of beef soup, and the only difference was that his had a few pieces of meat in it."

"Do you mean your soup didn't have any meat in it?"

"Who wants to eat meat, anyway?" Duoduo said.

"Not me," Lailai and Mimi agreed with their sister.

Overcome by a sudden sadness, Duanli was momentarily speechless. Her decision to eat vegetarian meals for two days flew out the window.

Every day she went to the market, and every day the temptation to buy cuts of meat and fresh vegetables was too great, so she wound up spending more than she had budgeted for food. She simply hadn't the will power to economize. Not being given to indecisiveness, she'd been accustomed to spending money and enjoying life, taking for granted a pantry stocked with things like dried shrimp, dried sea lettuce and mushrooms, and having a decent soup at every meal. She felt she'd put up with as many inconveniences and difficulties as could be expected of her, and yet the money just seemed to flow out, until finally it was gone. Feeling truly miserable, she talked things over with Wenyao one night. He was even more concerned than she, but ultimately it was left for her to come up with a solution.

"Let's sell off everything we don't need."

"Right, that's what we'll do!" Wenyao was pleased. Having been at the end of their tether just moments before, he now sensed that a catastrophe had been averted. They could press on again. So he rolled over and promptly fell sound asleep. At school he'd been known as a dashing young man whose good looks and elegant airs had captivated many coeds. On one occasion, when a movie studio had used the school as a setting, he'd been spotted and signed on as an extra. His field was civil engineering, and although his grades had only been average, he'd always been quite active in school: playing the trombone in the school orchestra, cheerleader at track and field meets, organizer of student outings, and one of the most active participants at evening social gatherings. Endowed with the gift of gab, he was a pleasure to be around. Of course, that was due in no small measure to the fact that the proud and beautiful Duanli had agreed to be his wife. But now that their lives were devoid of any enjoyment, Duanli discovered that enjoyment was the only thing he sought.

There was a soft noise at the back door, which opened slightly, then closed softly. That was followed by the sound of muffled footsteps coming up the stairs. Wenguang had returned home. He was like a ghost, coming and going like a shadow. He went out, he came back, and no one was aware, no one noticed; naturally, no one knew what he was thinking. At the outbreak of the Cultural Revolution he had come forward to make a clean break with his father, packing up his bedroll and moving to the school. But he was back home, crestfallen, in less than two months. No one knew if he'd been rejected by the Red Guards or if he'd declined to join. He came home haggard, gaunt, dirty and, someone said, lousy; in other words, like a beggar. His father neither yelled at him, drove him away, nor, as it turned out, paid him the slightest bit of attention. His mother's reaction was limited to saying over and over, "We're paying for the sins of our past life!"

And that must have been what it was, for a decent, close-knit family had nearly fallen apart, and Duanli bemoaned her cruel fate.

2

Duanli rummaged through her trunks and closet, digging out all the clothes that were no longer being worn, with the idea of selling them to a secondhand store.

She couldn't sell Duoduo's old cloths, since they could be handed down to Mimi. Lailai's clothes could be altered for Mimi, too. In fact, some of Mimi's old things were about the only children's clothes that could be sold. She dug out a little orange-colored overcoat and an off-white wool jumper. She could sell Wenyao's Western-style suit, although it probably wouldn't bring much, since no one was wearing Western-style suits these days. The most fashionable item she ran across, considering the times, was an olive-drab military uniform. Here, this satin brocade quilted jacket can go, so can these woolen pants. Every pair was a hundred percent wool and extremely well made; they had all come from the best dressmakers, like New World, and, since she had come in for several fittings, they fit her perfectly. Rummaging through these things like this was a painful experience. She'd always enjoyed wearing nice things, and wearing clothes that didn't fit properly or weren't just what she liked bothered her, made her uneasy, made her feel as though she were someone else, not herself. But she could take no pride in that now, and her mood was ruined.

She thought back to the wedding of Wenyao's cousin, and how she had begun making preparations a full two months ahead of time. Since it was to be a major event in her life, she'd gone out and bought some black and red patterned material, which she'd taken to New World to be made into a dress. Dark colors looked best against her fair, glossy skin. The dress was going to be ready on the morning of the wedding, which to her way of thinking, couldn't have been more appropriate. But when she went to pick it up she learned that it hadn't been sent over from the tailor shop yet, and that she'd have to come back at five in the afternoon.

Later that day, dressed in a pair of slacks and a shirt that she wore around the house, she and Wenyao returned to New World to pick up the dress, then took the number 26 bus straight to the Peace Hotel. Even at that they were late, which was nothing new for Duanli, who was always late for affairs like this. She had her dress, but to her chagrin, it didn't fit: the seamstress, who had measured it wrong, had cut the bustline an inch bigger than it should have been, making the entire dress so loose it was nearly shapeless. She could have cried. "If anyone says your dress looks too big," Wenyao consoled her, "we'll just tell them that's the newest fashion." He was always ready with a witty line, but this time Duanli didn't appreciate his humor. She was depressed all evening, saying nothing and not mixing at all, barely touching her food. She couldn't wait for the wedding banquet to end.

She held up that very dress now, then put it with the other things, and wrapped them all up into a bundle.

"Mama," Mimi cried out from the window, where she was keeping a playful eye on the lane outside, "a couple of trucks have pulled up downstairs."

Duanli tossed down her bundle and ran over to the window. Sure enough, the iron gate that opened onto the little garden downstairs was open, and there were two trucks parked in the gateway. Several men climbed out of the trucks and began moving some dilapidated furnishings into the downstairs apartment.

"They've got some kids," Mimi said.

"It's our new neighbors," Duanli muttered. This was always happening; several families had moved in to buildings up and down the lane recently. The new neighbors were all from working-class districts on the outskirts of town, and everything about them was different from the original occupants of the area.

Downstairs a woman carrying a rice vat called out, "Where'll I put it *at*?"

Duanli pulled Mimi away from the window and closed it.

"Don't watch them. People from up north are as mean as the devil. Don't you so much as say hi to them, do you hear me?"

Although Mimi stopped watching the goings-on, Duanli kept going back to the window to see what was happening downstairs. Each time she looked out the window, the load on the trucks had grown smaller, until all that was left were some briquettes and kindling. Finally, even that had been moved inside. The trucks drove away, leaving behind two men, two women, and a bunch of kids, boys and girls of varying ages, all dressed in drab hand-me-downs, going in and out of the building. It didn't take Duanli long to determine that the fat woman who had been carrying the rice vat and the skinny, hardworking, tight-lipped man were one family, and that the woman was called "A'mao's Mom". The other man—a big, burly fellow—and the woman wearing a textile-factory cap were also a couple, but it was impossible to tell who the children belonged to, since they all looked the same to her, filthy and rough.

Duanli was in a frightful state, wondering how she should deal with these new neighbors. She didn't know what kind of tempers these people had, since she'd never had anything to do with their kind before, although there were some borderline families in the next lane over, whose kids often came over to make trouble, calling them things like "rowdies" and even pelting them with stones. Once the Cultural Revolution got underway they came over and pulverized the glass shards that had been stuck into the top of the wall around the courtyard to ward off thieves. Then they straddled the wall and shouted slogans, cursing people and even throwing bricks through glass windows day after day, without fail. Things hadn't gotten back to normal until the downstairs was sealed up. That was the only experience Duanli had ever had with people like this, and she was worried. It was one more thing to fret over. Then she thought about the sealed-up third floor. If a couple more families like the ones downstairs moved in, she'd be surrounded by a "struggle" unit, which meant she could look forward to a struggle session every single day.

Duoduo came home then, just as Duanli was getting all worked up.

"Mama, a couple of families just moved in downstairs. Isn't that great! They've already scrubbed the floors, so you have to take off your shoes when you go inside."

"What's so great about it?" Duanli shot back out of frustration.

"Do they really walk around barefoot?" Mimi asked her sister excitedly.

"Go see for yourself if you don't believe me."

"Mama, I'm going downstairs," Mimi said, barely able to contain herself.

"No, you're not!" Duanli shot back angrily. Mimi stopped in her tracks and sulked, leaning up against the wall next to the door instead of walking back toward her mother.

"But Mama, what're you scared of? They don't bite," Duoduo said. "On my way upstairs, a fat woman smiled at me."

"That shows how much you know! The people who came to ransack the house and struggle against your grandfather had smiles on their faces too." Duanli sighed. "Anyone who wants to can take advantage of us."

Duoduo sat down at the table without another word and took

a little red book out of her quotations notebook, trying to memorize the contents. These were her lessons.

Duanli stood up and surveyed the pile of things laid out on the bed. Fording herself to get back to work, she began gathering them up.

"Duoduo!" she called.

"What's up?"

"Come over here. I want to talk to you."

"I'm trying to memorize the 'Three Venerable Articles'. We're going to have a spot test tomorrow at school." Duoduo said with a pout.

"Duoduo, I want you to go to the secondhand store for me. Here, take this stuff."

"What for?"

"This ... this worthless stuff just takes up space in the house. We're better off selling it!" Admitting their poverty even to the children embarrassed Duanli. To her, poverty was a sin, something to be ashamed of.

"You want *me* to sell it? Not me. *You* do it."

"I can't go. If someone sees me they'll assume we're holding things back, and there'll be another house search."

Duoduo, who was scared to death of house searches, kept quiet. But she still wasn't willing to take the stuff and sell it, no matter what. She paused, then said, "Let's not sell it, okay?"

"You little imp, why are you disobeying me?" Duanli was getting mad. "Why's it so hard to get you to do anything?"

Duoduo started to cry. "Let me do something else, okay?"

The tears softened Duanli's heart. "Duoduo," she leveled with her daughter, "Mama's money is all gone, honestly. I have to pay for the utilities the day after tomorrow, and I don't have the money. Be a good little girl and help Mama out." Her face was flushed, and she, too, was on the verge of tears.

"What if someone sees me, what'll I do then?" Duoduo sobbed.

"No one pays any attention to children." Duanli thrust the bundle and their residence card into her daughter's arms. "Mimi, go along with your sister."

"Sure thing!" Mimi, who was still leaning up against the door, shouted, her spirits soaring with the prospect of going downstairs. She came over, took her elder sister by the hand, and pulled her toward the stairs. Duoduo tagged along behind her sister, wiping her eyes as she went.

That brought a sigh of relief from Duanli. In truth, she was no more willing than Duoduo to go on this errand and, if anything, was more bashful about it than her daughter. How could she have sunk to this level?

Grandmother was talking in the next room, and the sound came through loud and clear. The old woman must be angry at something again to get carried away like this. If the new neighbors downstairs heard her talking this loudly there could be trouble, so Duanli decided to go in and try to calm her down.

"Mother, what's the matter?" Duanli asked. Wenying was brewing tea for her mother and Wenguan was slouching in the foldaway bed in the corner.

"Listen to this Duanli. This horrible son of mine says he's signed up at school for a combat team that's going to Heilongjiang to reclaim some wasteland. Do you have any idea where Heilongjiang is? It snows there in June. It's so cold, people's noses and ears freeze and drop off."

Wenguang didn't say a word. Having no intention of offering an explanation, he just lay there staring up at the ceiling.

"Don't get so upset, Mother!" Duanli urged her as she took the cup of tea from Wenguang and handed it to the old woman, then led her over to a high-backed rattan chair. "Maybe he was told to sign up. Maybe he had no choice."

"No, it was his own idea," said Wenying, who attended the same school as her older brother. Fu Zhigao was Wenguang's classmate, so the news was probably reliable.

"Signing up doesn't matter," Duanli said trying to console her mother-in-law. "That's a sign of the times. These days everybody has to sign up for one thing or another, but only a tiny minority actually get accepted."

"For people with our political background, if you don't volunteer, they drag you off!"

"Not necessarily. They may not approve *because* of our background! Even though it's Heilongjiang, we're still talking about a combat team, and the political requirements have to be pretty rigid."

"What sort of qualifications does anyone need to go to

Heilongjiang?" The old woman was distraught. In '58, Tiger's daddy, who lived in Lane 1, was branded a Rightist, and the whole family was packed off to Heilongjiang, weren't they?"

"Times have changed since then."

Her mother-in-law's face softened a bit as she sipped her tea. She was beginning to feel better about the family's terrible political background.

"Duanli, did you know that a couple of families from up north have moved in downstairs? I wonder what they're like."

"We'll stay clear of them," Duanli said reassuringly.

"They're from up north, so maybe they're decent folk," Wenying said hopefully. "Auntie Abao was from up north, wasn't she?"

"You wouldn't expect someone who's eating your food to get nasty would you?" the old woman remarked cynically, with a shake of her head.

"Daddy!" Wenying called out, hurrying over to fetch her father's slippers and get him some water to wash his face. The old man, who had just come home after a day's hard work, was covered with dirt and had a dark expression on his face.

Duanli stood up. "I'm glad you're back," she greeted him.

"Yeah, I'm back," he acknowledged halfheartedly. He was a big man who had always been stylish and full of life. Wenyao's bearing had come from his father, although he lacked his father's intelligence and ability. The old man was dressed in common gray work clothes, which made him look more slovenly than the people around him. He had, it seems, been born to wear nice things.

"Why don't you take a rest, Daddy. I was just leaving." Duanli left the room, gently closing the door behind her. Wenying followed right on her heels.

"The work assignments for the class of '66 have been announced," Wenying said softly.

"Are they all right?"

"Forty percent will remain in Shanghai, including those who have to take care of their families because of poor economic conditions or as eldest sons, as well as those with good political backgrounds. Second best are those assigned to farms just outside Shanghai, followed by Dafeng Farm in Northern Jiangsu. The worst assignments are to teams out of the area, in places like

Anhui and Jiangxi, where they really have to sweat in the fields."

"So Wenguang wouldn't have much chance of staying even if he hadn't signed up," Duanli said gravely.

"That's right! I wonder what the class of '68 assignments will be like."

"Don't think so far ahead. What happens, happens. Worrying about it doesn't help, and you can't escape it."

"God only knows what the future holds in store for me. Maybe I ought to go see a fortune-teller," Wenying said ruefully.

"Mama!" Duoduo shouted as she came running in. "We—"

"Oh, you're back!" Duanli cut her off. "It's nearly dinnertime. Wenying, don't let it get you down. Why don't you spend a little more time with Fu Zhigao while you're still young."

Wenying laughed sarcastically.

Duanli pushed the two children into their room and closed the door. "You're not to let Grandmother or anyone else know that we're selling off our things," she told them softly. " Grandmother and Grandfather would be mad."

The children nodded obediently. Actually, Duanli wasn't really afraid of angering her mother-in-law, but rather ... how could she put it? In simplest terms, the more monks there are, the less food there is to go around. Her in-laws, she was well aware, had not shown enough concern for her before. One year, when she'd wanted to buy a set of ash furniture, her mother-in-law had said there wasn't enough money, and had told her to wait a year or so. But not long after that she had bought Wenying a piano. Duanli didn't feel so badly about what she was doing now when she recalled this.

"How much did you sell it for?"

"Altogether a hundred and five yuan." Duoduo said as she handed her mother the money and receipt.

"Only a hundred and five?" Duanli was stunned. The two pairs of woolen pants alone had cost over seventy.

"That's right. Not bad, huh? I didn't believe it at first, myself.," Duoduo could barely control her excitement. "The clerk at the store said we could leave the stuff there on consignment and pay him when it was sold. That way we'd get even more. But I figured that a hundred was plenty, and besides, didn't you say you had to pay the utility bill the day after tomorrow?"

"Yes, that's right. But realistically speaking, you could have sold it for a little more than that."

"Then why didn't *you* do it?"

Duanli didn't say a word, but she was thinking that next time she would indeed have to do it herself. People are always taking advantage of children.

"Mama," Mimi piped up. "The new neighbors downstairs really do go around the house barefoot."

"Umm."

"The fat auntie told me she'd never seen such a nice apartment in her whole life. Where'd they live before? What kind of place could they have lived in?" Mimi was puzzled.

"They're from a slum district. They lived in a shack."

"Wow!" Mimi blurted out smugly.

After dinner, Duanli went downstairs to dump the garbage. The door to the apartment facing the stairs was wide open. Sure enough, the fat woman was sitting on the floor doing some sewing, while four or five kids were having a great time playing on the floor around her. Several pairs of shoes were lined up in the doorway. The room was virtually bare, with hardly a stick of furniture. On her way back from dumping the garbage, she noticed that the fat woman was sizing her up. Her eyes, which were big to begin with, protruded slightly. Duanli lowered her head and ran upstairs.

That night after everyone was asleep, Duanli told Wenyao how much they'd gotten from selling their things. When her husband, who was half asleep himself, heard that they suddenly had over a hundred yuan, he woke up fast.

"A hundred and how much?"

"A hundred and five."

"Let's give Mother fifty."

Duanli didn't say anything.

"We'll buy a chicken tomorrow, a hen, and stew it."

Duanli didn't say anything.

"And a kilo of oranges. I haven't had any fruit in the longest time."

Duanli still didn't say anything.

"We'll buy some ham and keep it around the house."

"Hah!" Duanli laughed. "Are you afraid I don't know how to

spend money? Are you going to teach me?"

"The best thing you can do with money is buy food with it. Once it's in your belly no one can tell. Take Daddy, who worked like a slave to accumulate some property and wound up as a capitalist. He'd have been better off eating up the profits."

"Are you saying that a hundred yuan or so is enough to get some property?"

"I was just giving an example."

"For Lailai's tenth birthday party we spent a hundred yuan for a single table at the International Restaurant."

"That's right."

"How can you know, since you don't pay the bills? Ask me and I'll tell you how tight money is."

That's right."

"I've thought it over, and I say we don't spend the whole hundred yuan on food. We have to save some, just in case. What if one of the kids gets sick, or if something else happens? This way we won't have to worry."

"That's right."

"I have to pay the utility bill tomorrow, and the day after that we're going to have to buy some bottled gas. You don't get paid for another ten days, and I don't know where the food money is going to come from. So we're going to have to spend at least thirty yuan before you get paid again. And even when you do, it won't be enough to live on. We really have to hold back thirty yuan to help us get through next month."

"Does that mean we won't be able to give Mother any?"

"It's up to you." She paused, then continued in a conciliatory tone. "Mother has a lot of clothes she doesn't wear and things she no longer uses. Who knows, maybe she'll consider doing the same thing. If we try to give them some of the money, they won't take it for nothing, and they'll just return it. All this politeness winds up being a burden to all concerned."

"Ai!" Wenyao sighed. At times like this, sighing was all he ever did. Duanli realized how totally useless her husband was. In the past she'd always depended upon him; no matter what she needed, or what difficulties she faced, all she had to do was take them to him and everything would be fine. Now she realized that the source of his ability had been the endless supply of money coming from his father, pure and simple. When the money ran out, he had turned into a useless clod who wound up depending upon her. He rolled over and hugged her tightly. "Ai!" It was Duanli's turn to sigh. She wished she had a job, even if it were teaching school. The year after she'd gotten married, a local elementary school had run short of teachers and asked her to fill in. She'd refused. How could she be a teacher? Especially in a class of small children! She'd managed to complete her secondary education only through the efforts of so many of her teachers, which had made her more marriageable. And yet, she'd never thought much of teaching as a profession. So she hadn't accepted the offer. After all, since she hadn't had to worry about food and clothing, who needed work like that?

But now, there was never enough food to eat or clothes to wear, and she couldn't help wondering what might have happened if she'd accepted the offer back then; maybe she'd have stayed with it, and now she'd be earning a monthly salary of fifty or sixty yuan. Just think, fifty or sixty yuan! Just the thought of it got her blood pumping, and she forgot completely how she used to be able to spend fifty or sixty yuan, or more, on one trip down Nanjing Road. But times were different now, and a little amount of money was something worth having.

She heard some soft footsteps coming up the stairs. Wenguang was home. What was he thinking? Why did he have to sign up to go to Heilongjiang? It looked as if he'd do anything to leave home. What had the family ever done to him? It had fed him and clothed him. He no sooner said he wanted to study art than they'd hired him a tutor. When he was tired of that he talked about all the benefits of studying a foreign language, and in no time at all he had a private language teacher. In the end, he'd learned nothing at all, and had neglected his studies so badly that he hadn't even passed the middle-school entrance exam, making it necessary to take a year of makeup classes. During that year the family had hired two tutors, one for language and one for math. But the tutors were more concerned about him than he was for himself, since they didn't feel right about taking any money without any results. If they couldn't be responsible for him, at least they had to be responsible to themselves. But Wenguang acted as if it were all a game, neglecting his studies and daydreaming all the time, even playing hooky. The family, concerned that he might overtax his brain, treated him as solicitously as they would a brand-new mother, until his so-called daily lessons consisted of nothing but milk, eggs, and longan fruit. Somehow he managed to pass the entrance exam the next year. Then when it was time to take the high-school exam, the same scenario was repeated. It took some work, but he passed. Next came the college boards, and Duanli, who didn't know what the others were thinking, was sweating it out for him. Then along came the Cultural Revolution and the end of entrance exams. That had saved the day for him, but had closed off all other avenues at the same time.

Duanli recalled what Aunti Abao had said: "The people in your family don't grow up; they're cast in gold."

That's right, cast in gold. Costly, but devoid of any life force.

3

As Duanli squeezed into the line of shoppers buying fish, she was pushed smack up against the broad back of the man in front of her. She'd managed to muster the courage to go shopping for fish since everyone in the family wanted some for a change; and since it was cheaper than meat, she gave in. She'd gotten up at three in the morning to stand in line, and if anyone had told her that God would be unmoved by such good faith she wouldn't have believed it. The line kept growing longer in front of her, nudging her farther and farther backward, farther and farther from the fish stall. Fortunately, the fish seller came out just then to assign numbers, the most effective deterrent against line-crashing. He walked up to the line, spread out his arms, and began pushing everyone over to one side, straightening out the bulges by squeezing people into line and packing them in so tightly they could barely breathe. He then removed a tiny piece of chalk from behind his ear and began writing numbers on the people's upper arms, shouting out each one as he went along:

"Number three, number four. . . ."

All this made Duanli feel very uncomfortable, sort of insulted. Having a number written on your clothes was like wearing a prison uniform.

"Number twenty, number twenty-one...."

Seeing it was nearly her turn, she decided to try to make a deal with the man.

"Comrade, write it here, would you please?" She folded back the lapel of her jacket.

"Be careful it doesn't get rubbed off!" he said obligingly. "Number twenty-seven." After calling out her number, he moved on without missing a beat: "Twenty-eight, twenty-nine...."

Duanli breathed a sigh of relief. Everything was fine now. All she had to do was wait her turn.

"Fifty-nine, sixty! Okay, that's it. That's all there is. The rest of you are out of luck, so don't waste your time standing in line," the man shouted.

Those who had numbers were assured of buying fish today. Duanli shifted her weight onto her other foot, her anxieties replaced by happiness. She never imagined that eating a little fish could be such a pain in the neck. She began to feel guilty about all the times she had chewed out Auntie Abao.

"Two *jin* per person, two *jin*'s the limit!" one of the fish sellers announced. They were open for business. The line began to inch forward. The progress was slow, but at least it was progress. Finally, it was her turn. A woman in an apron covered with fish scales scooped out a few fish and threw them onto the scales.

"Two *jin* one ounce," she shouted. "Seventy-eight cents."

Duanli thrust her shopping basket over, but the woman paused just as she was about to dump the fish into it. "Where's your number?"

Duanli turned her lapel inside out. "It's right here."

"Where?" The woman stared at her suspiciously. "These people have been lined up since three in the morning and won't tolerate line-crashers."

"I've got a number!" She turned her lapel inside out again, but this time she was flabbergasted. There was nothing there but some chalk dust. No number. The material was too shiny for chalk, and with all the pushing and shoving, the number had been rubbed completely off.

"Go on, get out of here!" someone behind her yelled. Others started to push or pull her out of line.

Duanli fell across the greasy counter in despair. She was nearly in tears, unable to say a word.

"She was in line there!" someone said hoarsely in a Northern Jiangsu accent. "I'm her witness. She was in line there."

Heads turned to see who was speaking. Duanli spotted her. It was Auntie A'mao, the new neighbor downstairs. She was standing ten or so places behind Duanli. She stepped out of line and addressed the crowd:

"She asked him to write her number under her lapel. You can see for yourselves. Check the numbers of the people in front and in back of her. Then you'll see."

The person ahead of her was number twenty-six, the one behind number twenty-eight. That made her number twenty-seven. By then some of the people nearby recalled her standing there without making any fuss, just keeping her place. The woman at the scales handed her the fish, but not before giving her a piece of advice: "Next time you'll know better. Don't have the number written inside your clothes. You think it takes away from your good looks? If that's what you're worried about you'll have to do without fish."

Duanli picked up her shopping basket and got away from there as quickly as she could, without so much as a backward glance. Nothing like this had ever happened to her before. But at least she got her fish. After she'd bought some greens and potatoes and was about to leave the marketplace, she spotted Auntie A'mao and another woman whom Duanli recognized as someone who did the grocery shopping for several families in the lane; everyone called her Auntie Golden Flower. Duanli felt obliged to go over and thank Auntie A'mao.

"You really saved my skin a while ago."

"I just did what was right," she responded warmly.

Auntie Golden Flower jumped into the conversation: "Do you do your own grocery shopping? Tough, isn't it!"

Sensing a tone of derision in her comment, Duanli said nothing. Auntie A'mao took up the subject:

"If you think it's tough doing your own grocery shopping, you should see what it's like when you can't afford to shop!"

Auntie Golden Flower took a look into Duanli's shopping basket. "Is that all you bought? How can that be enough?" She was just curious, not finding fault. Duanli's home, where the front door was always closed, was an unknown quantity where the other people in the lane were concerned.

Duanli, who was still uncomfortable about the embarrassing incident of a while ago, blushed as she shifted her basket to the other arm.

"It can't be all that bad when you've got fish to eat. The emperors themselves lived on meat and fish," Auntie A'mao said.

"You don't know how well off they used to be."

"Weren't they a bunch of capitalists?" Auntie A'mao said distastefully.

Duanli, who had heard enough, quickened her pace, but to her surprise, so did they.

"They can't depend on the old fellow anymore. It's tough going now!"

"What's so tough about it? They can work, can't they?" Auntie A'mao viewed life in simple terms, which was a blessing of sorts.

Duanli slowed down and said softly, "I'd like nothing more than a job."

"As I see your situation," Auntie Golden Flower said, "the best job for you would be baby sitting. You wouldn't even have to go outside. You could stay home and earn some extra money."

"How would I go about it"? Duanli asked, showing a bit of interest.

"They bring the kid over in the morning and pick him up in the evening. You'd be responsible for two meals."

"Oh." Duanli was perking up. Money was really getting tight these days, and their income fell thirty or forty yuan short every month. The hundred and five yuan was by now just a memory. Selling off their possessions had become a matter of public knowledge, and even several bundles of clothes belonging to Duanli's mother-in-law had been sold. A few days earlier, Fu Zhigao had borrowed a motorized cart to help them deliver a redwood octagonal table to the secondhand store on consignment, along with Duanli's cosmetic table and three-sectioned mirror. The hard times were teaching the children a lot about life. Duoduo no longer cried when she had to take things over to the secondhand store; in fact, she regularly went there with some of her friends after school to see if the things placed on consignment had been sold. If they had she'd run home and happily report the news. Duanli would then loosen her grip on her purse strings and buy some fruit or prepared food or snacks, knowing that within three days at most she'd receive notification in the mail that she could claim the money. And yet she was aware that they couldn't just sit idly by and eat up the profits, since living off the sale of personal possessions held out short-term possibilities at best. Watching someone else's child in her home wouldn't have any effect on her housework, and would produce some badly needed income. Mimi, who just moped around the house with nothing to do, could even help out, which was an added benefit. They walked on a bit farther before Duanli said haltingly:

"Auntie Golden Flower, could you, would you keep an eye open for me to see if anyone needs a sitter? I've got the time, and it shouldn't be too hard. . . ."

Auntie Golden Flower knew at once what she was trying to say: "Sure, no problem, leave it all to me."

Duanli breathed a sigh of relief.

Auntie Golden Flower reported back to her that very evening. She was more interested in being helpful than afraid to have dealings with Duanli's family, even though they had fallen so low. Duanli invited her in, but she begged off, preferring to stand at the top of the stairway and sneak an occasional look inside the apartment.

She had come to tell Duanli that she had located a family with an eighteen-month-old boy named Qingqing. Both of his parents were workers who were thirty-eight years old before their pride and joy was born, and who couldn't bear to send him to a nursery school yet. Having been informed of Duanli's situation and the somewhat worrisome fact of her bad political background, which could conceivably hold unpleasant consequences for them, they nonetheless felt good about the proper lifestyles of such people, with their attention to sanitation and manners. They felt that they could entrust their son to her without any misgivings, and after weighing the pros and cons they agreed to the proposition. A sum of thirty yuan a month, which included two meals and a snack every day, was settled upon. Additionally, they agreed to have a bottle of milk delivered to Duanli's home daily at their own expense.

On the following morning, when everyone was seated around the table eating breakfast before leaving for school or work, Qingqing was brought over. He was a fair, chubby, dark-eyed baby who didn't take to strangers right off. As soon as Duanli picked him up he squirmed and fought until she put him down on the floor. Wenyao, Duoduo, Lailai, and Mimi stood off at a distance watching him, observing him somberly, as though he were some sort of alien creature. Even Duanli was a bit tense, since this was the first time she'd ever had anything to do with someone else's child. Even her own three children had been taken care of by a wet nurse. She hadn't nursed them herself, even though she could have, because she was afraid it would ruin her figure. Qingqing wasn't intimidated by the family"s scrutiny. He scrutinized them right back, one after the other. All of a sudden, he squatted down and started peeing on the floor, loudly enough for everyone to hear.

"Yechh, that's filthy!" Duoduo shouted. "My God!"

Wenyao frowned.

"Why's he peeing on the floor?" Lailai asked his mother.

Duanli, who didn't know, kept quiet.

Just then, Qingqing started bawling, sensing everyone's disapproval and disappointment.

Mimi walked up and took him by the hand. "Don't talk about him like that; he's just a baby." As the baby of the family, she had no one to play with, and so was the only one who welcomed Qingqing's arrival. She had often pleaded with her mother, "Mama, how about giving me a little brother; even a sister would be fine, okay?" And if it hadn't been for the Cultural Revolution, Duanli probably would have had another child, since a second son was just what the family needed. Rearing children was her obligation, but now she was worried that she couldn't afford to feed the three she already had.

Mimi took the crying baby over to the bathroom and pointed to the toilet: "This is where you're supposed to pee." She reached up and pulled the chain to flush the toilet. Qingqing stopped crying. Breathing a sigh of relief, Duanli went over and got the mop to clean up the mess. When she finished she heated some milk. She was shocked at how quickly the boiling milk frothed up and spilled over the sides of the pot, nearly burning her fingers.

Feeding Qingqing was one of the most difficult things she'd ever had to do. He refused to eat, pushing the spoon or glass away with his strong chubby fingers. But after plenty of coaxing and trying to force it down his throat, she managed to get half a glassful of milk down him, when all of a sudden he gurgled and coughed, spitting up everything he'd just swallowed. All that work for nothing! The smell of milk nauseated Duanli. Then when it was time for lunch, she found he could hold a spoonful of rice in his mouth seemingly forever. But rice wasn't like candy, which sooner or later dissolved in the mouth. Getting him to chew his food and move it around with his tongue before finally swallowing it nearly wore her out. After saying every nice thing she could think of, she wound up pleading with him:

"Nice Qingqing, good little boy, swallow it. Qingqing's such a good little boy, swallow it now, swallow it, good boy!"

With his mouth stuffed with food, Qingqing just played with some chips of wood in front of him, completely ignoring Duanli's flattery. She grew desperate. Why was he refusing to eat? What she didn't realize was that her own three children had been a hundred times harder to take care of than Qingqing.

Mimi stood alongside watching with excitement. Finally, unable to contain herself any longer, she pleaded with her mother: "Mama, let me try, okay?"

"This isn't a doll I'm trying to feed, so what's there to try?" Duanli, who was by then thoroughly frustrated, refused any help.

Mimi didn't force the issue, but a moment or two later she reached over and tapped Qingqing's tightly closed mouth gently with her finger: "Knock-knock, open the door, I want in."

Qingqing blinked, then gurgled and started to laugh. His mouth was empty. Duanli hurriedly shoved a spoonful of rice in before the door slammed shut again.

"Knock-knock, is the little rabbit home?" Mimi changed the routine.

The door opened.

"Boom, boom, boom, there go the plane's bombs!"

The door opened.

"The car's driving in!"

The door opened.

Half a bowl of rice had made its way down into his stomach when Duanli heard that familiar gurgle in his throat again, the one that sounded like he was going to throw up.

"God help me!" she uttered prayerfully.

Mimi quickly picked up the pot lid and began pounding on it with a chopstick, so confusing the baby he didn't know whether to be frightened or what. But his disorientation quickly turned into excitement, and in no time at all he was thrashing his arms and legs, as happy as a lark. He didn't throw up after all. Leaving well enough alone, Duanli stopped feeding him, thus bringing mealtime to an end. From then on, she adopted Mimi's handy tricks when it was time to feed Qingqing, pretending that his mouth was a door and keeping him from spitting up his food by distracting him with strange sounds. The baby's meals turned into a real production.

Blessedly, this little defect of his was offset by an extremely positive trait. He took long naps in the morning and afternoon, and while the boy was sleeping, Duanli felt more relaxed and peaceful than ever, and was actually able to find some pleasure in the chaotic life she was living.

While she was enjoying a bit of that all-too-infrequent happiness, Wenying came rushing in, nearly panic stricken:

"Sister-in-Law, Wenguang's application to go to Heilongjiang has been approved! He leaves in a week! Mother's crying her eyes out and Daddy's ranting and raving. Hurry up and try to calm them down!"

The news shocked Duanli out of her contentment, and she rushed out of the room with Wenying, stopping in the doorway just long enough to say to Mimi:

"You watch little brother, and don't let him fall out of bed!"

It was sheer chaos in the next room. The bed was piled with olive drab clothes—a padded hat, padded pants, a padded jacket— all of which Wenguang was rolling up into a bedroll. Duanli's mother-in-law was sobbing so hysterically she couldn't talk, while her father-in-law, who had stayed home sick, was sitting in the redwood high-backed chair, his face purple with rage as he railed at his wife:

"He's not going to die out there, so what are you crying about?"

"So he doesn't die, he's still being banished!" she said. "This horrible son of ours is just looking for trouble, and he's going to live to regret it. But by then it'll be too late."

"Let him go! He's bored to tears here." With that the old man got to his feet and started out the door.

"Where are you going?" his wife shouted. "If someone sees you outside they'll say you're malingering!"

"I'm going to work!"

"We're paying for the sins of a past life! The sins of a past life!"

When Duanli saw the padded clothes on the bed she knew it was too late to do anything. So after reflecting for a moment, she bent over and helped her mother-in-law to her feet.

"Mother, don't let yourself get upset. Listen to me. Maybe it's a good thing his application was approved. It shows that the authorities have faith in him and that he has a future."

The old woman's sobs lessened a bit.

"You see those uniforms, that means he's in the army. He's going to an army reclamation farm. . . ."

"It's not army, it's state-run," Wenguang corrected her frostily.

"State-run is okay, too. As long as it's run by the government it's all the same."

Her mother-in-law dried her eyes. "He'll be so far away we couldn't call him back if we tried. A nice family like this—in no time at all it's scattered to the four winds."

"Don't think about things like that. Wenguang has a future ahead of him. Who knows, this might be just what he needs to find his calling."

"I don't care if he finds his calling, all I want is for him to come back safe and sound." His mother burst into tears again, and this time she was joined by Wenying. Even Duanli, who by now was as sad as the others, started to cry.

The women cried for a while before Duanli calmed down again. What good does it do to be sad? she was thinking. One way or the other, he's going. The week will pass before we know it, and there's so much to be done in the meantime. Mother's getting on in years, and she's in no mood to do anything, anyway. And Wenying's too young to have any experience in matters like this, so it looks like I'll have to take care of things myself. With that thought in mind, she dried her eyes and said to Wenguang:

"Open up your bedroll. Your comforter and sheet have to be washed. Wenying, wash those things for your brother."

Wenying came over and took the bedroll.

"Wenguang, I want you to make a list of things you'll need."

Wenguang just stood there for a moment, then took out a piece of paper and wrote down a single word—comforter. He couldn't think of anything else, apparently feeling that all he needed to make his way in the world was a comforter. Duanli sighed, took the pen from him, and made a list: washbasin, suitcase, mosquito net.... How could two brothers be so useless!

After the list was complete, Duanli checked off the items they already had and noted which ones they'd need to buy. A quick calculation showed that they'd need at least two hundred yuan to send him on the "road to revolution".

"Are you getting any help from school?" she asked him.

"No. They said we'll be able to buy things like mosquito netting and cotton blankets by showing our notices," Wenguang answered her.

"If that's the case," her mother-in-law said, "run over to the secondhand store and tell them to reduce the price of that octagonal table to sell it quickly. It doesn't matter how much, as long as they give cash."

"Let's not get ahead of ourselves, Mother. I think we ought to check with Father's work-unit. After all, going to Heilongjiang is a revolutionary act. They should be willing to help out. If they do, that's fine. And if not, it doesn't matter. There'll still be time to think of something else."

"Duanli, it looks like it's all up to you."

"Don't worry, Mother. I'll go." Duanli tried not to let her apprehension show.

Duanli spent most of the afternoon out on the errands, while Qingqing was taking his nap. She went to her father-in-law's work-unit and Wenguang's school, where she got sympathetic responses and donations of fifty yuan from the unit and twenty from the school. Since she hadn't held out much hope in the first place, the money boosted her spirits considerably. She took out the money she had received from the sale of her cosmetic table, since she was well aware that during times like this saving any money at all was next to impossible. Once she'd abandoned that pipe-dream, it seemed perfectly reasonable to part with the money. Poor people are always the most generous. With a little here and a little there, she managed to scrape together something over two hundred yuan.

It was Sunday, the day Qingqing stayed home, so she went out with her brother-in-law to get the shopping done. Many of the items in the crowded store were marked with tags that said "For sale only to people with notices." Most of the customers that day were buying provisions for long trips. The crowds intimidated Wenguang, who was incapable of asserting himself; after a couple of feeble attempts at pushing his way up to the counter, he'd just give up. It was a lost cause. Duanli couldn't help feeling a little sorry for him. A spoiled brat like that, a man cast in gold, was sure to be at everyone's mercy out on his own. So why had he signed up?

"Wenguang, you've gone overboard this time." She just had to get it off her chest. "Back when you broke with the family, you had your reasons and your own problems. But they never held it against you, so why did you have to spite them like this?"

"I'm not doing this to spite them, Sister-in-Law."

"Then why'd you do it?"

"I'm not all that sure myself. Maybe Daddy was right when he said I was just bored to tears."

"Isn't this a pretty ridiculous way to solve that problem?" Duanli couldn't believe her ears.

"No, Sister-in-Law, you don't understand."

Duanli didn't say anything.

After they had walked on a little farther, Wenguang said softly, "I don't know why, but I feel bored a lot of the time! I have no idea why we're put on this earth. Really, why are we put here?"

"Why? To eat, wear clothes, and sleep."

"No, those are just the things that keep us alive. I want to know what the purpose is."

"God only knows," Duanli said.

"Life seems meaningless. I can't think of a single function I perform."

"Was it because you were bored that you broke with your family back then?" Duanli was amused by the strange thoughts that went through his head.

"Maybe, who knows!"

"So why did you come back? Why didn't you stick it out?" There was a trace of cynicism in her voice.

Wenguang's expression darkened. "They were a bunch of barbarians. I couldn't take it. I honestly couldn't stand it."

Once again, Duanli felt sorry for him. She kept quiet, sensing the strangeness of a situation where he had nothing to do. "I wouldn't mind being bored for a few days," she muttered to herself. "I'm dead on my feet all the time. I'm really worried that I might just give out at any minute."

The week virtually flew by, and it was time for Wenguang to leave. His mother nearly cried herself sick, so Duanli refused to let her go to the train station to see him off, having Duoduo take half a day off from school to stay home and watch Qingqing. She and Wenying accompanied Wenguang to the station.

Once he was on the train, Wenguang huddled timidly against the window until he was nudged aside by someone else. Duanli stood there looking at him, as though she were in a daze, wondering how long it would take him to discover he couldn't stand it and would want to come home again. But this time it wouldn't be so easy, not from thousands of miles away. Tears started trickling slowly down her face; Wenying, who was standing next to her, had been blubbering from the very start. As the train eased out of the station, Wenguang's eyes were turning red; he turned his face away from them and didn't look back. The train increased speed, faster and faster, until, far off down the tracks, where everything was hazy, it made a turn and disappeared from view.

Duanli left the platform with Wenying, whose eyes were swollen from crying. After they had boarded the number 41 bus, Wenying breathed a long sigh and said softly, "Now that he's gone, maybe I'll be able to stay in Shanghai."

"What do you mean?"

"The policy is 'take one, leave one,'" Wenying explained. "That friend of mine," she continued softly, "has been assigned to the Shanghai Division of Industry and Mining. His is a special case, since he's an only son."

"Oh. . . ." Now Duanli understood. "Do you like him?"

Wenying blushed, but didn't try to dodge the question. "He's let me know several times already how he feels about me."

"Is he a decent fellow?"

"He has a good head on his shoulders, and whenever I'm with him I know I've got someone I can lean on."

"That's wonderful!" Duanli suddenly envied her younger sister-in-law. If her husband could only be a little more like that, her life would certainly be a lot easier.

"Sister-in-Law, what do you think of him?" Duanli's opinion was important to Wenying.

"It's hard to say, since I've only seen him a couple of times. I've heard Duoduo and the other kids call him Fu Zhigao."

Wenying punched her sister-in-law playfully.

"I've seen that movie. Fu Zhigao is a pretty handsome fellow, real refined looking."

Wenying punched her again. "That sounds terrible."

Duanli smiled and took a good look at her sister-in-law, noticing that she had indeed grown into a woman. Her broad, fair forehead gave her a cheerful appearance. She had a dainty nose, lovely lines around her mouth, and even though her eyes were still puffy from crying, they radiated youthful hope, possessing a luster that stirred one's heart. Duanli was moved by what she saw and wished her a life of happiness. A happy marriage was what she needed to make up for all the bad times.

They didn't get back home until six o'clock. Duoduo, who was holding Qingqing and pacing excitedly, informed them that a schoolmate had come over to tell her about a major new directive that was to be announced that evening; she said she had to be at school at seven o'clock to participate in a celebration march. She was growing frantic that Mama was late coming home to make dinner and Qingqing's parents still hadn't been by to pick up their baby. She thrust Qingqing into Duanli's arms, tossed her quotations bag over her shoulder, and started out the door.

"It's only six o'clock," Duanli reminded her. "Eat some dinner first."

"I don't want any. I'll be late!" Duoduo, who was nearly in tears, turned and rushed out the door. She was always getting upset over the slightest little thing

She didn't return home until nine o'clock. Duanli brought her dinner in for her.

"What was the directive about?"

Duoduo, who was wolfing down her food, answered between bites, "Educated youths have to go to the countryside...."

4

Duanli returned home after doing her morning grocery shopping, stopping before going inside, as always, to bend down and pick up the milk that had been delivered to the door. But this morning all she found was some broken glass and a puddle of milk. It must have been the work of those little hooligans who always came over to make trouble for the family. They'd stand in the doorway downstairs and yell, "Zhang Wenyao, bring your personal seal down here!" So he'd come running downstairs, all for nothing. Or else they'd bang on the door like Red Guards, throwing a scare into everybody. They'd even come over late at night and throw rocks or bricks through the upstairs windows. By now everyone had gotten used to it, writing it off as just one of life's tribulations. But this time they'd carried their little game too far. That milk was meant for Qingqing, and she'd have to pay for it. A bottle of milk cost seventeen fen, plus a twenty-fen deposit on the bottle. For that much money she could buy two boxes of the crayons Mimi wanted.... Duanli just stood there staring at the broken glass as though she were transfixed.

The back door opened, and Auntie A'mao came outside to light a fire in the charcoal brazier she was carrying. Since they had moved in as squatters without a rental contract, the gas company wouldn't install a gas stove for them. So they were forced to use charcoal briquettes, and every time they fired up their brazier, the lane was filled with so much thick black smoke that no one dared open their windows or hang out the wash.

"What's wrong?" Auntie A'mao asked.

"Some kids smashed a bottle of milk," Duanli said as she snapped out of her daze, bending over to clean up the mess.

"Whose little brats would do a thing like that? Find out and make them pay!"

Duanli just shook her head and smiled cynically.

"You don't know who it was? Then just start cursing. Curse up and down the lane. Put a curse on the guilty family's whole line!"

Duanli shook her head again.

"You don't know how to curse? Or you don't dare? What are you afraid of? Your father-in-law is your father-in-law, you're you. The Communist Party places more importance on how you perform personally than on your family's history," she said to Duanli, trying to set her straight.

Duanli just smiled.

"You'll never get through life being a softy. You've got to be tough." This was Auntie A'mao's philosophy of life.

Duanli looked up at her. What she was saying had gotten through, and it made sense.

"Like taking a bus to work. The more you let other people push you around, the less your chances of getting on. You've got to push and shove right along with everybody else."

Duanli nodded.

Wenyao and the children had gotten up, and Duoduo, who had already taken over some of the housework, was cleaning up the room. She didn't do a bad job either, if it weren't for her constant grumblings that sometimes drove Duanli to distraction. "I'd rather do it myself than listen to you complain all the time!" "Then you do it!" Duoduo would snap back, so angry she could barely talk. But the next day she'd be at it again, working and grumbling. Duanli got used to it pretty soon and just let her grumble, since the new arrangement did make life a little easier for her.

"Mama, did you buy any oil fritters?" Lailai asked her.

"Yes." Duanli took them out of her basket.

"Mama, I don't want mine," Duoduo said. "Give me four fen instead."

"I already bought them. I don't have any money to give you."

"No, you have to! I'm not going to eat mine, so give me the four fen. Be fair about it," Duoduo insisted stubbornly.

"Mama, Qingqing wants his milk," Mimi said as she brought Qingqing over.

Duanli had forgotten all about the milk. She banged her forehead with her hand. "The bottle of milk was smashed by those little hooligans. Mimi, hurry up and finish your breakfast so you can go stand in line at the provisions store and buy another bottle. If you don't hurry they'll be sold out."

Buying milk by the bottle was difficult. Since there were only a few bottles available every day, you had to get there before the store opened at nine o'clock. Mimi was perfectly suited to lining up to buy things: she didn't get flustered and never left her spot. She just stood there like a good little girl, without complaint, for as long as it took. Besides, she had a good head on her shoulders for such a youngster, and whether it was five or six yuan for the utilities bill or two fen for a box of matches, she never came back with the wrong change or lost any money. She had a far better sense of what hard living was all about than either her older brother or older sister, and it was just her bad luck to have born at the worst possible time, for no sooner had she started figuring out what was going on around her than everything was suddenly all topsyturvy.

But even if Mimi left now, she wouldn't be back till at least nine-thirty, the time that Qingqing usually took his morning nap, and Duanli had to feed him something before he went to sleep. But what? She looked down at the little fellow, who was staring openmouthed at Mimi as she ate her bowl of rice porridge. She had pushed her oil fritter over to the side to concentrate on eating some pickled vegetables with so much enthusiasm it made you hungry just to watch her. Duanli had an idea: "Mimi, give him a spoonful of rice porridge and see if he likes it." Qingqing surprised her by not only letting Mimi put in his mouth, but even swallowing it. Duanli quickly filled a bowl half full of rice porridge, sprinkled some crumbs from the oil fritter on top, sat down, and started feeding him.

"Duanli," Wenyao called out to her, "Wenying's school sent notice that there's a parents' meeting tonight. Mother wants me to go in her place because of her bad hearing. I'm afraid they're going to talk about mobilization to go to the countryside and since I'm not very good at things like that, why don't you go, hmm?"

"How can you be so useless?" Duanli said resentfully.

"Things are different now than during Daddy's time, when you had to be on the ball to survive. Thanks to the Communist Party, everyone's got a job, no matter what, and even if there's no meat on the table, at least no one's going hungry."

"I think Daddy's money ruined you. You can't do a blessed thing."

"I had Daddy's money, all right, but I don't believe that people who didn't have any money had more abilities than I. The only thing they do better than me is complain."

"You know how to talk, I'll give you that much." Duanli never could out-argue him. Just then she remembered that he had been a star on the debating team in school.

"Okay, that settles it. You'll attend the meeting tonight, right?" Wenyao put down his bowl, gently stroked Duanli's hair once or twice, and walked out of the room. Mimi finished her rice porridge, then started nibbling on the oil fritter she'd saved till last as she went out to get a place in line. Lailai was still eating, having unobtrusively picked up the oil fritter that Duoduo had refused and eaten it himself. Duoduo was standing next to her bed, doing something with her head lowered. Duanli watched her out of curiosity. She saw her put some money into a clay jar.

"Duoduo, are you saving money?"

"Umm. One of the kids at school gave me a piggy bank. Once you put money in it you can't get it back out. Then when it's full you have to smash it."

"What are you saving for?"

"I want to buy a pair of stretch shoes," Duoduo told her. All the girls were wearing boys' stretch shoes.

Her daughter was growing up. There was already the hint of a bustline, which made her clothes look too tight on her. As soon as girls entered puberty they began paying attention to their appearance, always trying to make themselves look pretty. Duanli couldn't help feeling that she'd shortchanged her daughter, and vowed to herself to make her some new clothes. She recalled all the clothes she had owned at that age.

Duoduo very carefully slid the piggy bank under her bed, so Qingqing wouldn't start playing with it and break it. "That's the only way to save money!"

This gave Duanli an idea. Naturally, she wasn't a child any longer, and since she could take care of herself, there was no need to force herself to save by using a piggy bank. She dug out a little embroidered purse she hadn't used in years, into which she'd start putting a portion of the money she didn't need to spend. No matter how little it was, it'd soon add up.

While she was making dinner, she discovered that they were

out of MSG. She caught herself just as she was about to tell Mimi to go out and buy some. This would be a good place to make a little savings, since standards for taste varied from person to person. She put the sixty-two fen she had saved into her purse. Then when she went out to buy some toothpaste, she decided to switch from the expensive brand she'd used since childhood to a tube of Shanghai Toothpaste instead, at a savings of twenty-eight fen. She began to experience the joy of saving, and once she'd started there was no turning back. All she could think about was filling up the purse. Wenyao began teasing her by calling her "the cheapskate".

While Qingqing was sleeping, Duanli opened the trunk to look for some old blouses that she could alter for Duoduo. At one time there had been more lengths of fabric, of every imaginable color and design, than they knew what to do with. Buying fabric had been one of the real pleasures in Duanli's life. Whenever she'd gone out shopping, she would never pass a fabric store without going in and buying several lengths of material, whether she needed them or not. Sometimes she'd buy because the patterns struck her fancy, sometimes because the quality was exceptional, sometimes just because she liked them, and sometimes for no better reason than she felt like it. More than once she'd gotten home with her purchase and put it away, only to forget it completely until the moths got to it. When the house searches began, all this stuff had been taken from her and piled up in the courtyard as a lesson in class privileges, and even she had been shocked to see how much there was.

Duanli dug out two nearly new Chinese dresses whose patterns and color were still attractive: one had a yellow design over a brown background and the other was sky-blue. She turned them both over and over, but didn't know where to start cutting. After mulling it over for a while, she used one of Duoduo's shirts to make a pattern on a piece of newspaper, but slightly bigger. Then she laid the pieces of the pattern on top of one of the dresses, marked it with chalk, and began cutting the material, taking care to see that there was enough for all the pieces. She worked at an unhurried pace, as excited as a child playing house. By the time she began stitching the pieces together, she was inexpressibly happy. What admiration she felt for herself, how smart she was! Coming up with an idea like this had given her a taste of what it was like to be creative.

As soon as Duoduo came home from school, Duanli told her to try it on. Duoduo put it on and was speechless, her excitement revealed in the blush on her face as she looked at herself in the mirror from every angle. Back when she had owned more new clothes than she could ever have worn, she'd been little more than an innocent baby; then as she grew into young womanhood, when appearances were so important, she'd not been able to wear a single new blouse. Since there'd never been anything to dress her up in, Duanli had tried to compensate by weaving purple and red silk threads into her braids. She alone could see the subtle changes caused by using different colors of thread.

Duanli told her daughter that the blouse wasn't ready yet, and that she couldn't actually wear it until she'd finished the fine stitching. But Duoduo, who couldn't bear to take it off, said that she could do the invisible stitching herself. Duanli wouldn't hear of it. This job had been so absorbing because it was the first thing she had ever created with her own two hands. Mother and daughter spent an exciting afternoon together. While Duanli sewed the blouse her thoughts were already moving on to other projects. She decided to make something for Lailai and Mimi next.

As they had expected, the parents' meeting at Wenying's school had been called to discuss student assignments. This graduating class was going to be revolutionary red all the way: one hundred percent of the students were being resettled in far-off villages, places like Heilongjiang, Yunnan, Inner Mongolia, Guizhou, Anhui, and Jiangxi. There were to be no exceptions, not those in financial straits nor only sons or daughters; all were to be educated by poor and lower-middle-class peasants.

Duanli's family held a meeting when she returned home, and were unanimous in their resolve to fight the directive. "I've raised her for eighteen years," her mother said, "and it's not as simple as having one less mouth to feed." Duanli voiced her opinion: "What's the big deal! As soon as I graduated from college I became a housewife." Wenying was crying throughout the discussion, nearly breaking everyone's heart. Duanli felt sorry for her, for she was probably the only one in the room who knew all the reasons why her sister-in-law was so unhappy. Fu Zhigao had already begun working in one of the big factories. Duanli recalled how happy she'd been when she was a young woman in love. For her it had been the most carefree time of her life, but for girls like Wenying, all their youthful golden years had brought them so far was grief. She decided to do whatever she could to get her sister-in-law off the hook, no matter what it took. Having a directive and carrying it out were two different matters.

First the teacher came over to carry out the mobilization order, but Duanli sent him packing with ease. She wasn't particularly well informed of the way things worked, but when she saw his patched and tattered clothes she knew he was a small-fry, and easily manipulated. That was followed by a parade of cymbals and gongs up and down the lane to put the propaganda campaign into motion. Some of the local hooligans took advantage of the hubbub to break a couple of windows. The next phase was a study session at the school, which Duanli attended, leaving Wenying at home to watch Qingqing. "Study session" turned out to be a misnomer, since the real purpose was to get everyone to declare where they stood; no declaration, no going home. Meals consisted of a bowl of hot water and a roll. Duanli didn't eat the first day, but on the second day she was told she had to pay for her food, so, holding her anger in check, she ate what she was given. Somehow she managed to get through this phase, but then someone pulled strings to have Wenying and Daddy's subsistence pay cut off, and Daddy was subjected to a struggle session. Wenying and her mother did little all day except cry, while Wenyao did nothing but sigh.

Duanli tried to get him to do something, but he just said, "Wenying's too delicate as it is. I refuse to believe that it's some kind of hell out there. What about all the thousands of people who live their entire lives there?" His own comments made his chest swell.

Finally the school sent an ultimatum: If Wenwen didn't come and sign up, they'd cancel her residence registration. Not only that, the longer it took, the worse the assignment; she'd have to put up with Inner Mongolia, Yunnan, or Tibet, where the living conditions were the worst. For people who had spent their lives looking up at clouds in the Shanghai sky, these places might just as well have been foreign countries, utterly unimaginable places. Realizing that her back was up against a wall, Wenying finally decided to sign up for Jiangxi. It was farther away than Anhui, but the people in Anhui lived on coarse assorted grains, and she knew she couldn't handle that.

Scraping together everything they could lay their hands on, the family bought her what she'd need to take with her. Unlike Wenguang, who was far more able to cope, she took everything she could think of, all of which had to be purchased: a toilet, a wooden basin, a kerosene stove, a steel wok, Shanghai cabbage, sausage, canned food, toothpaste (ten whole tubes), and toilet paper—a whole carton of it. If there wasn't enough money to satisfy one of her demands, she cried so pitifully that she eventually got what she wanted. Ultimately, they had to sell some more things, and Duanli contributed the money she had been saving in her purse. Even Duoduo, who was sensible beyond her years, handed over her piggy bank, saying to her mother as she looked away, "You smash it. I won't buy those stretch shoes. They're not popular now, anyhow." Duanli took it from her but didn't have the heart to break it. Ultimately, however, Wenying said she wanted to buy five kilos of flour to make steamed rolls, and Duanli had no choice but to break the piggy bank. It contained more than four yuan, more than enough for a pair of stretch shoes. She held back a little of the money to buy some shoe-top material and try to make a pair of shoes herself. She was struck by how useless and selfish all the second-generation adults in this family were. Auntie A'mao's eldest son from downstairs had been assigned to Anhui, and Duanli saw what he was sending: a small trunk and a bedroll that he tied onto his bicycle rack and delivered to the debarkation point.

Wenying's send-off was a sad affair. Since she was going at the height of the down-to-the-countryside movement, which over-taxed the facilities at North Station, she had to leave from the Pengpu cargo station. There was no platform, so the people were forced to see off their friends and relatives from the gravel road beneath the tracks, which was so far from the train that they couldn't even touch each other's hands; everyone felt that it was a sort of last farewell.

Not only was Wenying leaving Shanghai for the first time in her life, but the thought of leaving the city had never so much as occurred to her, even though her father had been born in a small rural town in Zhejiang and had only come to Shanghai at the age of eighteen to start a business. Besides, how long a history did Shanghai itself have? When all was said and done, she belonged to Shanghai, and, it seems, Shanghai belonged to her. But just because she'd never been away didn't mean she hadn't heard horrible stories about the places out there, including some from Duanli, who had expressed her fears and hatred of the world beyond Shanghai. And yet, when Duanli saw the forlorn look on Wenying's face, in addition to feeling sad, she couldn't help but experience a sense of bewilderment as well. Could it possibly be that bad? Is she the first person to ever be sent out there? It struck her as funny, a feeling that included at least a trace of self-mockery.

Wenying's father came along to see her off, since he felt partially responsible for her being resettled. If he'd been content to just be one of the workers back then, instead of the boss, Wenying might have had a chance to get out of this. The train pulled out of the station. Fu Zhigao was the first to leave, since he had to work the night shift. Duanli walked slowly out of the station, holding her father-in-law's arm as he shuffled along. After they'd walked in silence for a while, he said to her sorrowfully, "It's all my fault. I've caused you all this trouble."

"Daddy, don't say that. Just think of all you've done for us."

He didn't say anything.

"Don't let yourself get upset, Daddy. Wenying is a delicate thing who's never been out on her own, and I know how that scares you. But maybe once she gets where she's going, everything will be all right."

"Wenying *is* too delicate. None of my three children has amounted to anything!"

Worried that she had spoken too fast and had angered her father-in-law, Duanli kept quiet.

"Duanli," he said to her, "I've been watching you these past couple of years, and I've seen you get stronger and stronger. I don't know why, but none of my children takes after me. Maybe they were spoiled by my money. The only thing they know how to do is spend money. I had a friend in industry before Liberation who took all his money back to his home in Zhejiang and used it to put up buildings, make roads, build bridges, open schools, and set up factories. By the time he was finished he'd spent a million US dollars, including the money the villagers had wheedled out of him. We all laughed at him for being naivee, but he said that the truly naive people were those who left their money to their heirs. I can see now that he was the one who had vision."

Duanli didn't know what to say, so she said nothing.

"Thank God we're living in a new society where everyone at least has food to eat. A lack of ability is just that, a lack of ability, and nothing more. I'll be able to close my eyes in peace if they manage to live decent, peaceful lives," the old man said sorrowfully.

"Yes, a peaceful life is about the only thing we can hope for," Duanli said softly echoing his sentiments.

5

It was time for Qingqing to leave Duanli's home and enter nursery school, and the family was taking it hard. Duoduo no longer said anything about the trouble the baby had caused her, like having to fan him so he'd sleep on hot summer days when she didn't even have time to mop her own sweaty brow, and still he wouldn't sleep. She'd fanned him until her arm felt as if it were going to drop and she was in tears. She'd carried him outside and spent some of her hard-earned money to buy him a popsicle. Lailai had treated him like his own brother, even though the baby had once torn up some of the stamps in his collection, and he'd even drawn him some pictures of aircraft carriers. Mimi had gotten along with him from the very beginning, but on one occasion she'd smacked his hand when he was sneaking some food, and she was forever asking him, "Qingqing, do you hate me?" Even Wenyao, who was always complaining about how much trouble Qingqing was, had something nice to say about him: "He's not a bad kid. He doesn't cry much, and any kid who doesn't cry isn't a bad kid." The last few days Qingqing was with them, everyone fought over who was going to dress and feed him and who was going to hold him.

Qingqing was a sensitive child, so that after spending two years with Duanli and the others, he saw things the way they did. Whenever some of the little hooligans came over to make trouble, he would scold them tersely and solemnly: "Bad!" If there was fruit in the house, he'd take it over to Duanli and say, "Auntie, eat." When Duoduo was angry, he'd be just as frightened as Mimi and would stick by her, not saying a word as he came and went cautiously.

On the day he left he threw his arms around Duanli's neck, to her surprise, and bawled, making her so sad she didn't know what to do. Duanli had a hard time getting used to his absence, feeling empty inside for the longest time. Often, when she returned home from the market, she'd reach down in the doorway, out of habit, for the milk that wasn't there; or when she was cooking, she'd leave a little rice in the bottom of the pot to get it nice and soft for Qingqing; or when she was just sitting and sewing something, she'd sense that Qingqing had awakened and was crying. When these things happened, she laughed at herself without quite understanding why.

She had three children of her own, but she'd never appreciated them like she did this one. She'd gone through it all with him—good, bad, and indifferent. Her own children had been reared by a wet nurse, and since she'd never fed or slept with them, they had never wanted her, only their wet nurse. But this had seemed reasonable to her; since they had been reared by a wet nurse, naturally they were closer to her than to their mother; nothing unusual there.

Qingqing had been gone a month before Duanli discovered a more realistic void: Their monthly income was cut by nearly twenty yuan. She had no choice but to go see Auntie Golden Flower again and enlist her help in finding another child. Bothered by the thought of how much she had troubled the woman, she brought a box of fruit and pastries along as a gift. Auntie Golden Flower immediately agreed to help her find another child, but refused to accept the gift. "Not after what I've done," she said, "not after that." What she meant was that she had originally doubted the poverty of Duanli's family, suspecting that they were just covering up their real situation when they sang the blues. But now she was convinced that they were genuine. "For a proper young lady from a wealthy family like you to be willing to baby-sit other people's children must be a last resort."

She dropped by a couple of days later, and although she didn't have any news, she brought over some yarn.

"Daughter-in-Law Zhang (that was always the way she addressed Duanli), do you know how to knit sweaters?"

"I do, but not well enough to show them off."

"You're just being modest. I know an old woman who needs a sweater to keep her warm, and she's not concerned with how it looks. If she sent out the yarn, it'd be machine-knitted, which is a waste of good yarn, so she'd like someone to knit one by hand."

"I can give it a try."

"The measurements are here, and all you have to do is knit one of those sweaters that all the older women wear. You can use whichever stitch you like. She'll pay—"

"I don't want any money. I don't have anything to do, anyway, and knitting's as good a way to pass the time as any."

"This is no time to get polite. She asked me to arrange it for her, and we've already discussed the amount. What do you say to four yuan?"

"I really don't want any money."

"If you won't take the money, I'll have to get somebody else," Auntie Golden Flower said as she laid down the yarn and left.

By working on the sweater day and night, Duanli finished it before the week was out. The four yuan she earned came just in time to pay for the bottled gas. Although she was feeling somewhat awkward about this turn of events, she was, after all, being productive, and that felt good. She became aware of an inner strength that somehow had lain dormant for all these thirty-eight years, but was now coming to life. This inner strength gave her courage, and she was no longer afraid to bicker at the market. On one occasion some young hooligans crowded in front of her while she was in line to buy some fish, then accused her of line-crashing. She very uncharacteristically grabbed their shopping bag and threw it as far as she could. As they walked over to retrieve it they threatened her, "You just wait!" But nothing ever came of it. On another occasion, just after Lailai had entered middle school, one of his schoolmates picked on him at school. Duanli rushed over and demanded that the teacher and the head of the propaganda team make the child apologize to Lailai, and she got her way. She stopped being a shrinking violet and regained her self-respect, but it was a different kind of self-respect than she had felt before.

After knitting the sweater for the woman, Duanli went out and bought a knitting manual, which taught her how to make several different weaves. Then she went over to ask Auntie Golden Flower to help her find some more knitting jobs. But when she saw that Auntie Golden Flower herself was wearing Duanli's sweater, the request died on her lips.

But Auntie Golden Flower knew why she had come without her having to say so. "I've been asking around for you," she said apologetically, "but so far I haven't found the right family. But I've heard that a local workshop is looking for workers. You could go over and apply."

"A local workshop?"

"It's light work. Naturally, the pay isn't very good, but I don't know all the details."

"Who should I talk to?"

"Go see your neighborhood section head."

"All right, I will, and thanks."

"For what?"

"Well, I'd better be going." Duanli took a step or two, then stopped and turned around. As she reached over and touched the sweater Auntie Golden Flower was wearing, she said softly, "I shouldn't have...."

Auntie Golden Flower pushed her hand away. "She said it was too small, so she sold it to me for the cost of the yarn."

Duanli's eyes reddened.

She mulled over Auntie Golden Flower's recommendation on the way home, finding it more and more attractive. Mimi would be starting school soon and wouldn't be able to help around the house anymore. Duoduo was out in the countryside helping with the harvesting, plowing, and sowing, and even though she'd said at the time that she'd be home in a couple of weeks, she recently sent word that with war preparations underway, there was a general dispersal, which meant that she wouldn't be returning to Shanghai for six months or a year. The whole idea of war was far too remote for Duanli, who knew only that Duoduo was not home and therefore could not help out; taking care of a child at home required that someone be watching him at all times to avoid any accidents. This wasn't a matter of a broken milk bottle, which could be compensated for, but the responsibility for a human life.

Since Duanli was no longer tied to home, she was free to go out and find work, and even though the production team wages were low, they did provide a measure of security. While she was mulling over the pros and cons, not once did she consider her bad political background or her college diploma. Her only thoughts were of practical matters like rent, utilities, gas, and provisions. If Wenguang knew this he would be crestfallen! What had previously been no more than necessities to sustain life had become life's very goals. He had always considered basic survival as being in the service of some magnificent ideal, but anyone could see that we are put on this earth only to survive and to improve the quality of that survival, if at all possible. We eat to have the strength to work; we work to eat a little better. The methods and the goals move in endless cycles, with no beginning and no end. Ai, in a word, life is a mystery. Some people say that man is born to suffer, others say that man is born to enjoy life; some say that man lives to atone for sins, others say that man lives to sacrifice ... but these are matters for people who have plenty to eat and clothes to keep warm to ponder. Duanli had but one thought on her mind: finding a way to get hired at the local workshop, thereby assuring herself of a fixed income, and of regaining control over the family's expenses. The thought possessed her, fulfilled her. Instead of going home, she went straight to the neighborhood office.

Duanli didn't know if it was because the workshop was so shorthanded that they would take anyone or if this provided them with an opportunity to re-educate the daughter-in-law of a former capitalist, but she quickly received approval to begin as a temporary worker in the production unit.

Duanli went to work for the first time.

The local workshop occupied the basement of a gatehouse in a stone warehouse. The proximity of the buildings on either side of the narrow lane allowed for very little sunlight to enter the rooms. The rooms were normally cold and dark, so when sunlight did stream in, they turned hot and sticky. The workshop was a relatively small room with a slat bench-table stretching from one end to the other beneath a bright fluorescent lamp. Workers were seated along its length on both sides. Duanli sat at the seat assigned her and looked around at her co-workers. Most were middle-aged women, but there were some older women among them, and a few young men and women with physical disabilities, urban graduates who were unable to participate in the general resettlement. There was one man, whose age she couldn't determine, who moved clumsily back and forth, a foolish grin on his face as he brought over the parts and picked up the finished work, breathing heavily and fawning over everyone. They called him A'xing and openly made fun of his clumsy movements. But he just grinned, and drooled. He was a simpleton.

The workers were fitting coils into transistor radios, a simple operation that required no skill, but demanded care and patience. If the metal coils were put in slightly off center, or unevenly, or too loosely, or too tightly, the job was rejected and had to be redone.

Duanli worked hard and carefully, getting through her first hour without a single reject. The work interested her, as she watched one radio part after another leave her hands and stack up neatly in a cardboard box. The sight excited and pleased her. When A'xing came over to pick up her work, she didn't much like the idea of parting with it. At ten o'clock a speaker on the wall began blaring calisthenics music. The people around her laid down their work, got to their feet and stretched, then strolled outside. Auntie Liang, whose workstation was next to Duanli, told her that there were fifteen-minute calisthenic breaks in the morning and afternoon, and that anyone who didn't want to participate could take a fifteen-minute rest-break. Either way, no one worked during those fifteen minutes. Duanli laid down her work, but she didn't know what to do during the break. So she just sat there on the bench and examined her fingernails. The youngsters were out in the lane whooping it up so much they were beginning to sound like rowdies. The older women just stood in the doorway looking here and there and gossiping. Duanli sensed their frequent gazes in her direction.

"Isn't that the daughter-in-law of the capitalist family in the big lane? She's a pretty little thing, looks like a young girl."

"That 'little thing' is the mother of three or four children. But she knows how to take care of herself. She looks young for her age."

"... must really be in bad straits for a well-bred daughter-in-law like that to sign on as a worker."

Duanli felt like joining them, but when she heard what they were saying about her, she was too embarrassed to walk over there. Not knowing what to do with herself, she picked up another coil and started working again.

"Ouyang Duanli, whose good side are you trying to get on?" Auntie Liang yelled over to her. "Come outside and relax a bit."

With an embarrassed smile on her face, Duanli got up and walked over.

"Are you getting into the swing of things all right?" one of the shorter women asked her.

"It's pretty good, just fine," she said. She recognized the woman as one of those who had come to her house during the campaign to root out the "four olds". She had watched her smash several four-foot-tall Ming vases.

"No trouble getting here on time?" one of the others, a tall, heavy woman, asked her.

"A little hectic, that's all, but nothing that getting out of bed a little earlier can't solve," she answered. She had gotten up well before dawn, swept the floors, cooked breakfast, and gone grocery shopping. While she was at the market, the loudspeakers had announced six a.m., and she knew she had to move a little quicker if she was going to be on time. It had been a long time since she'd had to live by the clock; previously, if something that needed to be done by seven was put off till eight, there had been no harm done. But no longer; she had to be at work at seven-thirty, not a minute later.

"Are your children old enough to help around the house?" a dark-faced woman with a noticeable mustache asked her.

"The oldest one, who's fifteen, does a few things. But she's off in the countryside with her class making preparations for war." Duanli recognized this woman as the mother of one of the boys who frequently came over to make trouble.

"My daughter went, too, but I sent her older brother to the countryside to bring her back. If there's going to be a war, then there's going to be a war, and we'll all die together. But while we're still alive we've got to eat, and we can use the money she brings in from her cotton work," Auntie Liang said loudly.

"It's one thing after another! One minute they're cutting shoe tops, the next they're being resettled in the countryside, then they're making preparations for war. One thing after another, until all they've got to show for it is going hungry!"

"It's getting harder and harder to buy any food. . . ."

Duanli stood there listening to the old women talk, sharing their sentiments without daring to make her feelings known. It was strange how these people who had so zealously ransacked her house during the campaign to root out the "four olds" could feel the same frustrations with daily life as she. It seemed to her that they were all in the same boat, that the Cultural Revolution hadn't brought them any benefits either.

At noon they were given an hour for lunch. Not many of them went home to eat. The majority had brought lunch from home and sent it over to the canteen to be warmed up, so they could eat in the workshop during the lunch break. Duanli ran home as fast as she could, vowing to bring her lunch from now on, both to save her an extra trip and to allow enough time to take a short nap at the workshop before getting back to work. The only problem was what to do about lunch for Wenyao and the kids. Ai, if only Wenyao weren't so useless!

The four hours in the afternoon were harder to get through than the morning. All that repetition was starting to get to her, especially since she had caught on to the job so easily. Once the novelty was gone, boredom set in. Her back was starting to hurt her and her neck was getting stiff. And her eyes, well, after all that time under a fluorescent lamp, they were starting to get tired and sore. She kept looking at her watch, but time seemed to be passing so slowly that she began to wonder if her watch had stopped.

At last it was time for the afternoon break. She quickly laid down her work, got to her feet, and walked outside with the others. Just standing there in the lane was a treat. Some of the youngsters were teasing A'xing, first making him sing a song, then having him do a dance, altogether treating him very meanly. Everyone was laughing at the spectacle, Duanli included. She knew it was wrong, and was sure that it would upset his family if they knew, but she just felt like laughing, loud and hard.

A couple of the girls were trying to drive a motorized cart, which took them all the way out to the main street, as they screamed frantically that it was going to flip over. One of the boys rushed over and, taking advantage of their predicament, said to them, "Call me Elder Brother and I'll show you how to ride it."

"We'll call you Baby Brother!"

"Fine, you just try it!"

"Baby Brother!"

How he did it no one knew, but the air was suddenly pierced by high-pitched screeches like a brood of baby sparrows whose nest was being ravaged, followed by several obedient shouts of "Elder Brother". The boy then jumped up onto the driver's seat, the girls sat down behind him, and the three of them rode the cart back looking very happy and excited.

As recently as the day before, Duanli would have scoffed at this as frivolous and boring, but today she was laughing right along with everyone else, enjoying the spectacle and having a fine time. The work was so monotonous that any little diversion was welcome. Simple work produces simple people.

The fifteen minutes were up in no time, and it was back to work. Every joint in Duanli's fingers ached, and by this time her actions were completely mechanical. She could hear every tick of the clock. Outside in the lane, children were yelling and shouting, a few of whom came tramping through the factory, their schoolbags thrown over their shoulders, on their way upstairs; their families lived above the workshop. The quitting bell rang at last. Duanli walked out the door feeling relieved all over. The rays of the setting sun were gentle, painting the edge of the sky a bashful pink. The bells on passing bicycles made a chorus of happy, light-hearted music. An obviously naughty child who had been kept after school by his teacher was threading his way through the crowd of pedestrians, toting his schoolbag on his head and earning angry shouts along the way. Life was like a flowing stream, and Duanli was a single drop of water in that stream. She was in a good mood, feeling more free and easy than ever before.

When she arrived home, Mimi informed her that there was a letter from Duoduo. Since Duanli had to hurry up and prepare dinner, she told Lailai to read it to her. Duoduo's letter read like a grownup's, opening with: "Dear Mama, Papa (notice that Papa followed Mama), Brother, and Sister: How are you all!" That was followed by greetings to her grandparents. Then she wrote about their lives in the countryside, saying that in the main they weren't working too hard, so they got plenty of sleep and were having a wonderful time. They had eaten some meat that week; their teacher had taken them on a twenty-*li* walk to a little town called Chen River Bridge, or something like that, where they had feasted on won tons, flatcakes, and oil fritters, and had a wonderful time. At night, after they were all tucked into bed and had put out the lamp, they told ghost stories, scaring each other so much that no one dared to go to the toilet alone at night, and they were having a wonderful time. The only drawback was that they were all homesick, and everyone had cried at least once. But their teacher let them in on the secret that they'd probably be going home soon, according to some distant, mysterious directive. He told them not to breathe a word about it to anyone, so Duoduo admonished her mother not to tell a soul (and here was Lailai reading it at the top of his lungs!). Duanli told him to lower his voice. Duoduo closed her letter by urging her mother to take care of herself, and to keep from getting too tired, and for her brother and sister to do as they were told. By this time, tears were streaming down Duanli's face. She knew that all her hardships had not been in vain. More than that, these few sentences written by her daughter made all her own suffering seem altogether worthwhile.

That very night, out of the blue, Wenying returned home. She had come back with a schoolmate, but this other girl didn't even stop long enough to sit down; after dividing up the peanuts, bamboo shoots, and mushrooms they'd brought home with them, she said "See you tomorrow", picked up her share of the food, and was off.

Even though Wenying had only been away five months, it seemed to the family that it had been a good three years. They all got out of bed and threw wraps over their shoulders to greet her. She was much more tanned than before, and slimmer, but as vital as ever. Her mother was delighted at first, making some eggs and bringing her a basin of water to wash up in; but her thoughts soon turned to Wenguang, who was still up north, so far away she didn't know when she'd ever see him again, and her tears began to flow. Wenying was in fine spirits, talking and laughing up a storm, far more talkative and lively than she'd been before she left. She told them about the mountains where she'd been, and the trees and springs; about how the people in the collectives would bicker over a meal or a bucketful of water; and about how the peasants in the area were called bumpkins. Fascinated by everything she had to say, they let her talk for the longest time before anyone thought of asking her how she'd managed to get home. Was she on official business or on a family visit? Wenying told them she'd come back for medical reasons. What was wrong with her? Everyone was speechless. Wenying winked slyly, but said nothing, and everyone assumed it was some sort of female problem, so they didn't press the matter. By then it was already two in the morning, so they called it a night and went back to bed.

But Duanli couldn't sleep. Something didn't seem right to her. She nudged her husband. "Wenyao, don't you feel there's something different about Wenying?"

"Like what?" he asked quizzically.

"She can't stop talking, and she was never like that before."

"She's been out in the world and has come back a stronger person! People change, you know!"

"But I can't help thinking that something's wrong. What kind of medical problem could she have?"

"You're making a mountain out of a molehill!" Wenyao rolled over and went back to sleep, leaving Duanli alone with her confused thoughts for a long time, until she finally drifted off into a troubled sleep.

On her way home from work the next day, she ran into Wenying's traveling companion as she was coming out of her house, but all the girl did was greet her casually and brush past her. When Duanli walked in the door at home she saw her mother- in-law sitting there with a worried look on her face. She quickly greeted Duanli, then started in with her "I'm paying for the sins of my past life!" routine.

"What's happened, Mother?" Duanli was alarmed, and her suspicions of the night before grew deeper.

"Oh, Duanli! My daughter has a problem here!" She pointed to her temple.

Just as she had feared. Duanli's heart sank.

"Wenying didn't want to go in the first place. She never accepted it. She cried in bed every single night. Then her boyfriend here wrote to tell her that everything was off, and when she read his letter she didn't even cry, because it drove her off the deep end!"

"What kind of person would do a thing like that! He was the one who was chasing after her! But then, with one in Shanghai and the other out in the countryside, it does complicate matters."

"They call it a broken heart. They say she won't get better till she gets married. How are we ever going to manage that?" Duanli's mother banged the table and burst into tears again.

Duanli ran over and closed the door. "Mother, don't let her hear you. You mustn't upset someone in her condition, or else she'll go off the deep end again."

"So what are we going to do? Oh, Duanli, I'm just a useless old woman, and your father-in-law has his own troubles, so he can't just come and go as he pleases; and since all Wenyao knows how to do is enjoy himself, it's all up to you."

"Mother, this sort of talk doesn't accomplish anything. What's important now is for Wenying to see a doctor."

"But what if she sees a doctor and the word gets around? That'll ruin her."

"We can't just ignore it. I'll go ask around, and you stop worrying."

"When you ask around make sure you say it's for someone else. You mustn't give anything away."

"Not to worry, Mother, leave everything to me."

Wenying's problem became more and more apparent each day. She was always hearing Fu Zhigao call her, and would run to the head of the stairs to wait for him. She'd wait and wait, until she couldn't wait any longer, then just sigh. Then she'd walk back inside and sit down, but before long she'd start to squirm again, and would go in and take a bath, change her clothes, brush her hair and make herself up, telling everyone that she had a date that night with Fu Zhigao to go for a walk or take in a movie. The schoolmate who had come back with Wenying and felt she'd done her part by seeing her home, never returned. But Wenying's problem kept her family hopping.

Duanli checked out the mental hospital, but her mother-in-law was hesitant about sending Wenying over there to see a doctor, afraid that word would get out and make things difficult for Wenying in the future.

Meanwhile, Duanli had to go to work, prepare the meals, and do the laundry, and still find time to comfort Wenying, until all these duties nearly ran her ragged. Duoduo came home just when things were at their worst. The minute she saw her mother she rushed over and threw her arms around her in a warm embrace. She had really grown up, and although she was more deeply tanned than before, she hadn't lost much weight. She looked incredibly healthy. The sight of her daughter delighted Duanli. This was the first time in her life she had truly experienced the joy of reunion. She rushed into the kitchen and fried some eggs to welcome her daughter home, and the others shared the unexpected treat. Wenyao took advantage of the situation by sending Lailai out to buy some wine; his greatest talent was milking the maximum enjoyment out of any situation. Duoduo insisted on sleeping with Duanli that night, so Wenyao was forced to sleep in Duoduo's little bed on the other side of the screen. Mimi crowded into her mother's bed along with her sister, and the three of them, mother and daughters, talked and giggled late into the night. They exhausted every imaginable subject, even sharing some of the ghost stories Duoduo and her girlfriends had told at night in the countryside. Lailai, who was feeling jealous about being excluded, punctuated their talking and giggling with frequent comments of "You're all crazy!" Their laughter woke up Wenyao in the middle of the night, who thought it was time to get up. But when he sat up and noticed the moon overhead he just shook his head and lay back down.

They talked and giggled until Duoduo and Mimi finally fell asleep. Duanli had an arm around each of her daughters, luxuriating in the joy of motherhood. She suddenly thought back to the family's so-called good old days; they had been comfortable, trouble-free times, but there was so much more to life now.

Now there was a bit of everything—good, bad, and indifferent. Duoduo rolled over and wrapped her long, full arm around her mother's neck. Duanli was deeply touched: we'll never let anyone part us again, she thought. We're going to stay together as a family from now on; nothing and no one will ever break it up again. She loved her family at this moment more than at any other time in her life. That love embraced every one of them: the headstrong and unpredictable Duoduo; Lailai, who was always hungry; kindly and honest Mimi; even her useless but somehow lovable husband. She sensed that she was the family's protector, and that made her proud—proud and happy.

6

On Saturday evening, Duanli's mother-in-law said she wanted to talk to Wenyao and her about Wenying's condition. She wanted them to come up with a workable idea, although she closed the door on one option as soon as she began: "As I see it, a mental hospital isn't the place for her."

This made it virtually impossible for Wenyao or Duanli to offer any opinion.

"If we commit her to a mental hospital, they'll tie her up and put her in a room with rubber walls, and they'll give her electric shocks, so if she doesn't have a problem when she's admitted, she'll have one soon enough."

There was no denying that stories about mental institutions were pretty frightful, even though none of the people telling the stories had ever been inside one. But whenever there's a shortage of facts, the imagination takes over. All Wenyao and Duanli could do was hold their tongues.

"We had a case of a broken heart in our hometown village near Ningbo once. No medication was prescribed or taken, and as soon as the patient got married, everything was just fine."

At this point, Duanli began to get an inkling of what her mother-in-law was driving at, so she said very cautiously, "Wenying isn't a child any longer, she's reached the age when we ought to be talking about her wedding plans. But for the time being she's been resettled in the countryside, which means she's no longer registered here, and since she doesn't have a job, it's going to be hard to find a suitable husband."

"That's right, Mother, and we can't forget about her problem. There's no way something like that can be hidden, and if you let it be known, who knows what they'll . . ."

Wenyao's mother cut him off in mid-sentence:

"That's why I need your help!" she said, her anger rising. "Why do you think I'm talking to you now? I'm looking for some answers. Are you trying to tell me that Wenying is unmarriage-able? Don't make me laugh."

"Who's saying she's unmarriageable? It's just that we have to find someone reliable," Duanli, the peacemaker, said. "Let us give it some more thought, Mother, okay?"

That night Duanli and Wenyao discussed the problem from every angle, finally agreeing that her only chance was to find someone in the countryside.

"Who would have dreamed," Wenyao said ruefully, "that a daughter in this family would ever fall so low."

"Whose fault is that? It's your mother's fault for sticking to her old ways. Getting her married instead of taking her to see a doctor is a sure way of bringing her down in the world," Duanli said indignantly.

"Mother's lived for more than sixty years, and I doubt that she knows any less of the world than you or I. Once you've been committed to a mental hospital, you've got a stain on your history. Can you understand that?" Wenyao said with authority. Only when he was sure he could speak on the side of authority would Wenyao state his opinion or make a recommendation in a dispute. At school, the authority was the workers' propaganda team; at home, it was his parents.

"Then you go ahead and obey orders, but don't go blaming everybody else if it doesn't work out." She had nothing more to say.

"Are you angry?" Wenyao asked her anxiously after a while.

"No, I'm thinking. If you're set on finding her a husband in the countryside, at least find her a good one. And you ought to try to find someone who lives as close as possible, some place like Shaoxing or Kunshan. That would make it easier for her to be reassigned here after she's married. The lifestyles keep getting better the closer you get to Shanghai, and communications are easier."

"You're right, of course!" Wenyao nodded his agreement eagerly, pleased to have such a smart wife.

Wenying's mother greeted the suggestion with enthusiasm and decided to send letters to some distant relatives in the Ningbo area. Even though there hadn't been any contact with them since the Cultural Revolution got underway, in days past they had received their share of benefits from her, so they ought to be willing to help out now. Besides, whoever the family was, they'd be getting a Shanghai girl as a daughter-in-law, which, as far as she was concerned, was something worth fighting over. Although Wenyao wrote the letters, they were actually dictated to him by Duanli. After dispensing with the pleasantries, they mentioned Wenying's situation in general terms (they included a photograph), then got down to the matter at hand—they wanted to arrange a marriage for her, preferably with someone who didn't live too far from Shanghai. As for her illness, that was dispensed with in a single vague sentence: "Her physical condition has been hampered by her having gotten upset." The letters were sent, and the family began to count the days until they received a response. The postman, who came twice a day, soon became the most important person in their lives. When nothing arrived in the morning mail, they looked forward to the afternoon; when nothing arrived in the afternoon mail, they looked forward to the next day. Meanwhile, Wenying's problem seemed to be getting worse.

One event followed on the heels of another, and soon Duoduo's three years in middle school had passed; it was time for job assignments. Like the class of '68 before her, this one was also to be revolutionary red. According to the people at the resettlement office, revolutionary red was the goal for the next ten, even the next hundred, years, one generation on top of the other. This was all the women at the local workshop talked about, day in and day out, and it seemed that the resettlement movement was going to affect every single family.

"My daughter's school sent over someone from their mobilization team," Auntie Liang said. "I told him not to waste his time, because we weren't going. That's all I said before leaving him sitting there by himself. I sure wasn't worried that he'd steal anything. After sitting there for a while he left."

"My daughter's in the same boat. Her elder sister just left for Anhui, so the school didn't have the nerve to send anyone over. She tried to argue with me when I told her I wasn't going to let her go, but I reminded her that I was the one who raised her, so what right did she have to argue?"

"Even if she does resettle, you still have to raise her. They can't take care of themselves, since they spend all their own money before they're even off the train."

"Do they think that keeping these kids at home means they'll never get a job the rest of their lives? For the last two classes the policy was 'take one, leave one,' and now for these two classes it's revolutionary red. Who knows what it's going to be for the next two. They're afraid that if they don't change national policy at least once a day, the people won't be on their toes."

Duanli kept her mouth shut, but just listening to all these complaints not only provided her with an outlet for her own personal anger, but gave her an idea as well. Her brain was really working now. Maybe this was the time to try to find a way to keep Duoduo home. Back when Wenying had received her assignment, maybe if they'd stuck to their guns and tried harder, they might have come up with something. From an emotional standpoint, she hated the idea of being separated from Duoduo. Now that her daughter had grown up, the two of them were much closer, and sending her off now would be like driving a knife into her own heart. In economic terms, this time there was no way she could manage to scrape together all the travel necessities. Sending Wenguang and Wenying down to the countryside one after the other had completely drained the family's meager resources.

"Ouyang Duanli," Auntie Liang called to her, "are your children facing resettlement?"

"The oldest one is in the class of '69—revolutionary red!"

"Are you going to let her go?"

"To tell you the truth, I'd rather not. She started school younger than most kids, and was in a five-year school, so she's not even fifteen yet. But I'm afraid that a family with a background like ours doesn't have much chance of getting out of it," Duanli said sadly.

"Anyone can get out of it! What are you afraid of? Since resettlement's the end of the line, how much worse could it possibly get?"

"We'll see what happens," Duanli said, but now her mind was pretty much made up.

When Duanli got home, Duoduo was waiting to tell her that the school was sending someone over to interview the family, and she was supposed to stay home to wait for them.

Not long after they finished dinner, sure enough, there was a knock at the door. It was the head of the workers' propaganda team from the school and one of Duoduo's teachers. After taking a seat, they looked around the room, then amiably asked some questions about the family:

What were Duoduo's father's wages, and her mother's?; how old were Duoduo's brother and sister?; how was Duoduo's health?; and so on. Then it was time for the matter of mobilization. Duanli's heart was racing as she thought about what she'd say when she refused them. Before long, without even waiting for them to finish what they were saying, she blurted out in exasperation:

"Duoduo's too young. You have to be eighteen for military service or for entering the job force, but she's not even fifteen. She's not going."

"Li Tiemei is young, too," the head of the propaganda team said.

"Li Tiemei is three years older than Duoduo!"

"What's wrong with getting a head start on the road to revolution and making her strong?" The propaganda team head frowned, but Duoduo's teacher just lowered his head and remained quiet.

"She can join the revolution in Shanghai, and she can get strong here, too! Besides, she's the eldest child, and her brother and sister are still little children. She can't go. Wait until her brother's eighteen, and I'll personally deliver him to the countryside." Maybe she had let her emotions carry her away, for it sounded as if she were having a real argument with them.

The head of the propaganda team and Duoduo's teacher exchanged glances, but didn't say anything right away. Then one of them turned and asked Wenyao, "How does Duoduo's father feel about this?"

Wenyao stroked his chin and tried his best to dodge the issue: "Going to the countryside, that I support. But Duoduo's awfully young...."

"Duoduo's political background isn't very good, so she has a greater need for thought reform than most of the others."

That did it! Duanli jumped up from her stool and said angrily, "Duoduo has a bad background because of her grandfather. Even if her father has to bear some of the responsibility, what's that got to do with the grandchildren? Doesn't the Party place importance on individual performance? You're here tonight to mobilize, and the down-to-the-countryside campaign is supposed to be done on a volunteer basis, so don't try to pressure us with that background stuff. If you really think that Duoduo has to go because of her background, then why come on the pretext of mobilizing? All you have to do is transfer her household registration!"

This outburst left them speechless. Duanli was delighted with herself, surprised to find that she could say what she had to say when she knew she was right. She was so excited she was blushing.

As soon as their visitors were downstairs, Duoduo came flying out from the closet, where she'd run fearfully when her mother had begun her outburst, locking herself inside, even if she suffocated in there. She ran up to her mother and yelled:

"What have you done! By treating a member of the propaganda team like that you've really gotten me into trouble."

"What kind of trouble? Resettlement's the end of the line, so how much worse can it get?"

Wenyao stood there watching her with his arms folded, shaking his head. "Aren't you a fireball! When did you learn that? You sounded like one of those women who do people's shopping for them."

"It's all stuff she's been hearing from those gossipy women at the workshop," Duoduo grumbled. "A bunch of barbarians!"

"You have to be a fireball to get by. Otherwise, that capitalist cap they put on your father will bear down on generation after generation of this family until it squashes us."

Wenyao had to agree with her. "You've got a point there."

"So what am I going to do?" Duoduo asked anxiously.

"What are you going to do? You're going to stay home and let us raise you as we should!"

"When Mama jumped to her feet just a while ago," Lailai interjected, "she scared the two of them so much they nearly fell over backward!" He gave a short demonstration that got them all laughing, Duoduo included, despite herself.

Within a few days Duoduo began to waver, saying how all her classmates were going, and she was constantly arguing with Duanli. "Let them go," Duanli yelled at her. "Are you afraid there won't be any place left for you to join up later?" She ignored her daughter's arguments. Duoduo had never seen her mother feel so strongly about something, had never seen her act so stubbornly. And yet she was more content and more at peace than before. She spent her days around the house, buying groceries, cooking, taking care of her brother and sister, and playfully referring to herself as "the little housewife" or "the little worker". She was a big help to her mother, making it possible for her to go to the workshop without worrying about what was happening at home. She began receiving praise for her fine work, not to mention the forty yuan or so in wages that she brought home every month, of which she gave her mother-in-law fifteen to help out with Wenying's expenses.

Contact had already been made with someone in Ningbo, but so far nothing had been arranged, and it wasn't until early August that a family with possibilities was found. Their name was Wang; the father was an accountant for a production brigade, and his son was twenty-six this year, three years older than Wenying, which was just about right. He was a high-school graduate, which made their cultural levels suitable. Like his father, he too was an accountant, and since he only had an eighteen-year-old sister, the potential for family disputes was lessened considerably—that was a good sign. After a family meeting, they asked Wenying what she thought, telling her only that the marriage would give her the opportunity of being assigned in the south. After all, when a girl grows up she's supposed to get married and go to her husband's house. Wenying agreed. So Duanli wrote to the Wang family, agreeing to a meeting and saying they would consider the match.

The young man arrived on the first day of autumn, accompanied by a relative of Duanli's mother-in-law. He wasn't bad looking, was tall and husky, and had lively eyes. His hair was neatly parted on the side, and he wore three fountain pens in the breast pocket of his jacket. Since it happened to be a Sunday, Duanli managed to put together a meal for their guests.

Wenying's mother seemed satisfied with the young man, while her father expressed his opinion in a low voice with a terse "rustic," without actually objecting. Naturally, Wenyao and Duanli had no say in the matter. But that didn't keep Duanli from thinking that he somehow didn't seem like the kindly sort. Wenying obviously liked him a lot, for her spirits were higher than they'd been in a long time, and she was a real chatterbox. Since they had no way of knowing what she was feeling inside, they had to be content with watching her behavior, which was lively. But there was still plenty of anxiety among members of the family that her problem would manifest itself. In truth, a problem like hers couldn't be hidden forever, but for the time being, they put those thoughts out of their minds, choosing instead to keep up the deception, to no one's benefit.

Lunch was ready. Since their guests were from the countryside, there was no need to be formal, so Duanli's father-in-law excused himself. Duoduo and the other children, on the other hand, were seated around the table, looking as serious as they could manage. Duanli was in the kitchen, her hands full with getting the food ready, when all three of her children came bursting in, closed the door behind them, and broke out laughing. Duoduo was laughing so hard there were tears in her eyes and Mimi was rolling on the floor holding her belly.

"Have you kids gone crazy? Where are your manners?" Duanli scolded them.

"Mama, you should see the funny way he eats," Duoduo said, trying to control her laughter.

"What's so funny about it?" Duanli's curiosity was aroused.

"Like it's the first meal he's ever eaten," Duoduo said.

"When he eats, his eyes are opened this wide, and he keeps

looking from one bowl of food to the other," Lailai said, imitating the man. Duoduo and Mimi exploded into laughter again, bending over and holding their bellies. Even Duanli started to laugh, but her jocularity soon turned sour, as she began feeling bad for Wenying.

After lunch was finished, Wenying's mother told her to go in and take a nap, apologizing to the guests, "Since she hasn't been well, we can't let her get too tired." After a while, she gave Duanli a sign with her eyes, and Duanli, who caught her meaning, chased the children out of the room. She knew it was time for her mother-in-law to talk business, so she walked out, too. But her mother-in-law called her back just as she was closing the door:

"Duanli, come in and sit with us."

As she walked back into the room, she noticed the look of panic on her mother-in-law's face, and she knew at once that the older woman was having a case of stage fright. It looked as if it were going to be up to Duanli again, and she was troubled, since she didn't know where to start. She busied herself with brewing a couple of glasses of tea, nervously trying to think of something.

"Have some tea, Auntie." She handed the woman a glass.

"Oh, gosh, my fault, it's my fault!" the old woman responded politely.

"Here, Younger Brother, have some tea." Duanli sat down and began with some small talk:

"How's the harvest been this year?"

"It's worked out to be one yuan ten fen per man-day," the accountant reported.

"That's very good. When Wenying was out in the countryside, it was only forty or fifty fen per man-day, and one man-day was too much for her."

"Poor, much too poor!" the old woman commented.

"That's why my sister-in-law was so unhappy. And her health showed it. A person's mood has quite an effect on her health."

"Of course, of course."

"What exactly is wrong with Zhang Wenying?" the young man asked.

Duanli and her mother-in-law shot quick glances at each other. After a pause, Duanli said, "It's not really an illness, and she's fine as long as she's happy. It only shows when she's angry or upset."

"What's it like when it shows? She's not crazy, is she?" he asked directly.

"No, she's not crazy, nothing like that. She just gets real quiet, or she cries, or she laughs a lot."

The young man looked over at the old woman and asked no more questions, but his expression had darkened.

Duanli changed the subject. "How many families are there in your production brigade?"

"Over a hundred," he said perfunctorily.

"What's your major crop?"

"Rice."

The atmosphere in the room had grown cold. They just sat there for a while, until Duanli's mother-in-law left the room to have Mimi go out and buy some refreshments. Duanli also stood up and went out to get some hot water to fill up their glasses. Just as she was walking back into the room with the water she heard a muffled conversation:

"As soon as someone like that gets married everything's fine," the old woman was saying to encourage the young fellow.

"I'm not some sort of medication," he said, in obvious low spirits.

"As soon as she's better, you'll be a lucky man. Do you know what sort of family she comes from?"

"What difference does that make now? These days everybody has to work to eat."

"You're too young to understand. Have you ever heard the saying 'A starved camel is still bigger than a horse'?"

Duanli felt a chill grip her heart. She stood in the doorway rooted to the spot.

"Duanli, what are you doing?" her mother-in-law said as she walked up, looking at her strangely.

"Come over here, Mother." Duanli turned around, took her mother-in-law's hand without saying a word, and pulled her back into the kitchen, closing the door behind her.

"What's going on?" her puzzled mother-in-law asked.

"I think we should call off the match! It won't do anyone any good for her to marry this fellow," Duanli said urgently in a low voice. "Besides, there's no guarantee that marriage is going to solve Wenying's problem. I understand that it's your hometown, but it's been years since you left, and everything's changed. Wenying won't know a soul there. What if her in-laws start to talk? Don't you think that might make her problem even worse? Not only that, if he's such a good catch, why does he have to come all the way to Shanghai to find a wife? I'm afraid there might be a hidden agenda here." Then Duanli told her mother-in-law everything she had just overheard.

Duanli's mother-in-law was panic-stricken. Before long, the tears started to flow. "I'm paying for the sins of my past life. The sins of my past life!"

"Listen to me, Mother. Even though I'm not Wenying's sister, I wouldn't do a thing to hurt her. We can't keep ignoring her problem; she has to see a doctor," Duanli said earnestly.

"I'm an old woman," her mother-in-law said tearfully, "and I'm all confused. I'll leave everything up to you. You may only be my daughter-in-law, but you're stronger than my sons. Daddy was saying nice things about you just yesterday."

Now that Duanli had been given the go-ahead, she translated her words into action, and without delay. She took Wenying to see a doctor, who said she needed to be hospitalized. But since there was a shortage of beds, he told them to go home and wait for notification. Duanli had no choice but to go looking for help again. Now that she was working, she had some new social contacts, and although the older women at the workshop were an unrefined lot, they had kind hearts, not to mention plenty of curiosity, which made them even more kindhearted. Duanli's inquiries here and there finally paid off when she was introduced to the chief nurse in charge of admissions at the mental hospital. In November, a bed opened up.

Duanli took Wenying to the hospital and had her admitted.

The women's ward was a huge room with twenty or thirty beds, all of them occupied by women in white smocks, with every imaginable expression on their faces. Some looked absolutely cheerless, others had surly looks on their faces, while others were bundles of energy, constantly on the move, and yet others just lay there in a dazed sleep. There was even one who roamed the ward like a ghost, from one end to the other and back again. Wenying was deathly quiet, quiet and afraid. She stuck as close to her sister-in-law as she could, like a child needing protection. Duanli held her hand and talked to her encouragingly in a soft voice, as much for her own benefit as for her sister-in-law's:

"It's nice and quiet here. Now, you just rest and don't worry about a thing. Mother and I will come visit you this afternoon."

Wenying nodded obediently.

When all the paperwork had been completed, the nurse told them about the regulations regarding visitors, then helped Wenying change into her hospital clothes. Putting one of those white, medication-stained hospital gowns over a slight frame like Wenying's was like covering her with a sack, making her seem smaller than ever. She suddenly looked ten years younger: her face was pale and there was fear in her eyes, which kept darting all over the place, as though she were looking for a source of protection. At the same time she looked a good ten years older, with thin lines appearing at the corners of her eyes and on her forehead. She was slightly hunched over, and as she walked she sort of shuffled along.

Duanli told her to lie down and not move around, but she got out of bed and wordlessly followed Duanli all the way to the door. Duanli turned and said:

"Go on back in."

Wenying didn't say a thing as she leaned against the door frame and sadly watched her sister-in-law make her way downstairs. Duanli began to have doubts that she had done the right thing. She had the strange feeling that everyone in this place was crazy, everyone except her sister-in-law. She under- stood what had caused Wenying's problem, and it seemed perfectly reasonable to her. As far as she was concerned, her sister-in-law was clearheaded and perfectly normal, and she had no right to put her with people like this. The more she thought along these lines, the more convinced she was that it had been a mistake to have Wenying committed.

That afternoon Wenying's mother went to see her, and when she came home she cried. From then on, everyone who went to see her came home and sighed deeply, and it was easy to tell by the way they talked that they resented Duanli's sudden action, as though she had delivered her sister-in-law into the bowels of Hell. Duanli could feel the pressure, and it was taking its toll. She felt an increasingly heavy and unshakable responsibility for

Wenying, which was wearing her down and setting her nerves on edge. Yet at the same time, it invigorated her.

Never before in her life had she shouldered this much responsibility for anyone. Whenever one of her children had been sick in the past, it had been easy to blame the wet nurse, thereby removing all personal responsibility. And now she was responsible for the well-being not only of Wenying, but of the entire family. It was a truly heavy burden.

She went over to the hospital nearly every day after work to see Wenying and find out how she was doing. And to earn a little extra money to buy some nutritious food for her sister-in-law, she asked Auntie Golden Flower to help her find another child to watch at home. This one would, in the main, be Duoduo's responsibility.

It was then that Wenguang came back from Heilongjiang on a family visit. After he'd been home a couple of weeks he sent off a letter to extend his stay two more weeks. When the month was up, he extended his stay again, and by the time three months had passed, he stopped sending letters and seemed to have no plans to go back. All he did at home was sleep in and go for walks, the same as before. Bored and unhappy, he came and went without a word, his newly acquired smoking habit the only difference in him. Duanli had a hunch from his first day home that he wasn't planning on going back, but she had secretly hoped that he was made of better stuff than that. Now she knew that he was beyond hope, and although she felt sorry for him, she had lost all respect for him.

Life went on without incident until 1973, when a directive was issued stating that anyone with valid medical authorization and children with no siblings were to be allowed reassignment to Shanghai. Duanli sprang into action, running from one office to the other to secure Wenying's reassignment on medical grounds. Since her problem was already common knowledge, everything went through without a hitch, until all that remained was one last trip to Jiangxi.

"Let Wenguang go for her! He doesn't have anything to do, anyway," Wenyao recommended. "Besides, since he's been out on his own already, he knows the ropes."

"Me? Not me! I don't speak the Jiangxi dialect, so how am I

going to get anything done?" Wenguang said modestly, as though he were the only person in the family who *didn't* know the Jiangxi dialect. "You should be the one to go, Wenyao. You're older and more experienced."

"I have to go to work!"

"Take a leave. Your research institute is a government unit, so you get full pay when you're away on business."

"I'd be better off if I didn't get full pay. But since I do I have to be extra careful!" Suddenly he knew what would work. "You go! You haven't got anything to do, and it'll be like a vacation."

"I don't get along with people in the countryside, and if I make a mistake I'll mess things up."

Watching her sons go round and round angered their mother:

"Either way, one of you has got to go. You don't expect your sixty-year-old father to go tramping off into the wilder- ness, do you?"

"Wenyao, you go, just go!"

"No, you go, Wenguang, you go, you go!"

Duanli, who was both irked and amused by the spectacle, had had enough of it. "It looks as if it's up to me to go," she said.

"You, a woman, go all the way out there alone? Do you really think that's a good idea?" her mother-in-law asked doubt- fully.

"Since it's come to this," she answered with a sneer, "there's not much choice, is there? Someone has to go!"

And, sure enough, it was Duanli who went. She was gone ten days. When she returned she brought with her Wenying's house-hold registration, her ration cards, and the trunk with all her clothes. While she was there she'd also disposed of the odds and ends Wenying had left behind, such as toilet paper, soap, towels, toothpaste, and other things that were too much trouble to bring home, like her thermos, her wok, and her portable stove. The money this stuff brought in had been enough to cover Duanli's travel expenses, with two yuan, thirty fen to spare.

She returned home to find everyone in a good mood. Her mother-in-law told her that Wenying was getting better, although there was still a chance that she'd have a relapse. The doctor had said that if her situation remained stabilized a while longer she could be discharged. Duanli was so relieved to hear this that her legs grew rubbery and she fell into a chair. The rest of the family crowded around her anxiously, asking her what was wrong. She smiled at them out of happiness and sheer exhaustion and said, fighting back the tears, "Our family is still safe and sound, and still together."

7

The next three years seemed to drag along, second by second, minute by minute; but in retrospect everyone wondered where the time had gone. Duanli's parents-in-law were older now; Duanli had become a regular worker; Wenying, as an urban graduate who was an outpatient, was teaching at a local nursery school; Lailai had graduated from middle school and had been assigned as a clerk in a small tobacco shop at the head of the next lane; Mimi was now in middle school; Duoduo had managed to slip through the net after all, had joined a local production unit that made dolls, and even had a boyfriend, a nice, good-looking boy from a working-class family. Even though it was a step down, at least Duoduo's child would not have to suffer under the label of capitalist, and that was a relief. Only Wenguang and Wenyao hadn't changed a bit: the one did nothing but sleep in, go for walks, and mope around in a daze, thinking neither of the past nor of the future, just getting by day after day; the other held on to his government steel rice bowl, expending neither thought nor energy, and even though he didn't have much, his sixty yuan a month was enough for him. He didn't seem to have aged a day.

Toward the end of 1976, an epoch-making event rocked and changed China. The most immediate effect on the Zhang family was the announcement of home transfers of educated youth back to Shanghai. This lit a fire under Wenguang, who rushed back to Heilongjiang and arranged to have his household registration sent back to Shanghai. As soon as the new policies were in effect, confiscated items were returned to their owners (in the case of the Zhang family, not much had survived), reimbursement for the interest on private property and salaries that had been cut off was made, their bankbook was returned, the third floor of their house was opened up, and pressure was put on the two families downstairs by the building superintendent to move out. But the families placed conditions on moving, and as soon as these conditions were met, they raised more—boats always float higher as the tide rises—and it was anyone's guess as to when the situation might be resolved. Since this was a rare opportunity for them to improve their living conditions, they couldn't just wait to let matters work themselves out. But the Zhang family believed that the arrival of this day, after those ten terrible years, was heaven-sent; they were both enormously grateful and absolutely content, and they didn't expect a one-hundred-percent restitution.

Every member of the family was in seventh heaven, including Duanli's parents-in-law, who suddenly seemed ten years younger, their faces beaming. Their grandchildren were ecstatic. Everyone, with the exception of Wenyao, had been working in units that were at the bottom rung of the ladder, and for them there had been no light at the end of the tunnel; a raise in wages had been out of the question, not to mention finding a suitable spouse. But now a comfortable life was possible even if someone were unemployed, which was a fitting conclusion to ten years of extreme hardship.

Duanli's father-in-law received a large sum of money that he had been forced to leave untouched in an account for those ten years. "I'm an old man," he said magnanimously, "and I can't take it with me to my grave." So he divided it among his children and Duanli. "It's been tough on Duanli these past ten years," he said, "and the family owes its survival to her. What she did for Wenguang and Wenying can never be measured in dollars and cents."

"I don't want it, Daddy!" she said. Things had changed so fast over the past six months that it was like a dream. But now, as the stack of bills lay there in front of her under the fluorescent light, so close she could see every pattern and design, she knew that it was no dream. Somehow that stack of ten-yuan bills filled her with a strange sense of foreboding. "During all those chaotic years, no matter how much I may have wanted to do something, I lacked the strength. I can't take this money. Besides, the children are all grown up, and I have a job, so money isn't a problem."

"Since Daddy's already made up his mind, there's no need to be polite," her mother-in-law said.

Still Duanli wanted to refuse it, but just then she felt Wenyao gently nudge her with his foot, so she didn't say anything. Nonetheless, she was determined not to accept the money, convinced that taking it would make it harder to be the person she wanted to be.

They went upstairs to the third floor, which had now been restored to them, leaving the second floor for the older couple. After he closed the door behind him Wenyao said to her:

"You're sure full of opinions. What's the idea of not even talking it over with me? You almost let Daddy's money slip through my fingers."

"Since Daddy gave it to me, it was my decision to make."

"And who do you think I am? I'm your husband, that's who, the head of the household, and my opinions are supposed to count for something." During all the family's troubles, he had hidden in the background, but now he was ready to reassume the mantle of authority.

"Then I'll tell you here and now that I don't want it. What do we need with all that money?"

"Don't go getting stupid on me, okay? We didn't beg him for it, so what's there to be polite about?"

"I don't want . . ."

"And just why don't you want it? You could quit that job of yours and enjoy life for a change!"

"Not work?" This thought had never occurred to Duanli, and she didn't know what to say.

"You'd think you'd been working all your adult life," Wenyao said sarcastically.

That made her mad. "No, it hasn't been all my adult life, only a few years. But if it hadn't been for that job, the family wouldn't have made it this far."

"I know, you're right," Wenyao admitted apologetically. "You've really turned into a formidable woman! You used to be so gentle, like a little pet. Why, you used to be afraid to cross the street by yourself. . . ."

The pitiful expression on his face made Duanli feel bad. With a melancholic tone in her voice, she mumbled under her breath, "Yes, I've changed. Who could go through ten years like that and not change?"

Wenyao reached over and tenderly pushed back the hair that had fallen over Duanli's eyes. "This has all been much too hard on you. It's aged you a lot. I know I'm a useless man, and that's why I want Daddy's money, to pay you back."

Duanli didn't say anything; she turned to look in the mirror above the chest of drawers. It had been a long time since she'd taken a good look at herself, and the face she saw in the mirror looked surprisingly unfamiliar to her: her hair was done up in a common manner befitting a much older woman, and there were bags under her eyes. And where had those deep wrinkles around her mouth and nose come from? Her skin had turned coarse, the pores were considerably enlarged, and the sight of her face caused her to reach up and touch it with her hand. Oh, that hand, the wrinkled, bony, unattractive fingers, and the unpolished nails surrounded by hangnails.

"I have aged a lot," she said, letting her hand fall to her side as she gazed vacantly at the ugly, unfamiliar image in the mirror. No matter how she hated to admit it, it was her, all right.

Wenyao walked up beside her and stroked her hair, saying to her softly, "Don't get too upset; we'll get those ten years back somehow."

Duanli turned her head and took a good look at her husband; she thought for a moment that she was looking into the face of the playboy-husband of more than ten years before. He was as handsome as ever, bright and witty, and filled with a zest for life that seemed eternal. She loved him.

That night they deposited the money in the after-hours service counter at the bank so as not to lose even a single day's interest, to let it begin compounding from the very first day. But she couldn't bear the idea of quitting her job. Just getting it had been such a struggle, and besides, who's to say that someday in the unpredictable future. . . . There were no guarantees, and that job would always be her security; that was one of the beauties of socialism. After thinking the matter over for a while, she decided to request some sick leave, for even if she received no wages during that time, as long as she had a job to go back to she'd be all right. The hardships she'd suffered through all these years had led to a mild vertebrae problem in the lumbar region, so getting medical approval for sick leave from the neighborhood clinic was easy, so long as the loss of wages didn't matter.

When she took over the medical authorization, Auntie Liang didn't so much as glance at it. "You take some time off. This isn't the sort of work you should be doing over the long haul," she said frankly.

There may have been some hidden meaning in Auntie Liang's comment, or perhaps Duanli was just being too sensitive; but she blushed and quickly defended herself: "I really don't have to take the time off, but I think I need to give my body a chance to heal completely. I plan to come back as soon as I'm better."

"Sure, no problem. Come back whenever you feel like it," Auntie Liang said.

The squat old woman who was standing next to them spoke up: "You sure don't know how to appreciate your good fortune. If I were in your shoes I wouldn't hold on to a dead-end job like this, where you have to knock yourself out all day for one and a half yuan or so."

"Daughter-in-law of the Zhangs," the fat woman said to her, "use your head. Anyone who doesn't spend the money she's got is a dunce."

"You'll never get rich on the wages from a workshop like this."

"No, you've got it all wrong. I plan to come back to work when my health is better." Duanli rushed out with a red face; she left the stone warehouse and walked quickly down the lane. When she reached the main street, a gust of wind hit her in the face, making her suddenly aware that the back of her blouse was soaked with sweat. She heaved a sigh and headed home running into Auntie Golden Flower at the intersection.

"Ah, Daughter-in-Law of the Zhangs!" Auntie Golden Flower greeted her.

"Oh, Auntie Golden Flower, how've you been lately?"

"Just fine. I ran into your husband yesterday, and he told me you're looking for an amah. What do you need? Half a day? All day? Or just someone to do the laundry and buy the groceries?"

Duanli was embarrassed. Sure, they'd talked about this over the past few days at home, and she did see the need for a housekeeper, but she had objected strongly to asking Auntie Golden Flower to help them find someone. She wasn't sure why, but it just didn't seem right to ask her to do this for them, not right at all. She and Wenyao had even had an argument over it. He was angry that she wouldn't listen to him, and longed for the old Duanli, who was afraid to cross the street alone.

"I know someone, a woman in her fifties who's easy to get along with and absolutely honest. The only problem is that she's a temporary resident here. Would you like to meet her?"

"We're not sure yet that we need someone," Duanli said evasively.

"Why don't you go home and talk it over with your husband? You mustn't take the narrow view. If you've got the money you ought to enjoy life!" Auntie Golden Flower advised her.

"All right, I'll go home and we'll talk about it. I'll let you know in a couple of days. I'll send Mimi over."

"No, I'll drop by."

"No, I'll send Mimi over."

After this polite exchange they went their separate ways. Duanli's back was bathed in sweat again.

Over the next couple of weeks, Duanli went shopping with Wenyao to buy things for the house: They picked up some new furniture, a TV set, a refrigerator, an electric fan, some fabric, new clothes, shoes, face cream, hair conditioner, even some hair dye, shampoo. . . . Duanli went to have her hair permed.

She sat in the beauty shop looking into the mirror, her heart racing as she wondered what she was going to look like. After the operator had curled her hair, let it down, styled it, blown it dry, and put on the finishing touches, she gazed at herself in the mirror for the longest time as though spellbound. The person she was seeing looked both alien and familiar at the same time. She was gratified to discover that she hadn't aged so much that her looks couldn't be recovered.

"It looks wonderful, just terrific!" Wenyao said with satisfaction as he looked at her hairdo from behind, bringing her back to reality with his compliment. She smiled bashfully and got up, standing as straight as possible and instinctively looking at herself in the mirror above the chest of drawers. She liked what she saw. She felt as good about herself at that moment as at any time in the past. There's nothing to keep me from living a life of fulfillment from now on, she was thinking.

There were so many people walking along Nanjing Road in

what seemed like a slow, orderly march that she couldn't have picked up the pace even if she'd wanted to. Fortunately, there was no need to, since everyone was content to stroll along, do a little window-shopping, and occasionally stop to buy something. There didn't seem to be any objective linked with this avenue; perhaps the avenue itself was the objective. As Duanli walked along slowly in the midst of that crowd, trying to control her impatience, her inability to stretch out her arms or speed up the pace began to make her feel a bit claustrophobic, and she was looking for a chance to weave her way through the crowd and move on. She couldn't avoid bumping a few people along the way, all of whom turned and scowled.

"Why so fast? Rushing to catch a train or something?" Wenyao said as he held her back.

"I can't stand this snail's pace," she said.

"What's the hurry? The amah can handle anything that needs to be done at home. You don't have to worry about rushing home to cook."

"I know that. But I've got nothing to do."

"So just relax and enjoy the outing! Look at this piece of fabric here, it's lovely."

"Too dainty for me, and too old for Duoduo. Come on, let's go!" She pushed on ahead.

"Who says we have to buy it! What's wrong with just looking? You don't have to buy nice things to enjoy them." Wenyao held on to slow her down.

"Those shoes are nice. Look, aren't those heels interesting?"

Duanli took a look at them. "Thirty purchase certificates. That's a fortune!"

"No harm in looking."

This was her first visit to Nanjing Road in a long time, and there seemed to be far more people out on the street than the last time she was there, ten years earlier. Every store along the way was so jammed with customers that it made her head swim. They walked from the east end all the way to the west, stopping every once in a while for something to eat to keep up their strength. They walked a while, then they ate, all so they could look at more things. They pushed and shoved until they made their way up to a sales counter to get a closer look at things. Maybe this walking, shoving, and eating was what they were there for, maybe that was all the fun. But to Duanli, it was a huge waste of time and energy. But she kept this to herself and continued to think. Since all she had these days was time and energy, she needed an outlet for both, and this was probably as good as any. She recalled how she had once dreamed about this sort of carefree, aimless stroll, instead of always having to rush home as though she were running to catch a train; there had been so many jobs waiting for her at home: meals, dirty laundry, Qingqing.... Her thoughts went back even further: She had often walked up and down Nanjing Road or Huaihai Road without a care to her name, often resulting in an unexpected reward, like a fashionable, hard-to-come-by pair of shoes, or a piece of fabric that would be sold out within five minutes of being put on display. In those days, friends and relatives, even people on the street she'd never seen before, would often ask her enviously, "Where did you buy that dress?" "Are there any of those left?" "You didn't buy those shoes here, did you?"

"Duanli," Wenyao called to her, "this TV stand would fit right in with our furniture, wouldn't it?"

"Umm, let me see." She took a good look at the TV stand in the show window. It was a seven-drawer stand made of Chinese ash painted a soft cream color. It had a simple elegance.

"Like it?"

"Not bad. How much is it? Wow, a hundred yuan! Too expensive."

"What do you mean, expensive? If you like it, we'll buy it. We need some sort of stand for the TV." Wenyao took her by the hand and led her into the furniture store to pick out the one they wanted. He walked over to the cashier and peeled off ten ten-yuan bills, which he deftly slid under the glass partition. It was all done with the airs of someone with real upbringing. The way Wenyao spent money was a thing of beauty. Duanli rubbed the stand with a sense of satisfaction. At least, she thought, the day wasn't a total waste.

Duanli frequently went out shopping after that, occasionally stopping to buy something; and even if she did come back empty- handed, she was so well informed on what the stores had to offer and what was in fashion that she was a walking shopping report. So she never considered her time wasted. It didn't take long for her to re-experience the pleasure of walking, shoving, looking, until shopping became one of the most important aspects of her daily life.

At about this time, some of her father-in-law's old friends in industry and commerce started getting active again, and many of the women from these families became Duanli's best friends, enriching her social life. Being given a new lease on life deserved a celebration, and one of the women (no one recalled who it was) began a round of luncheons. Nearly every week after that one of them hosted a meal at places like Xinya, Meixin, The International, or the Peace Hotel. After everyone had hosted one meal, they started another round: a wedding banquet; the third round: a birthday party; the fourth round: a luncheon for no particular reason at all.... Attending these luncheons and serving as hostess became another important aspect of Duanli's daily life. This latest activity in turn initiated the third important aspect of her life—having new clothes made, having her hair done, having her nails done, massages. Back in her workshop days it hadn't made any difference when she went in with her hair uncombed and a dirty face, but now that she was walking on floors waxed to a glassy sheen and sitting at exquisitely set restaurant tables, it was important for her to sparkle just as radiantly as her surroundings. What had been needed at the workshop was production; what was needed at these new places was an elegant appearance, proper table manners, and fashionable clothes. The women were constantly sizing up one another and comparing themselves.

Duanli's life was filled to overflowing with these activities, and she was busy all the time. She felt like a young woman again, full of vitality, and she knew that she could live a fulfilling life from now on. And she wasn't thinking only of herself, either; her children were just as important to her. They had suffered during those ten years right along with their parents, and they deserved to be compensated for that. She decided to buy each of them an imported wristwatch, although since Mimi was still too young, she'd have to wait until she graduated from middle school. By then the selection would be even better than now. Within three days Duoduo knew everything there was to know about imported watches, and she bought a Swiss woman's Roma watch. Lailai wasn't as enthusiastic as his sister, since he was concentrating on his studies before taking the college boards. He hadn't passed in '77 and was planning on trying again.

"Tomorrow's Sunday," Duanli said to him. "Go to Nanjing Road with your father and see if you can find a watch you like."

"I can't, I have to study tomorrow," he protested.

"Then let your father buy one for you, okay?"

"It's up to you!"

"How about an Endicar?"

"It's up to you."

"What about an Omega?"

"It's up to you."

Duanli was losing her patience. "How come all you can say is 'it's up to you'?"

"Because that's what I mean! All watches are the same, aren't they? What's important is getting into college." He lowered his head and ignored his mother.

Duanli stood there looking at her son. He had grown tall and thin, altogether different from when he was child. His earlier passion for food had turned into a passion for studies, although he was still as impatient as ever and couldn't brook any delays. He'd spend eight hours standing behind the counter at the tobacco shop, then come home and hit the books until eleven or twelve at night. Duanli told him to take half a day's sick leave so he could study without staying up half the night and ruining his health from lack of sleep. Lailai took his mother's advice and asked for half a day off, but he worked harder during that time than he would have otherwise, and Duanli wished he'd gone to work instead, which would have been less taxing on him. Although standing at the counter meant that he was on his feet for a long time, at least he didn't have to tire himself out mentally. That was the last time she recommended taking any time off.

"Why go to all that trouble!" Duanli said under her breath. "After suffering through ten years of the Cultural Revolution, why not relax and have a good time for a change instead of making things hard on yourself."

"You're really something, Mama!" Lailai said impatiently as he looked up at her. "During the Cultural Revolution people like us couldn't have gotten into college if we'd worked ourselves to death. Now, finally, they're choosing students on the basis of merit, and you're giving me a hard time."

"College? What good is college going to do you? I graduated from college, didn't I, and what good did it do me? During the 'cultural Revolution I was a nanny and an apprentice in a workshop, and I never accomplished a thing. After some hard thinking, I've come to the conclusion that as long as you've got money you've got everything." Duanli was thinking about their incredible poverty during all those years, about the torturous, exhausting struggle to earn a single penny, and her eyes began turning red.

Everyone had suffered during the Cultural Revolution in their own way, and even the suffering of a single individual varied from one time to the other. The only thing this ten-year period had given Duanli was a materialistic attitude. She'd made up her mind to live the best life possible. As Wenyao had said, they had to get those ten years back. For her, those ten years had been a complete waste.

8

Duanli requested one month's sick leave after another, although she no longer went over to the workshop herself, sending Mimi or the amah in her place with a note. One day Auntie Liang sent word to her that since there were so many young people looking for work these days, not counting those who had returned to Shanghai from assignments elsewhere and had to be taken care of, there was no shortage of labor at the workshop. She could give up the job altogether if her health was really a problem, and if she agreed that this was the best way to handle things, all she had to do was send her amah over with the message. The amah, who had recently arrived in the city from the countryside near Yangzhou and was an honest soul, stood there politely waiting for Duanli's answer. But Duanli only smiled and said, "I'll think it over!" then dismissed her, deciding to discuss the matter with Wenyao when he got off work. But when he came home he brought a four- speaker Sony tape deck home with him, to the great delight of the entire family: Duoduo's happiness was tied to the popular songstress Deng Lijun, Lailai's to English-language tapes, and Mimi's to both, plus a reason that she was embarrassed to reveal to the others—she wanted to hear what her own voice sounded like. For some reason, this youngest child of Duanli's was more like a country girl than an urbanite; her sister called her "the hick". She took every new dress that was made for her and put it away, feeling that it was too nice to wear; and whenever she went out for a snack, she always settled for a bowl of plain noodles.

Duanli was as happy as the others to have yet another electronic gadget around for the family's use. While they were discussing where to put the speakers, Duanli forgot all about the matter she was going to discuss with Wenyao. She remembered it the next day, but since the matter didn't seem all that important, there was no need to take it so seriously. Let them do what they want, she thought: if they felt like removing her name from the roster, that was fine with her; if they wanted to keep it on, that was okay with her, too.

There was plenty to do around the house, since everyone was busy trying to get Wenying married. Now that she had a respectable dowry by any standard, she never wanted for suitors, and could pick and choose. Wenying had a very high opinion of herself, but she'd never given any thought to the fact that she was nearly thirty, and that no matter how well she took care of herself, she couldn't avoid showing her age. And after all those years of taking medication for her illness, some side effects were beginning to show—specifically, a certain hormonal imbalance. Already starting to lose her figure, she was no longer the svelte young lady she had once been, even starting to look a little dumpy. So it became a matter of "not getting what she wanted and not settling for less".

A few days earlier one of Duanli's girlfriends had introduced her to a young man who worked in a scientific research institute. He was good-looking, tall and well built, robust, and from a very good family. Wenying was quite taken with him, but it was hard to tell how he felt about her. They saw each other a few times, and that was the end of it. Wenying felt terrible, and showed signs of having a relapse, which terrified the family. They tried everything possible to take her mind off the young man, including arranging a trip to Suzhou with her mother. She was a little better when she got back, so Duanli decided to talk to her. "Wenying," she said, "you're nearly thirty, and you can't put things off much longer."

"I don't want to put anything off, but I have to find someone I like."

"Of course, but don't set your standards too high. Try to look at things objectively."

"What do you mean by that? My standards aren't too high, but where men are concerned, I've got my integrity to consider."

"Naturally, but what's important is the kind of person you're looking for. All other considerations are secondary."

"I want a decent man, but he has to be well situated, too."

"How he's situated isn't as important as how you feel about each other." Duanli thought back to Wenying's unhappy experiences in love. She more than anyone should realize how disgusting snobbishness is. Why can't she open her eyes? Didn't she learn anything from her illness? But Duanli had conveniently forgotten what had happened with Duoduo, how she herself had broken off the marriage talks with that working-class friend of hers, saying to her daughter, "Given your situation, you can pick and choose." And eventually, she had made a good choice—a young man whose parents were overseas, and who sooner or later would be leaving China to claim his inheritance.

"Why isn't it important how he's situated?" Wenying said, with a peculiar look in her eyes as she stared at Duanli. "Didn't you marry my brother for his money?"

Duanli's face reddened. "Don't say things like that, Wenying. I've shared good days with your brother, but I've suffered, too. During the Cultural Revolution ..."

"Daddy compensated you for that, didn't he? All that money he gave you. I'm his own daughter, and I only got half again as much as you," Wenying said cuttingly.

The color drained from Duanli's face and her lip began to quiver. Without another word, she rose and walked out of the room. By the time she got back to her own room she was trembling. So that's what she's thought of me all along! Naturally, disputes like this had often occurred between them before the Cultural Revolution, and even though it had never become a direct, ugly confrontation, there occasionally had been angry feelings. But this time it took her by surprise, and she didn't know how to deal with it, how to respond to her sister-in-law. She felt injured and resentful the rest of the day, and was in turmoil as she waited for Wenyao to come home, so she could air her grievances. But her impatience got the best of her, and when Duoduo came home from work, Duanli told her daughter everything. Duoduo, in keeping with her personality, was enraged by what she heard, and wanted to set Wenying straight immediately. But just getting it off her chest had lessened Duanli's anger, so she cautioned her daughter, "Just forget it. We don't want to lower ourselves to her level." But Duoduo wasn't about to forget it, and was determined to show her aunt a thing or two.

As Duoduo was leaving for work the next morning, Duanli stood at the head of the stairs and shouted down to her when she reached the second floor, just outside Wenying's door, "Be careful riding to work." Duoduo had bought a new Taiwan-made racing bike, which she rode everywhere she went, even if it was no more than a hundred meters; this kept her mother in a constant state of anxiety.

Duoduo stopped when she heard her mother and yelled back, "There you go, worrying about things that don't concern you again. If you'd done less of that up till now, someone would already be a country wife, and wouldn't that be terrific!"

"Well, she didn't concern herself for nothing!" Wenying shouted from behind the door. "She got her reward, and who wouldn't do it for that much?"

Back and forth it went, with no one willing to give in.

The friction intensified as time went on, until Duanli began to tire of it, and, since she was stuck in the middle, she was always in a bad mood. Wenying was starting to get unreasonable; whenever Duanli or Duoduo bought something new, Wenying would raise a fuss as soon as she found out about it, not relenting until she got something similar or comparable for herself. And every time her parents refused to buy her something she wanted, she took her anger out on her sister-in-law, bringing pressure on her parents by complaining about the undeserved reward Duanli had gotten from them. She was getting harder and harder to put up with, harder and harder to please, until even her mother couldn't manage.

Duanli swore to herself that she wouldn't get involved any longer, that she'd refrain from saying a single word. But it continued to amaze her how Wenying could keep from comparing how things were now with how they'd been during her resettlement in the countryside. She should be rejoicing over the recent improvement in her life. Duanli hadn't been thinking of herself when she was trying to make her sister-in-law face reality; yes, Wenying really ought to be pleased with how much better off she was now than back then. They had put those ten unbearable years completely out of their minds, pretending they hadn't even happened. Sometimes Duanli would suddenly feel terribly disenchanted, without ever so much as trying to figure out why.

Everyone dealt with this conflict in their own way: Grandfather accused Wenying of being ungrateful; Grandmother was angry with Duanli for not giving in, particularly after all she had gotten; Wenyao was optimistic that everything would work itself out in due time, that everything would be fine as soon as Wenying got married; and Wenguang treated it as nothing but a reflection of the tiresome lifestyle of the idle rich. When he saw the effects of these disturbing events on Duanli, he gave her some advice:

"Why let it get you down? It's just another way to keep you people from getting bored after you've eaten your fill. Since life's meaningless, anyway, everybody's just looking for a little spiritual sustenance."

"And where do you get yours?" Duanli pinned him down angrily.

"I don't. I put in my eight hours every day and pick up my pay at the end of the month. I don't have to worry about a thing. Everything's taken care of for me. Our needs are simple—eat to work and work to eat."

"You're bored in your own way!"

"That's right, and that's why I'm thinking of quitting my job."

Duanli smiled and nodded. "That's right, when your belly's full, you're off thinking about something else."

"The money Daddy gave me is all the capital I need. The government is encouraging people to engage in individual economic enterprises, isn't it? Well, I'm thinking about opening a Western restaurant."

"You're crazy!" As Duanli knew, he couldn't even fry an egg.

"What's wrong with being a little crazy? The only reason we're living is simply to stay alive. We have no responsibilities toward anyone." Wenguang had fallen into a state of melancholy.

"You're lucky to have what you have today," Duanli reminded him slowly. "Why can't you be content with that?"

"I know," he said dejectedly. "It'd save me time and trouble. Eat to work and work to eat, just keep the cycle going. But life is supposed to be an upward spiral."

Duanli just shook her head and ignored him.

"Sister-in-Law, do you still remember that day you went shopping with me before I left for Heilongjiang?"

"I remember."

"All of a sudden I appreciate the wisdom in what you said to me while we were walking."

Duanli was shocked. "Don't make fun of me."

"No, no, I mean it. I asked you about the purpose of life, and you said it was to have food to eat and clothes to wear! At the time, I thought that was a vulgar way to look at it, but now I understand. Food and clothes, that's what it's all about. We work to eat good food and wear nice clothes; we eat good food and wear nice clothes to work harder, increasing the value of good food and nice clothes. Isn't that how mankind has developed all along?"

"You've got the right idea," Duanli confirmed.

"That's why I no longer want a steel rice bowl. I want to strike out on my own."

Duanli studied his face, then shook her head. "You can think about it and talk about it, but take my advice and leave it at that. You'll never see it through."

"What makes you think so?" Wenguang asked defensively.

"When you broke with Daddy, you didn't see it through, and when you went to Heilongjiang to build up the border region, you didn't see it through."

"I was young and immature then. I've grown up now."

Duanli just shook her head.

"You wait and see," Wenguang said.

Several days passed, and it was apparent to Duanli that Wenguang's routine hadn't change at all. He put in his eight hours every day, except for taking half a day off whenever he was in the dumps, and just sprawled on his bed and read a stack of magazines. So many literary magazines were coming out these days that he couldn't have gotten through them all if he'd tried. Perhaps his plan to open a Western restaurant had died as quickly and easily as it had been born, and maybe that was a sign that he'd grown up. Duanli was laughing inwardly at him, although deep down she still felt a fondness for him, sensing that he had apparently reflected on a number of things over the past few years, and was becoming a better person for it. Even if he was all talk and no action, that was at least better than those people who never even got around to the talking stage. Duanli was reminded of her sister-in-law, whose only progress over the past ten years had been from the spoiled attitude of a young lady of breeding to the spoiled attitude of an old maid, and she was getting worse every day. Whenever Duoduo and her boyfriend walked into the house, Wenying had some comment to make, but since Duoduo knew without being told that she was superior to her aunt, she simply ignored her and refused to argue. Knowing that sooner or later she'd be leaving the home, Duoduo had lost her sense of permanence. She was often late to work, or came home early, or even took off without permission. Duanli, who was upset by her daughter's attitude, said to her, "You're supposed to request time off if you don't want to go to work, either sick leave or personal business. You can't just take off without saying anything. Whenever I run into your co-workers I'm embar- rassed to even talk to them."

But Duoduo only snapped back rudely, "What about you? You don't go to work, either. They can fire me if they want to."

Duanli was speechless with anger. She discovered that Duoduo hadn't changed at all in the last ten years: She was still as spoiled and headstrong as ever, still as devoted to having a good time and worrying about her appearance. Oh, how Duanli longed for the Duoduo who had come home from the country-side during the Cultural Revolution, her face deeply tanned, and had called her "Dear Mother". She sighed. The family had certainly suffered during those ten years, but their emotional ties had remained strong. Now that they had come through it, there should be lessons there to be learned. Was it possible that things were to be exactly as they had been before?

Life was returning to the way it was, including the social dances from an earlier time. Although there were no dance halls, lots of dances were taking place in universities, factories, institutions, even in private homes. Wenyao often took Duanli and the children to dances in the homes of friends, and occasionally even held them at their own home. Lailai, whose studies for the college boards were at a critical stage, never attended, while Mimi just sat off to the side and watched with a silly, countrygirl grin on her face. She looked absolutely rustic, with her hair done in braids and black cloth slippers on her feet. She owned plenty of new clothes and shoes, but she never wore them. "If you don't wear them pretty soon," Duoduo warned her, "they'll be out of fashion, and then you won't dare wear them out of the house." But they remained in her closet. She was acting more and more like a country girl, like someone from the lower classes.

It didn't take Duoduo long to learn how to dance, although she introduced her own variations to the traditional steps; she swayed and moved to the rhythms of the music, finding the traditional steps too restrictive. All the young people were trying out new dance steps, but Duanli and the others of her generation didn't go along. She stuck to old-fashioned steps— traditional, subtle, elegant, somewhat languid yet lithe. When she was dancing a waltz she forgot that she was a middle-aged woman, imagining herself to be a college student out on the dance floor again, and she and Wenyao always held the center of the floor as they swirled together.

The dances invariably went on late into the night, sometimes not breaking up until just before dawn. Their excitement fell into a sort of inertia, and when this inertia ultimately dissipated, a loneliness set in that made them aware of their exhaustion, which in turn made them irritable. Duanli was frightened by this loneliness, and as a result hated for the dances to end; but the longer she tried to prolong them, the greater the sense of loneliness that followed, and the more profound her exhaustion. It soon became so bad that she dreaded even being invited to one of the dance parties. For no matter how strong the attraction to attend, the fear of that inevitable loneliness and exhaustion was nearly overwhelming. She didn't know what to do.

Once the dance parties became a big part of her life, Duanli started going to bed late and sleeping in the next morning; actually, she was just resuming her night-owl habits that pre-dated the Cultural Revolution. After rising at ten, she'd have a cup of coffee and a couple of pastries for breakfast. Then instead of getting dressed, she'd walk around the house in her nightclothes. Since her biggest worry was that guests would drop in at this hour, she began to feel that the house was too small for her. So she went to her mother-in-law.

"Mother, it's already been two years since the "Gang of Four" fell, so why don't we go to the building superintendent and try to get the downstairs rooms back. We could use them to entertain guests. Now that Wenyao and Duoduo's friends are always coming over, not having a place to entertain them is an inconvenience."

"Your father-in-law's been grumbling about the same thing the last few days, but I'm not sure we can get them back. The people downstairs don't know when to leave well enough alone, and they're making more and more demands. They seem to have forgotten that they used to live in a shack."

"It certainly wouldn't hurt to try."

Duanli's father-in-law went over with their request several times, putting the superintendent's office in a position of being forced to exert pressure on the downstairs tenants. After about a month the people finally agreed to move out.

Thoughts of how good Auntie A'mao had been to her in the past brought Duanli pangs of guilt, so she went out and bought a cake to congratulate the family on their good fortune of being assigned new lodgings. But Auntie A'mao refused the gift, saying cynically without so much as looking at Duanli:

"So the boss-man's money still rates a nice big house, while we working stiffs get tossed out on our ear."

Duanli didn't know what to say, so after standing there for a moment she put the cake on a table that had already been placed on the truck. She walked upstairs and stood silently at her third-story window, watching crate after crate of briquettes and kindling and piece after piece of dilapidated furniture being put on the truck. Finally, with a blare of its horn, the truck drove off.

She walked back downstairs, opened the door and walked in. The empty room was spotless: the floor had been scrubbed clean and the white walls were neatly plastered, while a lone photograph of a popular movie star hung on one of the walls. Not only had they taken excellent care of the place, they had even tried to spruce it up. She recalled hearing Auntie A'mao tell her how they'd never lived in such a nice place before. She also recalled Mimi's smug reaction to learning that they had lived in a shack before moving here. "Wow!" Fully aware of how shabbily she had treated them, Duanli wondered where they were being sent to live this time. She hoped it wasn't back to the workers' ghetto.

Within a few days the building superintendent sent someone over to restore the lower floor to its original condition by reconnecting the two rooms. After the walls were papered and the floors waxed, they bought some new furniture, including a sofa, a love seat and some stuffed chairs, plus coffee tables and end tables, lamps, curtains . . . everything. Once again they had a dining room.

They had now come full circle, for the place was exactly the same as before the Cultural Revolution.

By the time Duanli got used to all of this again, her feeling of rebirth had nearly disappeared. She no longer thought herself blessed to have been given this new lease on life. She had a sense of deja avu, sometimes feeling that she'd suddenly been transported back ten years in time, although the mirror didn't lie; she had aged considerably. Melancholy and depression usually followed. What a strange feeling it was, one that even she couldn't trace to its origins, nor get a handle on.

Duanli's boredom was increasing: she was sick of all the luncheons; she found the dancing tiresome; she'd gone for all the walks she could stand; and she had lost her desire to shop. She desperately wanted to do something, but what? It was then that she began to envy Wenguang. He managed to lose himself in all the fiction he was reading, suddenly getting an inspiration to write some himself. All the things he had lacked the courage to do were now realized by the fictional characters he created. To everyone's surprise, one or two of his stories were published, and he even received a few fan letters from some silly middle school students. His spirits renewed, he took an extended leave from his job to stay at home and write. The problems that had tormented him for so many years were solved, just like that. After all those ups and downs, he now had something to do, something that was custom-made for him. He no longer felt empty inside, and he stopped moping around the house. At first Duanli viewed his activity as a form of escapism, but she soon changed her mind; he not only had plenty of imagination, but he knew how to put his thoughts down on paper, and that was not to be taken lightly. She read some of his stories, and even though they were sheer fantasy, they provided the reader with a measure of comfort. Duanli wished that she, too, could find something to do, for her boredom was taking its toll on her.

In the midst of these troubling times, Lailai's college admission notice arrived; he had been accepted into one of the top national universities. He held up the notice in a trembling hand, but everyone else's happiness was controlled, more subdued. There had been no lack of college graduates in the Zhang family, with nearly everyone in the family receiving at least a college education in times of smooth sailing. When August rolled around, and it was time for Lailai to report to the university, Duanli helped him put his luggage together. She bought him a mosquito net, some sheets, suitcases, a bedside radio, and in no time at all she had spent three hundred yuan. She couldn't help thinking back to those chaotic days when she had done the same thing for Wenying and Wenguang. How difficult it had been then! Duoduo had even contributed every penny of her savings. Duanli collapsed into a chair, her energy spent. Just thinking about those times exhausted her, frightened her. She'd been so efficient then, and so strong. Where was that efficient woman now? Could she even say that it had been she? She felt lost, as though she were in a dream world. Like someone who has just laid down a heavy burden, she was overwhelmed by a lightness so complete she felt she could simply float away, as though she were totally weightless.

A powerful weightiness always follows on the heels of lightness; a life of trials always follows on the heels of a life of ease.

Lailai left for the university in an exuberant mood, and Duoduo got married in the same sort of mood, but their departure left a cloud over the family. When Wenyao saw how depressed Duanli was becoming, he assumed that she was just worn out from entertaining the steady stream of guests. So he recommended that they take a trip to Hangzhou over the three-day National Day holiday. Duanli did feel tired, and she liked the idea of getting away for a few days. It might do her good. So she agreed to the idea, recommending that they take Mimi along.

"Everyone says she's acting more and more like a girl from a lower-class family because we never take her anywhere."

"She's had a rough life from day one, since the Cultural Revolution broke out when she was still a baby. I think she deserves a chance to enjoy life a little," Wenyao agreed.

But Mimi didn't feel like going. "I don't want to go. I have schoolwork to do. I only got an eighty on the last math test." Schoolwork had never come easy for Mimi, perhaps because of the way she went about it, and her grades were mediocre. Duanli felt sorry for her, wishing she didn't feel that she had to work so hard at her studies.

"You'll still have plenty of time for schoolwork when we get back. You know you've never been to Hangzhou."

"We're starting new lessons after the holiday, and this is the year I have to take the high school entrance exam. If I don't score a hundred in math I won't have a chance of getting into one of the top high schools."

"What does that matter? We don't have to compete with other people. Now that the bad times are behind us, you'll never have to worry as long as you're a member of this family." Duanli was speaking from her heart; Mimi and her brother were different people, and it seemed to her that her youngest daughter wasn't cut out for school. Since it cost her so much effort without doing her much good, what was accomplished by forcing the issue? She stroked Mimi's hair affectionately. "You suffered right along with Daddy and Mommy, but now that things are better, why not have some fun!"

Mimi raised her head and looked very earnestly into her mother's face. "Mama, how did we get rich so fast?"

"Your grandfather had his property restored to him."

"So you mean it's all Grandfather's money?"

"Grandfather's money is Daddy's money . . .," Duanli said evasively.

"Did Grandfather earn it?"

"Yes, Grandfather earned it. But he can't spend it all by himself. Later on, if you don't like your job, we have enough money for you to live on for the rest of your life."

"What kind of life can anyone have without working?" Mimi asked. Having grown up in poverty, the idea of a life of ease was totally beyond her comprehension.

Duanli had no answer. She just stood there speechless for a moment. "You don't have to go if you don't want to," she said meekly.

"Okay!" As though she'd been liberated, Mimi lowered her head and threw herself back into her schoolwork. Duanli walked out, stopping in the doorway to take another look at her daughter; her braids were pointing up to the ceiling as she worked on her math as though it were the only thing in her world. She'd been like that all her life, doing everything with un- bridled earnestness, care, and interest. Always happiest when she was busy, she did everything her mother told her to do as though nothing in the world could be more interesting than those odd jobs. Once, when Duanli had told her to go out and buy a watermelon, she'd stood in line under a blazing sun for two full hours before Duanli came to relieve her. Even though her face was bathed in sweat, her interest hadn't abated a bit, and when she saw her mother walking up she said excitedly, "Only ninety- eight people to go." Ninety-eight people. that was quite a line, but since it kept getting shorter, little by little, the objective was drawing perceptibly nearer. Mimi had grown used to being outside from her earliest childhood, sweating under the sun, drawing nearer to her objective, step by tiny step, until she got what she came for. Those ten years of suffering had left their mark on her. Time does not simply vanish without a trace; it always leaves something behind. Having everything restored to the way it was before the Cultural Revolution was impossible. Duanli's heart was flooded with an emotion she couldn't name. While it seemed to be comforting, it was also very sad, and she was quickly losing her enthusiasm over the trip to Hangzhou.

The three days in Hangzhou turned out to be pleasant ones, after all. They took a tour bus in order to travel worry-free and concentrate on enjoying themselves. The tour bus returned to Shanghai after three days of sight-seeing. As the bus pulled out, some newlyweds sighed as they commented:

"So long, Hangzhou. Tomorrow it's back to the grind!" But there was no sadness on their faces. Duanli envied them, for at least they were returning to something, even if it was a hard, dirty, tiring job. There was no need for her to worry about hard work, since there were no jobs waiting for her at home; she could schedule her time any way she cared to and do anything she pleased. But what was there to do? She gazed silently at West Lake as it rapidly receded into the distance, her heart empty.

"Yes, tomorrow it's back to the grind," Wenyao echoed the others. "See how lucky you are."

Duanli glared at him, assuming that he was making fun of her, or that he was displeased. But she soon realized how silly she was being, silly and overly sensitive. Could it be, she wondered, that she was so bored she was becoming neurotic? Frightened by the thought, she tried to cheer herself up:

"Let's take a trip to Ningbo over New Year's," she said to lighten her mood.

"Sure! The Ningbo countryside has a flavor all its own. We can climb Putuo Mountain and burn some incense there." The well-traveled Wenyao was already planning their itinerary.

Several of their young traveling companions put their heads up close to listen to him.

"Putuo Mountain is a sacred Buddhist spot. I've heard it's been restored lately, and that countless numbers of people go there every day to burn incense."

"Let's go there, too," one of the bridegrooms said.

His wife, a delicate young woman, gave him a cold stare. "And where's the money going to come from?"

"If I work overtime and don't slack off, my year-end bonus should be enough to cover it."

Exercising her wifely responsibilities for the first time, she made some quick calculations before nodding her approval: "We should be able to manage it."

Duanli's sadness returned. She couldn't stop envying other

people, and it affected her mood.

As soon as they walked in the door at home, their amah told them that Auntie Liang from the workshop had come over to get an answer regarding her plans. No matter what, she needed a decision within the week.

"Auntie, go boil some bath water!" Wenyao told the amah. He turned to his wife. "Quit the job," he said, "and be done with it."

"If I quit," Duanli said panicking, "I won't have any more work."

"So what? We're talking about less than a hundred yuan."

"It's not just the money."

"Then what is it?" Wenyao took off his coat and put on his slippers.

"What if there's another Cultural Revolution?"

Wenyao laughed. "Then we can say good-bye to the Party and good-bye to the nation."

"That's right."

"The Cultural Revolution is over, it's history, and we'll never have another."

"Yes, it's over," Duanli agreed. But, she thought, if it was over without leaving a trace, if there was nothing to show for it, then it was worthless history. Could ten years of suffering have been wasted? The people should have derived something from it. Is it possible that we adults have less understanding of that than a child like Mimi?

"There's no reason to worry about it."

"Sir, the water's ready, and the bathtub's been scrubbed," the amah reported.

"Fine, fine," Wenyao acknowledged. "Auntie, go over to the workshop and tell them—"

"No!" Duanli shouted.

"What's wrong? You want to go back to work? You don't know how to enjoy yourself, do you?"

"Don't you worry about me," Duanli said irritably. "I can take care of my own affairs."

"You've got too high an opinion of yourself. Everything's got to be done the way you want it."

"I used to want nothing more than to hear an opinion from you, but you never had any."

This really upset Wenyao. "All right, I don't want to argue.

Auntie, go tell them that Ouyang Duanli is coming back to work tomorrow."

"Auntie, I'll go tell them myself." Even though Duanli stopped her, she was filled with doubts. Could she go to work tomorrow even if she wanted to? That cold, dark, stone warehouse basement, the pale light of the fluorescent lamp, those endless coils, the vulgar conversations, all those silly games, A'xing's drooling smile. . . . "I'll go tell them tomorrow," she said weakly.

Unable to sleep that night, she sat alone out in the garden in front of the living room, gazing wistfully up at the distant stars. The autumn-night sky, which seemed so far away, so tran- quil, gave her a hollow feeling.

"Sister-in-Law," someone behind her called out.

"Oh, it's you, Wenguang. You frightened me. Why aren't you asleep?"

"I was lying in bed, when something suddenly occurred to me, and I couldn't get to sleep." He was leaning against the French door, smoking a cigarette, which glowed brightly every few seconds.

"Did you get an inspiration?"

"Maybe. There's this person who's spent his whole life looking for the meaning of life, when one day he suddenly figures it out. The true meaning of life is simplicity itself: supporting yourself through your own labor."

The stars in the sky glimmered, and Duanli felt like crying. She hadn't cried in a long time. Her life was filled with pleasant, happy things, so there was no need for tears.

"Use your own strength to row this little boat called life to the other shore. . . ."

Tears flowed down past her dainty nose and into the corners of her mouth, salty and brackish. She hadn't tasted them in such a long time. These days she tasted nothing.

"On the stormy road of life, with all its twists and turns, he tasted it all—good, bad, and indifferent. That, he discovered, was the flavor of life. . . ."

It sounds good when you say it, but in real life it's not so easy! Duanli thought to herself.

Duanli's hair was getting wet as the evening dew began to settle. It was getting late. The scent of lilacs was stronger than ever. The living-room clock chimed. Time was passing, making the silent transition from yesterday to tomorrow, leaving in its wake dew, fog, and flowers that were blooming or dying. But it always left something behind for mankind. It never made its passage in vain.

Translated by Howard Goldblatt

Biographical Note—My Wall

I was born and raised in a lane off Shanghai's wealthiest and most prosperous thoroughfare, Huaihai Road. A modern, roomy neighborhood, this lane had two rows of buildings, front and back, ten three-story sextuplexes altogether, each with a little garden in front. Our family lived on the ground floor of Building Number Four and therefore had the run of the diminutive garden. To my little eyes, it was a vast wilderness which I slaved barefoot to cultivate, never once reaping a harvest but never giving up hope. Whenever I planted some seeds, the next morning I would eagerly push aside the dirt covering them and search hopefully for signs of sprouting. The oleanders and loquat tree in the next yard leaned luxuriantly over the wall, bordering my tiny wilderness with clouds of pink flowers and bunches of little green fruits.

Outside my wilderness, every afternoon when school let out and sunlight was spilling over the wall casting a latticework of shadow, a bunch of naughty schoolboys would come running and shouting, kicking a ragged old ball back and forth through the air, shattering the courtyard's tranquillity. These were boys from the lane next to ours. Originally the two lanes had been separated by a wall that was, however, torn down during the drive to increase iron and steel production in 1958. After that, the two lanes were no longer separated, but they remained two completely different worlds. One was exquisite, elegant, the other coarse and common. From my flowery wilderness retreat, I listened with curiosity and not a little trepidation to the boys' rough, wild rompings and their uncouth shouts so full of life and energy. Thus passed my childhood and early youth.

Long after my childhood and youth passed and I had begun to write, I always wrote about life on the two sides of the base of that wall. These were stories that had been with me since birth. Stories from the two so different sides of the wall constantly competed to occupy my thoughts, like two streams rushing toward each other, always engulfing me in their crashing whirlpool. I could never devote my entire attention to writing a pure and simple story. Wild shouts from over the wall's base mingled with and transformed my pure, light, transparent rain into a turbulent storm. These wild shouts possessed limitless power, the power of a steaming lava flow, of oceanic undertows, of hurricanes and thunderstorms—the most elemental forces of Nature. They had tremendous destructive power, and equally tremendous creative power. Bursting through my affected bourgeois sentimentality, they merged with my life force, whose roots were growing deeper and deeper. This life force, it seemed, was precisely that same eagerness as that with which I had once pushed aside the dirt to see whether my seeds had sprouted. I could not sing my lovely song undisturbed, so in the spirit of adventure I set out to explore the regions beyond the wall, even though my song entreated me to stay.

Once I had seen the bitterness and bleakness of life on the other side, even love and sympathy no longer sufficed to calm and relieve me. Rather, I began to see the falsity and hypocrisy of my love and sympathy. I was disappointed, regretful, even enraged. I should be a much better person!

I feel I have a duty to make myself and others better and better.

Walking along the footing of this wall, I am like an acrobat walking a tightrope. I don't want to lose either side—indeed I cannot—and this has become an indispensable part of my life and my fiction.

In this collection, "And the Rain Patters On" and "Lapse of Time" may be said to be stories from the near side of the wall, while "The Destination" and "Between Themselves" belong to the far side. "Life in a Small Courtyard" and "The Stage, a Miniature World" begin on the far side but end up even farther away. "The Base of the Wall" is just that—the base itself.

The Author

The Translators

Yu Fanqin, translator, *Chinese Literature*, Beijing.

Michael Day, editor and consultant, New World Press, Beijing.

Hu Zhihui, translator, *Chinese Literature*, Beijing.

Song Shouquan, translator, *Chinese Literature*, Beijing.

Daniel Bryant, University of Victoria, Canada.

Gladys Yang, retired senior editor of *Chinese Literature*, Beijing.
 Her many translations include *A Dream of Red Mansions*,
 The Scholars, etc.

Howard Goldblatt, professor of Chinese literature, San Francisco
 State University.